A Woman POSSESSED

MARILYN HERING

A WOMAN POSSESSED

PROMINENT
BOOKS
EDGE

5830 E 2nd St, Ste 7000 #9983
Casper, WY 82609
USA

For Walter, with love

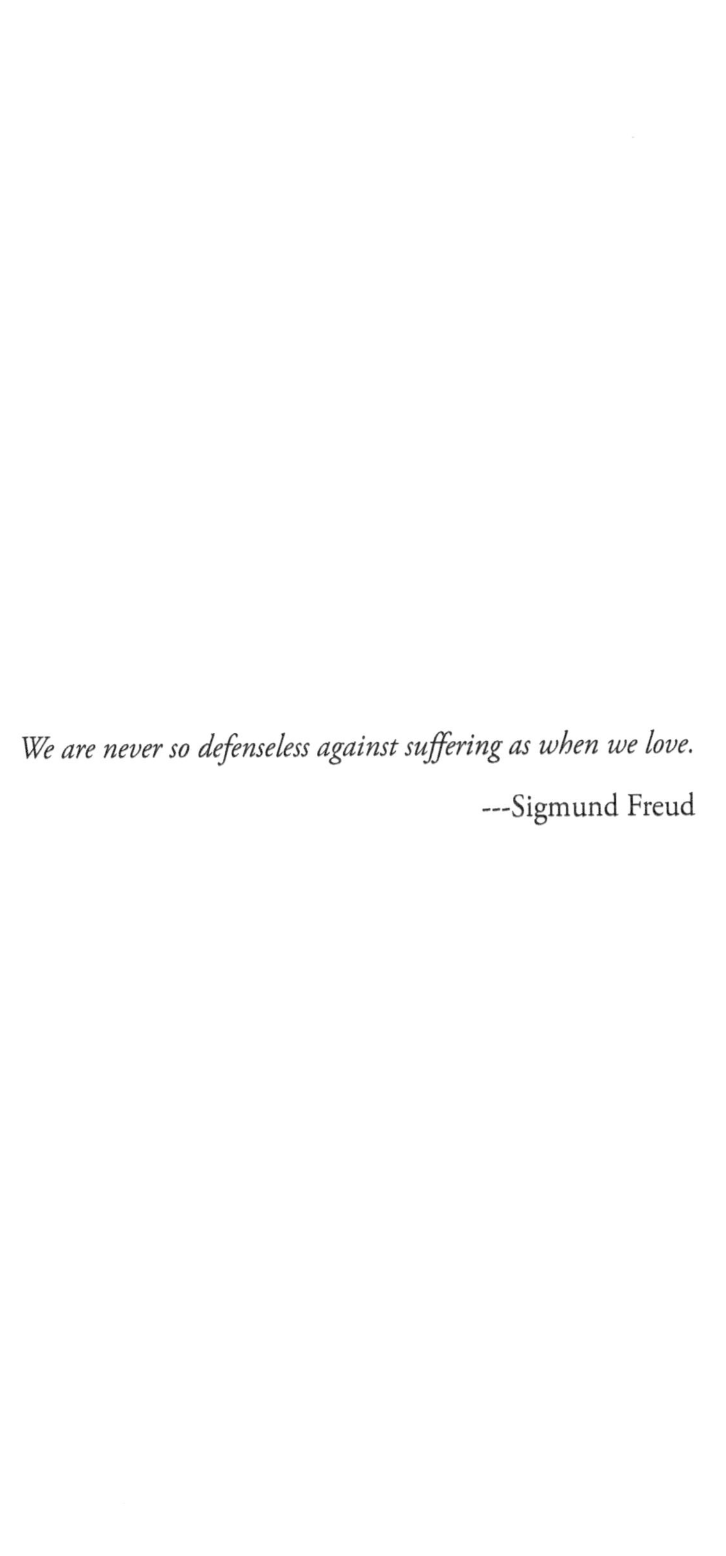

We are never so defenseless against suffering as when we love.

---Sigmund Freud

PART I

The Strike

Eleanor O'Bannion stared at the snow whisking against the windows of the third floor tenement she shared with her parents. She thought of its whiteness, so pure, so unobtainable. Especially by her.

She clenched her hands on the arms of her chair and turned, eyes riveted to the door of McNamara's Bar across the street at the corner. Now and then she heard clicking of horses' hooves on the gray cobblestones and strains of "After the Ball" floating from the bar's out-of-tune piano. The door mesmerized her as much as the snow had, though for different reasons. She twisted in the rocker, its squeaks sounding like explosions. She trembled, forced herself to fixate on the gaslight at the corner, emanating its soft glow. It did not calm her. Again she succumbed to her obsession with the door.

The clock at Paterson's City Hall tolled two in the morning. She turned. Her mother, Elizabeth, sat on the floor across the room, surrounded by bolts of emerald taffeta faconne, sapphire moire, magenta jacquard, picking it for flaws before bringing it back to Lafferty's Silk Mill. Now and then she caught her mother staring at the flapping soles of her worn shoes as she rocked. Finally she rose from the floor, winced, grasped her left hip, and limped into their matchbox kitchen.

Eleanor tightened her lips and stared once again at the oaken door of the bar.

Her father finally emerged, his hulk staggering through the doorway onto the snow-covered cobblestones. He slid, grabbed the lamp post, puked a geyser of brown chunks that splattered on the snow. She caught her breath. This time she and her mother would be spared the task of cleaning up after him. She could hardly wait for the time when they would never again wash urine or vomit-stained sheets until their hands became raw. Or have to lie when asked about their bruised arms and faces, saying they fell down the stairs or walked into the door. She clenched her hands, her flesh so taut it seemed to crush the bones of her fingers.

Her father wiped his face with the sleeve of his coat, staggered and slid across the street, disappearing into the tenement.

Seconds passed. Her breath quickened.

The clunk of his feet grew louder and louder as he climbed the stairs to the third floor. Every Friday night for years she hoped he would tumble down them, break his neck. He never did.

Her mother turned from where she stood near the stove, limped to the wall closest to the back of the apartment, huddled against it. Eleanor stopped rocking, faced the door as he tumbled into the room, stumbled towards the nearest chair, clutched it for support. He caught his breath, squinted until he finally saw her mother, pointed his thick finger at her.

"Take my shoes off."

Elizabeth limped to the chair he managed to drop into, bent down, began to loosen one of the ties of his boots.

"No, mother," Eleanor said.

Her father lifted his paw of a hand, thrashed the back of it against her mother's face, threw her to the floor. Then he lifted himself from the chair. Over two hundred pounds of flesh hovered over Eleanor.

"Don't talk back to me, girl!"

He lunged at her, but she knew her moves by heart. She crouched a second before his hand sliced the air to hit her, then darted to the far end of the room, towards the door leading to the back porch.

"You'll never catch me," she yelled. "You dirty pig!"

She stood with her hands plastered to her hips at the door of the back porch, her heart somersaulting. But she held her ground. He tottered a few feet away from her. The stench of stale beer and puke assaulted her. She winced at food clumped between his teeth when he laughed at her.

"You're no match for me. You know it."

"Come on then. Get me. You dirty coward!"

"You'll regret those words, girl."

He squeezed his hand into a fist, lunged at her. She flung open the porch door, backed out onto it. The cold penetrated like needles of ice. Snow stunned her toes between the broken soles of her shoes.

He stopped. She saw by his face he couldn't understand why she ran to the porch in such freezing weather. Then he grinned.

"You think the porch is safer? I won't come out there with the cold? Is that it? We'll just see about that, you stubborn bitch."

He lunged at her, a giant bear slipping on the snow-slicked porch, puffing and panting. In a heartbeat she stepped aside, her back facing the end railing of the porch. He continued to slide and shake, regained his balance. She moved backwards, closer to the railing, her dress brushing it lightly.

"You can't get me!"

"Oh, can't I now?"

She expected him to lunge forward. He didn't. She had not counted on this.

He stood fighting for balance on the slick floor. She had to act now or his hands would be on her. She ducked, slipped behind him. She could feel the ropes of muscles in his back through his worn coat. She lifted her arms, and shoved him forward with all her strength.

He slid, lunged onto the wooden rail. Its left side splintered and he plunged through.

His scream penetrated the air. Then silence. "Dear God! Eleanor."

Her mother stood in the doorway, hands pressing against her heart, eyes wild. Eleanor had no idea how long she'd been watching.

She slid across the slippery floor and embraced her mother. "He's dead. We don't have to be afraid any more."

Her mother held her hard a few minutes, then loosened her hold, dragged herself back through the doorway.

Eleanor stood at the edge of the porch, staring at her father's body lying face down, legs and hands splayed, in the blood-soaked snow. Then she placed her hand in her pocket and caressed the nails it had taken her so long to remove from the right side of the railing.

She smiled.

* * *

Billy Donnelly, Kevin O'Connor and Colin McCarthy, friends of her father from the silk mill and union, carried the body upstairs. It lay on the living room table, its stiff arms dangling from under the bloody sheet covering its bulk. She and her mother sat in silence, waiting for the undertaker.

Tony DeLuca, huffing and puffing from the three-flight climb, faced Eleanor at the door, his satchel in hand. He fixed a look of dutiful sympathy upon her and offered his condolences.

"Go downstairs, mother," she said. "To Mrs. Bleet. I can handle things here."

Elizabeth obeyed without a word.

They could not afford Bennett's Funeral Parlor on Market Street. Her father's body would be embalmed at home and waked there as well, as was most often the case when an immigrant working in the silk mills died. She began to lift the sheet covering her father's body.

"You don't have to do that, Miss O'Bannion." DeLuca set his satchel on the floor, snapped it open, began to check his instruments. "I'll take care of it all. Don't you worry about anything. I'll call you when the--procedure--is over."

"I want to stay."

He frowned. "I don't think you realize what--. It's not a pretty sight, Miss O'Bannion. You wouldn't want to see your father that way."

"Yes, I do."

"It would be an exception."

She crossed her arms around her chest.

He sighed. "All right. But don't feel ashamed if you have to run out or--"

"I won't."

"I'll need a few pails to catch the--um--"

She returned quickly with a pail and basin. She watched him examine the body, wondering if it were still warm. He began to drain blood. She savored each moment, watching him stab the vein and artery near her father's armpits, then the jugular vein in his neck, then the one near his groin. She continued to stare as he injected a needle into an artery near her father's heart, inserting forceps in the vein leading directly to it. Watching the blood spew from his battered body into the pail invigorated her. She stepped closer, studied his bashed face, clotted with dried blood, his nose a piece of pulp.

DeLuca kept glancing at her. She knew he expected any minute she would faint.

"You'll do what you can with his face, I suppose."

"Of course," he said. "But I can't possibly repair it decently. I'm sorry. It would be best if the coffin stayed closed."

"Whatever you say."

She sounded as emotional as a girl telling a waiter she did not care if he brought her apple or blueberry pie for dessert. She knew it would generate talk. She didn't care. Let them assume what they liked about her and her father. Whatever they thought, it would never approach the truth.

But there were her mother's feelings to consider.

She sighed, left the room, knowing tomorrow night she must use all her acting ability to survive the charade, hear the words of admiration from her father's many friends. They suspected nothing. Her mother wanted it that way, so that's the way it would stay.

She felt a chill when she returned to the parlor, saw the porch door open. Colin McCarthy, her father's closest friend, returned no doubt to comfort her and her mother. She stood in the doorway to the porch, watching him. His back was to her. He was examining the cracked railing, rubbing his fingers across its right edge, where it had split clean away from the post, searching for the nails still in her pocket. He rubbed his fingertips along its smooth edge again, deep in thought. Finally he faced her.

"I'm glad you came back," she said a little too quickly. "Mother's upstairs with Mrs. Bleet. So upset. I'll get her. You'll be such a comfort."

He moved towards her, his boots crusted with snow, puffs of breath trailing him. He seemed about to speak.

She met his look straight on. "Why don't you come in so I can close the door? It's freezing out here. We're losing the little warmth we have."

"I--"

"Mother needs you. More than ever now."

He put his hand to his mouth, but no words came.

Michael O'Bannion's body lay in a cheap pine box on the kitchen table, which now sat in the living room. It was flanked by two household candles flickering in their wooden holders. Colin McCarthy sent a large arrangement of white lilies that lay across the lid. Eleanor and her mother tied a black ribbon around the sleeve of their darkest dresses. Her mother insisted she tie her hair back to look more demure, but she refused, letting it hang in a copper cascade down her back. They quietly accepted condolences from mourners from the silk mill: jacquard weavers, loomfixers, throwers, mill boys and girls, each praising Michael O'Bannion.

Eleanor saw her father's death affected Colin most. She thought the world of him. He had met Eleanor's father on the ship to America, his destination Paterson, New Jersey. His cousin worked in the silk mills there, and they all hoped to get a job thru his influence.

And so it happened. Yet, even after nearly two decades in the new world, they never lost their political concern about Ireland. They still sent every penny they could back to Ireland to be used towards efforts to free it from British rule. Perhaps that need to see justice done was why Eleanor's father and Colin emerged as the strongest union voices at Lafferty's Silk Mill, stirring the workers to fight for better working conditions and fairer wages.

Eleanor watched Colin squirming in his seat. With her father gone, the burden of organizing the rumored strike lay on him. She knew he was a member of the International Workers of the World, the IWW, and had secretly organized the workers. She also knew a strike would throw thousands of them into the streets and drive them to near starvation if it lasted. She felt certain these responsibilities lay on Colin's mind as she surveyed him.

And given that, what would he do with his discovery she removed the nails from the porch railing?

Colin's stomach churned as he sat on the hard chair and stared numbly at Michael O'Bannion's coffin, trying to avoid watching the tiny, flame-haired woman standing demurely next to Eleanor, eyes red and swollen, who now and then wrenched her hands and blew into her handkerchief as she stared at her husband's casket.

Elizabeth. He flushed with shame and sorrow when he finally studied her, could not stop himself from absorbing everything about her. Her hair coiled at her neck, her face gaunt, her eyes blue stones now--not as they were so many years ago when he first saw her on the Olivia during their voyage to America.

He forced himself to look away. How could he think such thoughts with Michael not yet cold in the grave?

He turned to Eleanor, watched her greeting the mourners. Not one tear had fallen from her eyes since Michael's death. Should he ask her about the nails missing from the railing, ask what he feared knowing?

No. How could he reproach her with part of himself feeling so glad Michael lay dead? Elizabeth would be free now. She might finally let him tell Eleanor, the one person who meant more to him than even Elizabeth, she was his child.

His head throbbed from the agony of love, the burden of guilt. He vowed once again to sit cemented to his chair, remember Michael with appropriate respect.

He stared at the coffin.

The hours moved slowly for Eleanor. She wanted the wake to end so she could focus on her future and her mother's. But after an hour or so, she noticed many of the workers clustered at the far side of the living room, circling a man she did not recognize. He was a tall man, with dark, thick hair, its longer style common among the Italian immigrants of Paterson. The others moved aside to let him pay his respects to her and her mother. There was a certainty in his stride as he approached them.

Colin quickly rushed to greet him, and they walked together towards the casket. She observed his finely-sculpted mouth, his dark, steady eyes. Not one muscle in his face moved as he stood gazing at the coffin. He did not kneel or pray. He finally turned to face her and her mother.

"Elizabeth, Eleanor," Colin said, "I'd like you to meet Dante Ravelli, our IWW representative. He's going to help us through the hard times ahead."

Ravelli offered his hand to her mother, then shook hers.

"You both have my sincere sympathy," he said. "Michael was one of our key organizers. We have lost an important man, so needed in our efforts to improve the conditions of the workers. But we must go on, of course."

Eleanor noted he had a slight Italian accent and could not help observing his frayed jacket, his shirt grayed from too many launderings. How could a man dressed this way emanate such an aura of strength?

"And just how certain are you there'll be a strike?" Her mother dabbed her eyes with her handkerchief. "I can't imagine I could get through that now, right after the death of my husband."

"We're here to help you, Mrs. O'Bannion. We'll be with you. Every step of the way."

Blood rushed to Eleanor's face. "We can't afford a strike. It would last for months and what we'd lose we would never get back. I know that isn't the popular opinion around here." She eyed the workers hovering around Ravelli as she spoke. "I heard my father talk about the IWW plenty of times. I know you'd use violence. That's the answer to everything with the IWW, isn't it?"

Ravelli did not flinch. "You misunderstand completely if that is what you believe the IWW is about, Miss O'Bannion. But you can be sure there will be a strike. What choice do you have when you see the mill owners bleeding you the way they do? I am so sorry. To have both of you lose your husband, father, your main means of support.

And the shock of such a tragic accident, as I understand. But, once again, I can assure you that we will be here to help you. You will not be alone."

She felt her mother's weak hand attempt to squeeze her arm.

"Eleanor. Please. Let's not talk about it here." She motioned to her husband's casket. "Not now."

"Let me take my leave," Ravelli said. "At such a terrible time I am so sorry I have upset you."

He bowed slightly to them, then turned to Colin. They walked to the far corner of the room, joined by Kevin, Billy, other weavers, throwers, loomfixers, talking a long while, until the wake ended.

He turned at the door before he left, caught her eye a brief moment. She looked away.

The ordeal of the wake ended at last. Eleanor sat with her mother in stillness, watching the flames from the candle stubs on the casket cover. Finally Elizabeth blew them out, then walked to the curtain blocking the entrance of the small room where she and Michael O'Bannion slept together eighteen years.

"Don't stay up too long now, will you, dear?" she said. "We've got a hard day tomorrow."

She closed the makeshift curtain, quietly began to undress, donned her nightgown, shivering in the darkness. Michael's youthful face and form, so handsome, came to mind unbidden.

She and her sisters had been on an excursion to Mayo when she was taken aback by a handsome, charming young man passing out leaflets on Irish independence. He smiled at her, gave her one. She felt her fingers had been touched by flame. He preached to her, telling her the only answer to Ireland's misery lay in rebellion, the end of British rule.

To her surprise, she let her sisters get lost in the crowd of shoppers and listened to him. To this day she could not believe that she, a quiet, religious girl, accepted Michael O'Bannion's invitation to dine at a local eating house. Or that she agreed to meet him the next day. He brought her to huts just north of Mayo where children with sunken eyes huddled in the corners, snuggling near scant embers of turf.

Elizabeth cringed in her bed, remembering others with matted hair, feet covered with dirt, digging for food, a few roots they dug up from the parched earth. And while she tried to take it in, Michael spoke about change, of violence as the only means to attain Irish freedom.

She fell madly in love with him, with what she saw then as his strength. She gave up her family, her comfortable life, to be with him. They emigrated to America where he learned silk weaving in Paterson, soon became a loom fixer, the best paying job. He made contacts, even sent money back to Ireland in the beginning. But how brief their happiness was. His drinking and violent nature finally destroyed their love and she could hardly make ends meet.

Elizabeth tightened her blanket around her chest, clutched her aching hip. She longed to run to Eleanor, shout her joy to her for having killed Michael. She thought of the night long ago when she had returned from bringing her picking to Lafferty's. Michael held her darling child on her cot.

With his hand under her dress.

She stood transfixed in the doorway, finally cried out. He lifted his heavy body, turned to her. She could still see the sweat on his forehead. He straightened out his clothes, went to the kitchen and drank a beer. She looked at Eleanor curled up like a snail, turned to the wall.

Elizabeth's only way of coping with the horror was to not allow herself to acknowledge the unthinkable. Silence became her defense. Now guilt ran over her like a tidal wave. Eleanor killed Michael. And she lay there in the darkness, knowing why.

She heard her daughter, the squeaking coils of her daybed, the rustle of her dress as she changed to her nightgown.

Eleanor.

Her eyes filled, remembering the countless times her child flung herself between her and Michael during his attacks of crazed drunkenness. How he beat her since she had been a little girl. Eleanor never cried. Not once.

How could anyone expect her to cry at her father's funeral?

* * *

The funeral service lasted an eternity for Eleanor, with Father Garrity droning prayers over her father's grave. The Monday burial meant the workers could not be there. They couldn't afford to lose the time. Only Colin attended. He was a loom fixer, a precious commodity at the silk mill, and knew the owners would not penalize him.

Eleanor told her mother she was not returning to school. Her mother's protests fell on deaf ears. She was going to Lafferty's Silk Mill to look for work that afternoon. She needed a job immediately, especially if the workers planned to strike soon. The few dollars in contributions collected in memory of her father would not last very long.

Lafferty's Silk Mill was only a five-minute walk from the tenements. She moved briskly, past the millrace that provided water power for the mill. She never tired of seeing the Great Falls which dominated the silk mill section of Paterson. They hovered over the district, water trickling in spots, mostly in frozen silence now until spring. The clacking from the machines grew louder as she approached the building, as weavers created the fabric that would adorn dresses of the wealthy, the watered silk, moires, taffetas, satins her mother spent hours examining for flaws at home.

Lafferty's sprawled across most of Straight Street, its worn clinker brick structure surrounding high vertical windows covered with thick dust and grime. She took a deep breath, entered, the looms bellowing around her, her stomach churning at the stench of neatsfoot oil used to take gum from the silk skeins. It enveloped the room, even though the throwing process took place in the basement.

"And what do you want, miss?"

She startled, then turned. At the bottom of the stairs stood a ferret-faced man, his stomach hanging over his belt, trousers stained with oil. He trudged up the wrought iron staircase, stopping once to catch his breath.

"I need work," she said when he was close enough to hear.

He led her over to the glass-enclosed mill office where the owner overlooked the floor of the factory.

George Lafferty, dressed in a gray woolen suit and silk tie, his moustache trim, greeted her but remained seated.

"I'm looking for work, sir."

He gestured to the fat man. "Take her down." Then he returned to his examination of a ledger he had before him on his desk.

The odor of neatsfoot oil worsened as she descended the stairs to the basement, grasping the rail for balance. On this lowest floor women bent over giant wooden vats filled with water, its surface coated with oil, plunging skeins of silk up and down. On the far side of the room other women transferred dry silk to whirling, eight- sided wooden reels. In the center of the area giant steel monsters, the weaving machines, pounded.

"Here's the first part of throwin'."

The man, who had still not bothered to introduce himself, pointed to ropes tied near the ceiling from which hung the silk, some wet, some near dry.

"See here? After these dry, they go to them swifts." He pointed to the women monitoring the wooden reels. She saw now they had long, pointed spindles emanating from their center to twirl the silk onto the swifts.

"Here's where most start." He gestured to the vats in front of them. "Soakin' and then hangin' the silk skeins. Then they go to them swifts. Then to the machines. Some's here, but most is upstairs."

She watched the women grab the skeins of dull, lifeless silk removing its gum residue by plopping it into the large tubs, lifting and soaking, again and again, muscles in their arms bulging as the skeins grew heavy from the bulk of water. Over and over they crouched at the vats, raising the silk with swollen fingers, scabs and infections on their hands.

"Not an easy job, young lady," the man said. "But I know you from the wake. You're Michael O'Bannion's girl. The workers think his daughter's special. All that man tried to do for us. So you'll start out learnin' to weave ribbons. It's cleaner, and the money's better."

"I don't want to be considered special." She didn't want any favors because of her father. Though her feelings wavered when she thought of the prospect of being a soaker.

"Don't feel that way," he said. "The workers all agreed to it. They knowed you'd come here soon enough. It's their way of thankin' Michael, if you know what I mean." He bowed his head. "A shame he passed on."

She said nothing.

"So it's tomorrow you start then. Six o'clock. Six til six we work. Half hour for lunch."

"I'll be here, thank you. I didn't get your name."

"Oh, sorry, not thinkin'. It's Clegg. Angus Clegg."

She stepped carefully across the floor soaked with oily water, passing a thin, plain-faced girl walking towards the hanging skeins of silk. The girl smiled. Eleanor smiled back. The girl continued to look at her. And slipped on the slick floors. She stumbled onto the whirling picks of one of the skein-winding machines.

Her screams deafened even the noise from the looms. The workers stood frozen, then began to run across the room, waving at Eleanor, closest to the girl, pointing to the machine. "Pull the handle! The handle!"

Eleanor spotted a long, iron handle to the right of the machine, grasped it, her body shaken by the pounding of the belts and wheels. She pulled it toward her with all her might.

The machine stopped.

The girl had fallen on her left side. The machine tore the flesh of her arm, neck, side of her face and scalp. The muslin of her dress turned crimson. Clumps of her hair lay amidst the spindles of the machine. Splattered blood soaked the silk on some of the other spindles.

Eleanor lifted her carefully from the throes of the machine, lay her on the floor, tried to staunch the bleeding. The girl's arms waved involuntarily from shock. By then Angus Clegg and the other workers stood above her, a few bending down to assist.

"I'll call for an ambulance."

Clegg began to run toward stairs leading to the first floor of the mill.

The girl attempted to rise. "No. Please."

Clegg stopped. It was a moment before Eleanor realized what the protest meant. She would not be able to pay for an ambulance let alone a hospital stay. And doubtless Clegg would not want the notoriety of an accident having occurred as he supervised.

"Are you all mad," Eleanor said. "Do something!"

Clegg pushed a young boy towards the door. "Go get a nurse from the Alliance."

The boy, slipping and sliding himself, finally managed to get through the door.

A few minutes later George Lafferty descended from his glass- enclosed office. He stared briefly at the girl.

"A pity," he offered. "I'll send her home in my own carriage. She'll be all right. The nurse from the Alliance can accompany her, if need be."

He surveyed the ruined skeins of silk, broken from their spindle, flaccid hanks of fiber stained with blood, examined them closer in his hand, noted the other spindles splattered as well. He clicked his tongue against the roof of his mouth, glared at Clegg, tramped back to his glass-enclosed office.

Eleanor stood in delayed shock. After the nurse from the Alliance arrived, she broke away from the workers and bolted up the stairs, anxious to emerge into light and air.

She turned to take a last glance at George Lafferty in his glass- enclosed office, where no stench of oil or sweat permeated.

He was pounding his desk, shaking his arms. Fury at the lost silk? No. Standing in front of his desk was the stranger who attended her father's wake, Dante Ravelli. He faced Lafferty squarely. She continued to watch him, his body straight, shoulders back, lips moving, face expression-less while Lafferty fumed. She wallowed with pleasure at Ravelli's ability to rouse Lafferty. Then her smile froze. His presence could have only one meaning.

A strike.

The bells of St.John's Cathedral on Broadway tolled 5:30 a.m.. Eleanor stared at her wall covered with painted flowers on paper bags her mother saved for her--jonquils, roses, daisies, orchids, violets, lilies, so many others. Their beauty comforted her each morning as she faced the day.

She removed her nightgown and bathed quickly, feeling the cold of the room assault her. She threw her clothes on, gooseflesh lessening when she donned her dress, woolen coat and cap. Frayed as they were, they warmed her until she got last night's coals glowing in the stove. She grabbed a newspaper, folded it around the broken flaps of her shoes to keep her feet warm and protect her from the snow, then shoveled the daily ration of coal into the stove to warm the room by the time her mother awoke.

She listened to her mother's quiet breathing behind her curtained doorway. Bolts of cloth lay on the floor ready for Elizabeth's daily picking for flaws, a job she knew would end if there were a strike. She drank some watered milk and grabbed a slice of bread she chewed on the way to Lafferty's.

Thewinterof 1913 seemedrelentlessasmid-Februaryapproached. She pulled her cap down further as she turned off Market, trudging past the behemoths of Dexter Lambert, Barbour's Flax Spinning Mill, Frankes, Whatley's, Passaic Rolling Mills, Hamil and Booth, until she finally reached Lafferty's. Her feet felt numb by the time she arrived, although she only traveled a few blocks.

Most of the mill workers had arrived by the time she entered the cavern where she would spend the next twelve hours. Brisk chatter prevailed until a minute or so later when a bell clanged. Eleanor placed the piece of half-eaten bread in her pocket for lunch. She walked slowly to the loom assigned her, passing men and women at the vats, already dunking silk, the smell from the neatsfoot oil upsetting her stomach. She knew she must get used to it.

A gap-toothed woman with hands as delicate as feathers introduced herself only as Nora and began teaching her silk ribbon weaving. She showed her what she called a specialty warp, grasping silk from two beams, feeding it into a gravure printing press. Each color had one plate cylinder, which printed the pattern shades at various intervals along the threads as they flowed along efficiently.

Eleanor watched the process, dumbstruck at the beauty of the finished ribbons, works of art with their blazing color. When after an hour Nora completed the spool--fifty yards of ribbon-- she told Eleanor to place it with the piles of ribbons lying in baskets surrounding her--satin bayard, gros grain, taffeta warp print, satin beauvoirs, tinsel and Roman belts, taffeta millinery ribbons, tapestry Jacquards, every style a designer's imagination could conjure.

Eleanor felt grateful for her chance to learn ribbon weaving. As a woman she would never be taught the higher paying Jacquard loom process. It looked so deceptively simple as she glanced across the room observing seasoned weavers guiding their shuttles, the filling shuttle penetrating punched cards carrying the design, one card for each pick to pass through. Yet she knew it was more complex than it looked. How she admired the beauty of silks the weavers created, especially those incorporating flower designs. In spring she knew she would walk down Silk Road and see many of these ribbons and fabrics worn by wives of the mill owners--silk roses embedded in bands surrounding the crowns of their hats, lilies in decorative ribbon strips embellishing their watered silk dresses as they languidly descended their carriages.

Morning passed quickly. At lunch break she stayed with Nora and two soakers. They moved to the corner of the room, away from the vats and machines. Nora introduced Florrie. Dark pouches beneath her eyes dominated her face, all the more noticeable against her chalky skin. And Sarah, her teeth gray as granite when she smiled, her hair string.

Nora held Eleanor's hand. "You did a great thing yesterday, Eleanor, hittin' that switch."

"I was afraid. I don't mind saying it."

"Catherine Devlin's a strong girl. With a will like iron. Believe me. She'll be all right."

Florrie crouched closer to them, her voice barely audible "Did you hear about last night? The IWW and the other unions, they met with the owners. Nobody gave an inch. My Tony told me. He got it from Colin McCarthy."

Sarah pulled a piece of bread from her slice, chewed it quickly. "I know all about it. News travels fast around here. Heard it this mornin'."

Florrie placed her scabbed hand in her pocket, looked around, cautiously removed a small, red card, thrust it towards them.

"I joined the IWW. I'm proud to be a member now. Glad they're here."

Eleanor stared at the card.

"See?" She waved it boldly now, with no one in view.

Nora frowned. "I'm a member and I don't mind sayin' so. They say they're Commies. Agitators. With them here there's bound to be bloodshed. I don't believe it." She rubbed her back. "Oh, what I'd give for a chair."

"Don't listen to such talk. They care about the workers. They'd never get violent, unless there's no other way. That's what they told Tony."

Sarah raised her index finger, tapped in on Nora's chest. "Don't you tell me it's fair. Lafferty holdin' half of what we earn for a year. And if we leave before year's end, he gets it all." She transferred her finger to Eleanor's chest. "Didn't know that, I bet. And we get fined if we get caught talkin', or open a window. And docked a whole day's pay if we're outside and come in late from lunch. Even a minute. And they lock us out. I'll bet they didn't tell you all that when you got hired."

Florrie ran her tongue across her front teeth, removing excess bread from them, leaned toward Eleanor. "And don't make any plans for right after work. We have to stay to clean up. On our own time."

"The important thing is we have to go to the meetin' tonight. This is it. A strike call by the broad-silk weavers. I'm sure." Nora turned to Eleanor. "Will you vote strike?"

The women studied her, but she did not answer. Didn't these women know the hardship a strike could cause?

Nora bobbed her head. "We can win this time. I'm sure of it."

Hope was clear in her voice, but Eleanor knew Paterson's strike history too well because of her father's involvement with past strikes. She remembered the conflicts during the last one. The Jews of the WIIU and the Italians of the IWW refused to see eye to eye. The WIIU condemned violence against the authorities or any attempts to provoke violence on the part of the workers. But many anarchists in the IWW, supported by a group of militant Italians under the leadership of Carlo Tresca, Bill Haywood and Dante Ravelli, condoned violence if necessary and vowed a willingness to fight to their deaths for their cause.

Now the IWW had returned to Paterson. She felt certain it had not changed its views.

Then she remembered the accident. And George Lafferty's being more disappointed by ruined silk than by a ruined girl.

"Of course I'll support the strike," she said.

Eleanor still feared the probable bloodshed it would bring with the IWW at its helm. But her sense of justice told her the working conditions she now saw first hand must not continue.

The whistle blew loudly. They returned to work, Angus Clegg hovering over them, often standing next to her watching Nora explain the silk ribbon making. The room chilled when the sun went down. She buttoned her coat, donned her hat, and continued working. She dreamed of the blessed cup of tea her mother would make when she returned, her smile as she entered the door. Perhaps she had made her tasty potato soup.

Both would have to gulp it down so they would have enough time to get to the strike meeting at 8:00.

Eleanor arrived at the meeting hall on Fair Street, a fire-trap covered with peeling gray paint, windows caked with grime and frost, now bursting with mill workers. Almost as soon as she entered, she lost track of her mother amidst the crowd that kept pushing to and fro. She finally settled for a spot in the back.

From what she heard the workers blazed with fury having learned of the arrest of IWW leaders Carlo Tresca, Patrick Quinn and Elizabeth Gurley Flynn as outside agitators.

Eleanor's heart sank. The meeting centered around their appearance; and, in truth, she longed to see Elizabeth Gurley Flynn, the 'rebel girl' everyone talked of, who lived unashamedly outside of marriage with Carlo Tresca. She heard no mention of Dante Ravelli. Perhaps they were smart enough to have him stay separate from them away from the eye of the Paterson police many believed sympathized with the mill owners.

She stared at the hundreds of people wearing tiny flags on their coats, groups holding large signs above their heads.

"We wove the flag! We dyed the flag!

We live under the flag!

But we won't SCAB under the flag!"

"We stand United with the IWW!"

"Workers Unite! All for One!

One for All!"

She recognized some of the Irish IWW members who often visited her father, but the Italians predominated, shouting full force. Anarchists all as far as she was concerned. She hated the fact the city she loved had been nicknamed "Red City," a reflection of the newspaper anarchist Luigi Galleani edited. And the worst horror came when an anarchist from Paterson killed King Humbert of Italy. She boiled with anger watching the Italian anarchists dominating already.

Amidst being squeezed on all sides by workers she didn't know, she finally recognized a few faces from Lafferty's, saw Angus Clegg with a group of agitators nearby mouthing something, then spitting on the floor. Others, mostly men, stood with arms clenched across their chests.

Groups of women filled other parts of the hall. Most dressed as she did, in worn coats and caps, pale skinned and thin as the silk threads they handled each day. But one group stood only a few feet away in starched blouses with ruffles complementing their heavy tweed jackets and dark skirts, polished leather boots.

One woman in particular, her hair swept up with an ivory comb crusted with gold filigree flowers, caught Eleanor's attention. She pushed closer to her to examine the comb, noting the shapes of its flowers. Violets and something else, she wasn't sure what, done in exquisite detail.

She caught herself. She mustn't waste time on frivolous thoughts about combs when she had no idea where food would soon be coming from.

In that moment the woman turned, caught her eye. Eleanor noticed three ribbons of purple, gold and white pinned to her lapel. Others in her group wore them as well.

The woman, strong boned, tall, with arched brows above clear brown eyes, smiled at her.

"It looks like you're going to have a strike," she offered.

"Did you hear they arrested IWW leaders?" Eleanor said. "Is it true, I wonder."

"I saw it with my own eyes, just happened about twenty minutes ago. The horror of seeing a great woman like Elizabeth Gurley Flynn taken away to jail like a common criminal. All her life she's fought so hard for the workers."

Eleanor moved closer to the woman. "It's true then? They have a woman as one of their leaders? I can hardly believe it."

"And why not? We're just as intelligent as men, and, God knows, we've suffered enough to be as angry at injustice as men. It's about time we were recognized." She touched the ribbon on her lapel. "This is the symbol of our strength. Our desire for change."

The woman ran her eyes over Eleanor's shabby coat and broken shoes, then looked into Eleanor's eyes. Somehow this assessment of her poverty didn't embarrass Eleanor.

"But, my dear," the woman said, "you must be strong. There are women out there, strong women, fighting for you, fighting for the vote. That's where our power will truly be. Come to the rally March 3. Thousands of us will be there, even men and Negroes, all are welcome. It's the day before Wilson's inauguration, you see. A perfect day to make our point. Alice Paul will be there to lead us."

The woman assumed Eleanor knew who Alice Paul must be, though she had no idea.

"I'm so excited at the thought of hearing her. She's from Teaneck, you know. Not far from here. And to think of the fame she's gained." The woman's eyes widened. "And you needn't worry about transportation. We're going to provide it at City Hall on Market Street, 6 a.m." She placed a gentle hand on Eleanor's arm. "Won't you think about coming?"

"Do you think the strike will be over by then? You won't get many people if there's a strike. We'll be marching in the streets."

"Yes, I do think so. It won't last long. How can the mill owners hold out this time of the year? Spring is their busiest time for silk production, as I understand."

A roar from the crowd almost deafened Eleanor. The woman placed her lips closer to Eleanor's ear. "Will you think about coming?"

"I will."

She had no intention of going, but perhaps now the woman would stop discussing votes for women when a strike was imminent.

The noise of the crowd mounted. Those near the center aisles shoved back to let someone--Dante Ravelli--through. He seemed to have emerged from the cold like a phantom, still wearing the same jacket he had the night of the wake, the same graying shirt. He hastened down the aisle onto the side of the platform, his jaw set tightly, jumped on the dais next to Colin.

"We have the great pleasure now," Colin said, "to hear the man who will help us to victory, a great and courageous man, one of the leaders of the IWW. Dante Ravelli."

She watched him move to the front of the platform. He stretched his arms towards the workers. As he did, they began to stamp their feet, chanting "Justice for the workers!" amidst other howls of "Strike now! Strike now! Strike now!"

He stood motionless for a moment, then raised them higher, as though attempting to touch an elusive heaven. Slowly the chanting subsided. Then he surged at the crowd and swooped forward to the very edge of the platform.

"You know why we're here! We're at a crucial moment. The mill owners won't budge. They want you broad-silk weavers to work four looms. Four looms! You know what that means. It means you'll increase output, which will surely make the mill owners happy, but how many of you will lose your jobs when you have only one man now watching over four looms? There's nothing in it for you. Nothing! No working four looms!"

The crowd roared, "Strike! Strike! Strike!"

He paused, waited for the din to subside.

"And the mill owners must not be allowed to punish you for your union activities. Look what happened here tonight. Three of our greatest leaders have been arrested. Arrested! And why? Only because they came to Paterson to help you. Because they believe in justice for all men and women. Because they are unafraid to speak out when they see workers suffering. And for that they are in jail."

Once again the crowd roared and Ravelli let them.

"And now I want you to hear the most important point I will make tonight. You talk of striking? Before you decide to strike you must come together as one. Whether soaker or loom fixer, whether foreign born or native born, no matter what color, religion, sex you are. That is how you must enter this strike, if you decide to vote for it. That's how you will win it. United!"

A few boos sounded here and there.

"I know some of you feel you do not want to be part of the IWW. I know. But I'm telling you, we are your best chance to win. The bosses will try to use our differences to pit us against each other. They have done this before. But we must decide right now this will not happen again! We will march arm in arm on the picket line, as one, whatever union we represent. If we do this, if we unite and focus on our common goal instead of our differences, we will win!"

When the crowd moved aside to let Ravelli through, Eleanor managed to push forward and stood near the center of the room where she could see him more closely. His skin was flushed, a study in passion. She hardly recognized the cool and polite man who spoke to her so gently at the wake.

"What courage you showed when you left your homes in Europe," he said, "your villages and fields, often your parents, sometimes your wives and children, to establish yourself here in Paterson. You had such dreams, didn't you? Dreams of a new life in America, free from oppression, free to work, save, send for your families so they could come to America to find freedom." He punched his index finger into the air. "But what freedom did you find? Did you ever expect to be herded into the great prisons they call silk mills, into the slums of Mill Street? Did you expect strangers to greet you as "greenhorn" or "honkie," treated like dirt?"

Silence permeated the room. Eleanor glanced around, saw heads bobbing in assent, tears shining their eyes. Some workers gulped, attempting to swallow all their hurt.

Ravelli walked backwards a few feet, arms akimbo. She watched him breathing the silence into him.

"I've known it too. Known it all. I am not only your leader. I am one of you! I will be right beside you for the duration of the strike, as will Tresca, Flynn and Quinn. I vow to you they will be out of jail by tomorrow morning!"

Eleanor hardly heard the banners pounding on the floor, the workers shouting, the noise so deafening. She stood mesmerized, longing to hear him continue to speak. The roar finally lessened.

"Now I heard some booing in the audience when Colin here introduced me as being from the IWW. Unfortunately, I think some of you have bought the owners' lie that the IWW is a bunch of anarchists who believe the first step in any conflict is violence, that we'll use it at the drop of a hat to get our way. Well, don't you believe it! Do you know what to believe? Believe we live for justice. Fair wages for men and women. Believe we wish to end the terrible working conditions you have to live with at the mills."

Hundreds of fists pounded the air in unison.

"Strike! Strike! Strike!"

A woman carrying an infant in her arms called out. "And who's to feed my children if need be while the strike goes on?"

"If we do strike," Ravelli said, "we'll be setting up a food store on the corner of Prospect and Ellison for you and your families to turn to. And remember, the strike can not last. With spring coming, the mill owners will be having their busiest season. They can't afford a long strike. Now is the perfect time to act."

Another woman, her olive skin flushed by fear, confronted him. "But we can't afford to strike. None of us. We got no savings. You know that, Mr.IWW man."

"I ask you, madame, how can you afford not to? How can you ever possibly save any money at the pay rate the mill owners give you?"

"You said it, Mr.IWW. But what happens if we lose? Then where will we be?"

Eleanor turned to the back of the room, saw a burly man with a handle-bar moustache who seemed perfectly calm challenging Ravelli.

"You will not lose. You have to believe that." He began to rock his body back and forth as he spoke. "Do you know why? Because justice is on your side. What do you think will happen at the mills when you strike? All of you. Thousands of skeins of silk will be sitting in those mills during their busiest season. They can't afford not to meet your demands. But the main point I must make, once again, is that it can not be like all the other strikes when each union acted individually."

He frowned, shook his head. "That was your big mistake. And you know you paid for it. You all must stick together for there to be a complete, one hundred per cent shut down of all the silk mills throughout Paterson. If you vote strike, that's what you'll be voting for. Solidarity! Solidarity is the answer!"

A worker in the audience near the platform jumped onto the stage. "Enough talk. Let's call strike. Now! All in favor of strike raise your hand!"

The workers embraced his words, cried "Strike!" in unison.Hundreds of arms of the broad-silk weavers shot into the air.

The woman with the ribbon in her lapel grabbed Eleanor by both arms, caught up in the excitement. "Don't be afraid! You'll win, I know it. You heard what he said. They'll help you all the way."

Eleanor stood trembling, her attention still on Ravelli, the onrush of workers nearly knocking her to the floor. She stumbled, fell against the woman, who caught her. She finally regained her footing and just as quickly lost her in the turmoil.

Some of the workers grabbed Ravelli, lifted him onto their shoulders, carried him through the crowd. They moved by her quickly, their frenzy apparent. For a moment she thought he looked at her as he passed, but she must be mistaken.

She clutched her coat tighter, donned her cap, began to think about searching for her mother. She longed to get out of the hall and its acrid smell of hundreds of bodies. She hoped to avoid the woman with the ribbon in her lapel and the beautiful comb, fearful she would once again remind her of the women's march. But she could not move quickly enough to avoid encountering her again.

The woman grasped her sleeve. "Listen, I want you to know that if necessay, I'm here to help you. I'm down on Ellison Street. I'm a doctor at the Women's Alliance. I'm Mary Lafferty."

She extended her hand to Eleanor.

"Eleanor O'Bannion. I thank you for that. I can't help myself. I'm afraid of this strike. I don't think it will be as easy as they think."

"You'll remember what I said about help if you need it? You must fight the injustice at the mills whatever it may cost."

Eleanor nodded, then turned. "How strange. Lafferty's Silk Mill, that's where I work. And that's your name too."

The woman's face became rigid. "Not strange at all. George Lafferty is my father. Goodbye then."

Eleanor stood speechless, watching her disappear into the crowd.

Eleanor felt glad she did not encounter her mother for the walk home. She needed to think.

She decided to sit on the bench where she often sat, facing the Paterson Falls. She stared at them a long time, covered in icicles, hanging like deformed fingers. The sky of black velvet obliterated the stars. The only light emanated from the streetlamps casting halos along the path of the street. Needles of sleet began to fall, pricking her face. Yet, she would rather endure the cold than see the look of fright in her mother's eyes at the thought of the strike.

Her love for her mother saved Eleanor. Elizabeth fought for her to go to school, unheard of for a mill worker's child, her payments for her picking work making up for the wages Eleanor would have received at the mill. Because of her mother's determination, Eleanor could read. Stories Elizabeth told her during childhood flooded her mind. *The Little Princess, The Wind in the Willows*, Kate Greenaway's books.

Her mother's love of flowers also transferred to her. Even as a little girl she loved to caress the exquisite flower patterns on the jacquard silk her mother picked, Elizabeth identifying them while she stood amazed by their shape and color. As she grew older, she devoured every book she could about flowers and began painting them. If she could not buy the books picturing them, could not grow them in a garden, she would possess them on paper. Along with bags her mother saved for her, Colin brought her samples of dye used to color the silk at the mill and a paintbox. She loved the sound of their names: anemone, jonquil, periwinkle, peony, wisteria, so many others. She pasted their images upon the cracked wall above her cot, comforted by them in her aloneness.

The sleet began to soak the newspapers tied around her shoes. She must go home. Her mother would surely be worrying about her by now. Still she sat motionless.

Three men approached, two with woolen coats, collars up, caps nearly covering their brows. The third's dark hair glistened from wetness, his jacket collar pulleduparoundhisneck, soaked, inadequate for such a night. She immediately recognized Dante Ravelli. They appeared animated, absorbed in discussion. Two glanced at her as they passed, looked away. Ravelli paused.

"You should be going," he said. "It's such a cold night, you know. A young girl like you should not be out alone."

"I'm all right."

She stared at him, her clear, gray eyes meeting his. She felt glad her face must be red from the cold. She knew she blushed as he looked at her.

He stepped back. "Why, Eleanor, isn't it? Your father's wake. That's where I saw you. You showed a great deal of strength that evening. You seemed very brave."

She glared. If he only knew. "You don't have to compliment me, but thank you."

"I try never to say anything I do not mean." He sat down on the wet bench. "You don't like me very much, do you?"

"I don't like what you're doing, that's all. My father, as you know, he was in the IWW. He was a great believer in violence."

"I tried to make that clear tonight, that the IWW does not think that is the first answer in a strike. We'll do all we can to settle peacefully."

"But you know that won't happen. And if not, you'll use violence, won't you?"

He hesitated.

"If every other road has been taken, sometimes violence may be the only solution. There comes a time we must act on our beliefs, no matter what the cost. Or we are nothing."

"And what do you really care about us," she said. "Once the strike is over we're the ones who'll be left to pick up the pieces. We're the ones who'll never get back what we lose. Never. And you'll be gone to another place to stir up other workers."

"You will not lose. We are here for you. Sometimes workers need a voice to speak for them, a voice to help them eventually speak for themselves. Please believe me, I will do anything I can to help you gain victory."

She studied his face as he spoke, watching him now as he pushed back his soaked hair from his face with his chapped hands, each time wind and sleet blustering and blowing it awry again.

"You should have a heavier jacket. And a hat."

"What?"

"A heavier jacket, and a hat."

"Oh." He stared at his jacket. "Yes, I should. I don't seem to ever find the time to buy one."

"Well, you need to find the time." She rose abruptly. "Especially since I think it's going to be a very long winter for you here."

"We'll see." His voice lowered. "You've survived the death of your father. What could be worse than that?"

She wanted to cry as high as the sky that she thrilled at the knowledge of her father rotting in the earth, being devoured by maggots. Instead, she wiped her dripping nose, somewhat embarrassed.

"Are you sure you don't want me to accompany you home? Please. You can't continue sitting here in this brutal cold and sleet." She began to rise slowly. "I'm all right."

He offered his hand.

She turned away. "But I do thank you." She pointed to the end of the street. "Your friends are waiting."

"Will you support the strike, be there tomorrow with the other workers?"

"Of course I will. I'm not a scab, if that's what you think. Goodbye."

She trudged ahead before he could respond, in the sleet and slush, the flapping of her broken shoe soles clicking on the sidewalk, the newspapers tied around them now soaked and torn. She heard his friends call from the distance as she turned down Market to Ellison, to the tenement.

The broad-silk weavers were out less than a week when the dyers' helpers joined the strike. The proposed four-loom system did not affect them, but they desired an eight-hour day, not a ten-hour one they put in now, plus Saturdays. And they struck for improved working conditions as well. The broad-silk weavers, because of the special requirements to weaving silk with all its delicacy, had good lighting, cleaner working conditions. But the workers in the dye houses walked in dirty rooms filled with steam and fumes. In summer the steam suffocated, in winter it condensed quickly and froze. Moisture often saturated the ground, penetrating their feet when they trudged across the wet floor, even though they wore heavy clogs. Lung disorders prevailed. Stomach pains remained common. They often had to taste mixtures of dyes for consistency, dip their hands in boiling chemicals, blistering and then infecting their fingers. When Eleanor heard of these conditions, she realized the ribbon weavers should join the strike on principle.

Yet, at first she secretly hoped the ribbon weavers might hold out a little longer. She enjoyed her daily lessons from Nora, felt a sense of accomplishment at her growing ability to create ribbons without help. Then she discovered she was required to sign a contract withholding half her year's wages if she left before the year's end or went on strike. She found herself becoming more and more tense, fearful about the rule of being fined for laughing, talking, or opening a window. She stopped taking a few moments to catch a breath of air outside during lunch. If she forgot the hour and returned after the lunch bell, she would be locked out and docked a day's pay. She hated Saturdays when she was required to stay after work and clean up on her own time. The girls who worked at Lafferty's almost a year now had much more to lose if they struck, almost half a year's salary. She realized she must vote for a strike in sympathy and solidarity with them and the broad-silk workers and dyers' helpers.

In less than two weeks from the day the dyers struck, she, along with the other ribbon weavers, voted unanimously to join them.

Eleanor awoke to the sound of pellets of ice clicking on the window of their apartment. It would be a difficult day standing outside Dexter Lambert's Silk Mill, their focus of picketing today. She worried more for her mother, who joined the protestors without hesitation, though she worked at home as a picker, not fully employed. After a quick cup of tea, she and her mother tied rags around their feet, covered their heads down to their brows with caps, and buttoned up, readying for the picket line.

Before they left Eleanor paused, studying her wall of flower paintings. Their beauty distracted her from the room, its walls moaning from cold, its furniture threadbare, its floor boards buckling. Daffodils with verdant leaves, roses in shades of blushing pink, sunflowers surrounded by cinnamon centers, so many others. She whispered their Latin names, copied perfectly from the library book she borrowed, enamored by such beautiful words, *"Rosea americans, arthurium, botanicus, bellis perennis, calandrinia--"*

"Time to go, dear."

She clenched her lips. Her eyes became gray stones.

As they approached the mill, she could see that chaos ruled even at this early hour. The police shoved the strikers, especially the IWW members who wore their badges defiantly. One officer built like a butter churn smashed the head of a picketer with his club. The picketer fell face forward in the gray snow. The policeman raised the club again, but another officer restrained him.

"Dirty Commies!"

A few picketers bent down over the injured man. The rest of the crowd lunged at the officer full force.

Eleanor and her mother shoved themselves into the mass of bodies, pushing a stoop-shouldered officer who held his club tightly, arm raised. The strikers managed to knock him into the snow before he could bring it down.

She eyed a car moving through the crowd of strikers, forcing them to lurch out of its way. Eleanor immediately recognized the car of the National Dyeing Company, conveniently loaned to the police for patrol of the strike. Some of the strikers began pounding and shaking the car, chanting.

"Four looms. Never! Bless the IWW!"

"Four looms. Never! Bless the IWW!"

"Four looms. Never! Bless the IWW!"

Suddenly their rallying cry halted as the police clubbed three more men and women. Another woman with a smashed shoulder fought back, punching amidst her pain.

The foghorn sound of the police wagon blared in the distance, slowly growing louder as it plod along through the crowd of strikers.

Eleanor saw Dante Ravelli and five members of the Central Strike Committee they elected standing on the stone wall surrounding Dexter Lambert's mill, shouting to the endangered crowd, attempting to calm the growing storm.

A rubbery-faced woman rose from the ground where she was comforting her husband who lay in a pool of blood. She pulled a heavy stone from the wall surrounding the mill, threw it full force into the face of one of the police officers. "Dirty bastard, clubbin' my man! What'd he do? We was only standin'!"

The officer tackled her, her arms and legs fluttering in all directions as he threw her into the police van before it had even come to a full stop. The woman landed hard, face down.

Eleanor pushed forward as hard as she could, to get near the wagon, noted reporters from the Paterson *Evening News* and the New York *Call* frantically snapping photos. Dante and the others on the Strike Committee still stood on the stone fence surrounding the mill, attempting to calm the rioters, drowned by their cries.

"God bless the IWW!"

"God bless the IWW!"

"God bless the IWW!"

Police continued to punch and shove the workers, who punched and shoved back. A burly officer with a pock-marked face lugged Dante off the wall and hurled him to the ground. Eleanor could see the veins at his temples throbbing as he rose and hit the officer in the face. Another policeman locked his arms behind his back while the first one punched him in the stomach. Then he threw him to the ground. He dragged Dante across the slush and cobblestones to the lock-up wagon.

"Get in the wagon, you Commie scum!"

He shoved him onto the floor, next to other strikers headed for jail. Eleanor looked in, saw him rise. He began to pound on the window.

"Keep fighting! Keep up the fight!"

His voice was almost inaudible amidst the deafening roar of the crowd. But still he shouted. The workers stood aghast seeing one of their leaders receive such treatment.

Eleanor's blood sizzled. She found herself punching the officers on their arms, backs. "Let him go! Let him go!"

She might as well have been hitting stone.

She looked into the wagon through the bars. Dante stood, fingers squeezing his nostrils to stop the dripping blood. Then he bent down next to the woman they had thrown in earlier, took a handkerchief from his pocket, and wiped blood from her splintered hands. He placed his arm around her, lifted her to a seat on one of the fitted benches built on each side of the wagon.

Eleanor retreated from the crowd, watched as the police scrunched a few more members of the Strike Committee into the wagon, the workers clawing at the police the whole time. Finally two officers stood in front of the lock-up wagon, guns raised to hold back the crowd, then snapped it shut.

She saw one last vision of Dante Ravelli, crushed in with the others, sitting on the bench, comforting the woman.

Then he was gone.

Dante and the others from the Strike Committee refused food, and since the authorities feared they would cause even more sympathy on the part of the workers if they remained in jail, they were released after three days.

Eleanor and Elizabeth continued to picket from 7 a.m. until 2 p.m. when other strikers relieved them. Every day the police managed to lock up a few workers. And every day the anger of the strikers grew at the injustice of the lockups, and this made the IWW even stronger. After a few weeks with no end of the strike in sight, the broad-silk manufacturers, silk dyers' associations and the ribbon manufacturers began meetings to decide on a plan of action.

The strikers, now clearly led by the IWW, would not budge. During a strike a few years back, a few manufacturers agreed to conditions of the Socialist Labor party. When the strike ended, they renounced the workers' contracts. The workers remembered this, and the IWW remained adamant no agreements with separate mills would be considered.

The manufacturers, largely influenced by Catholina Lambert, the most powerful silk mill owner in Paterson, vowed they would risk everything rather than be defeated by a union. Many belonged to the National Association of Manufacturers, which decreed unions would not be tolerated under any circumstances.

The stalemate continued.

March passed as a succession of daily pickets. April slipped into Eleanor's life quietly, announced by the first crocuses blooming in the gardens of the mill owners' homes. She sighed. At least she would have some respite watching the gardens on Silk Road bloom.

Almost two months passed since the call for strike, but today she would not think of it. The warm sun uplifted her as she walked home slowly after another grueling day on the picket line. She looked for Dante every day but never spoke to him again. His attention was always riveted on the strike. Most of the time she watched him conferring with Elizabeth

Gurley Flynn, Carlo Tresca, and the most famous leader of the IWW, Bill Haywood, in Paterson to help organize and give encouragement to the strikers.

As usual, she held back from walking home to the tenements with the other strikers. She preferred to be alone. Most worshipped the IWW. She still had her doubts and didn't want to converse on the topic. The one week they said the strike would last was already close to two months.

As happened almost every day, she saw one of the O'Brien detectives, a Newark agency hired by Weidmann Silk Company as adjuncts to the police. They received five dollars a day to escort a group of strikebreakers onto the trolley after they finished work. She sighed, thinking of the food those men would be eating tonight.

An irate crowd of dyers' helpers booed the scabs as they entered the trolley. One flung a stone at the strikebreakers. She noticed that a number of other strikers from the dye houses and mills watched from their porches. One man, a tall, gaunt Italian, sat with his child on his porch step studying the brewing melee just a few feet from her. If the police and O'Brien detectives didn't act quickly to quell the strikers, those workers would become part of the fracas as well.

A few militant strikers blocked the steps of the trolley, refusing to let the scabs enter. Detectives, strikers, scabs began shoving back and forth.

"*Scumato!*" A bald man, eyeglasses too small for his fat face, grabbed a scab. "*Scumato!*"

The O'Brien detectives immediately attacked the strikers.

"Lousy wops! Get the hell out of the way!"

One clubbed the bald man. The rest of the strikers pounced on the detectives, and the scabs took those few seconds to break away, jump on the trolley.

The detectives refused to relent. One across the way from Eleanor pulled his gun from its holster.

The man on the porch with his child must have seen it as well. He stiffened, cradled the baby in his arms, and turned towards the shelter of inside his home.

A shot pierced the air. The immigrant slumped onto the porch. Blood gushed from his lower back. His child fell from his arms to the floor and began to wail.

She knew by the furor of the group attacking the O'Brien detectives they didn't realize what happenened.

The baby crawled to his father's body, touched him. Blood covered his fingers; he smudged his father's shirt with prints of crimson.

A woman ran through the door, grasped the baby, bent down over the immigrant. "Valentino! Ma *amore*! Valentino!"

Eleanor stood frozen. Someone should run to help the woman. She realized she was closest to her, yet her mind rebeled. The police would question exactly what she saw, and she felt uncertain about it even now. Had the bullet strayed when the detective shot his gun to frighten the strikers? Had he aimed at the Italian? Had he staggered, lost his footing for no reason before the gun went off? Her heart began to hammer. If only she had walked home with the other girls, she'd be almost home by now.

She ran.

As she fled, her mind whirled, nausea choking her at the vision of the baby bathed in blood, still trying to piece together the incident. But she felt one certainty. If the immigrant died, this senseless killing would be one more disaster that the strike brought.

She finally turned the corner of her street, staggered into the back yard. She caught her breath, attempting to compose herself before facing her mother. A few minutes passed as she stared at the languid river running parallel to the back of the tenement row. Green algae, still and stagnant, scalloped its edge. Little rain last summer and sparse winter snow had not replenished its usual gushing current, which would emerge soon with spring showers. Broken bottles, rusted cans, egg shells, torn bags of garbage lay naked on the banks, waiting for the strong rains of spring that would erase its stench, wash it away.

"Eleanor, what ever are you doing down there?"

She jolted at the sound of her mother's voice, saw her at the top of the stairs.

"Come on up. Good news. I stopped at the IWW store and they had some potatoes. We're having soup."

She felt certain her mother did not recognize any change in her, took her seat at the table.

"Do you know who was giving out food?" her mother said. "Dante Ravelli. You remember him, from the wake? Such an important man to take the time to help give out food."

Eleanor frowned. "Did you remind him the strike's lasted close to two months now, not the week he said?"

Her mother studied the kettle on the stove a moment, then carried the water for tea to the table. "Don't be like that. You know he's doing his best. We all are. And I saw Colin. I invited him and Mr. Ravelli for Sunday dinner sometime if he can come. What there'll be of it. Though Colin will help with food, I know. He's been good about that. He's become awfully close with Ravelli, I guess with the union and all."

Eleanor rubbed her teacup handle hard. "Why did you do that? He has friends he can eat with, from the IWW."

"I don't know why you feel like that. He's such a good man."

She rose abruptly from the table. "I'm too tired to talk about it."

"But the soup--?"

"I'm not hungry."

"Don't you want tea? You always have tea."

"I'm tired."

Her mother's stare penetrated her.

She sat back down.

"I'd never have invited him if I thought you--"

"I don't care."

If only she could leave the table, lie down on her cot, look at her flowers to calm herself. She sat in a heap of confusion at the thought of having dinner with a man she wanted to dislike yet hoped to see each day at the picket line.

But she could not arouse her mother's suspicion about her feelings.

"How's your cold? I'm sorry I didn't ask about it first thing when I came home."

"My cold? Better." Her mother poured more reviving tea. "I should be able to be back on the picket lines tomorrow. How did it go today?"

"All right"

"Did you hear anything new?"

Eleanor stared at her soup. "Nothing."

"Just another day then?"

"Yes."

She envisioned the repercussion the shooting of the mill worker would bring, lifted her cup with as steady a hand as she could, sipped her tea.

If only it had been just another day.

Valentino Modestino died that evening at Paterson General Hospital. The next day at the picket line all everyone talked of was the shooting. Not even the O'Brien detectives claimed one of the pickets fired or even possessed a gun when Modestino was shot. As it turned out, six picketing men identified a man named Cutherton, an O'Brien detective, as the killer. Some witnesses said they saw Cutherton and another special detective emerge from a bar, stumbling and looking intoxicated, just before the shooting. One striker said he thought Cutherton was dangerous and complained to the police about it at the time. They did nothing. Eleanor could not bear to attend the funeral and pleaded illness. Her mother returned that afternoon, red-eyed.

"So sad. The wife and child." Elizabeth squeezed her handkerchief. "We marched without talking through Paterson, past St.Michael's, down to Laurel Grove Cemetery. The IWW leaders, they gave each one of us a red carnation." Her mother's eyes filled. "The symbol of the blood that was shed. Each one of us put ours on the casket after Father Garrity spoke. It was flowing over with red carnations. You couldn't see the casket anymore. Thousands of them." Her mother paused, blew her nose. "I didn't know it was the IWW color too. Did you?"

Eleanor nodded.

"But they said with the evidence from witnesses at the shooting there will be justice for the poor man. Thank the Lord they came forward. He'll surely get his punishment now. After all, this O'Brien detective, he was identified. And being drunk. Don't you think?"

"I--hope so."

Her mother put her hand on Eleanor's brow. "Are you feeling better? Your forehead isn't hot."

She nodded.

"I'll heat up what's left of that potato soup. It'll fix you up. Rest for a while, til I call you."

She retreated to her cot, her crying muffled in her pillow, wet with tears. Why didn't she speak up? What was wrong with her?

Days passed. Still the strikers picketed, following their lack of progress in the Call. Colin often arrived for Sunday dinner bringing other bits of news along with a chicken or piece of bacon. Elizabeth accepted his gifts graciously, but only that, never money for daily needs, knowing his pocket must be beginning to drain as well.

One Sunday he arrived with a chicken, announcing Dante Ravelli would arrive soon for dinner. He hoped Elizabeth did not mind. Finally, he'd be able to spare a few hours to spend with them. Colin said Dante looked gaunt. He was limiting his food intake as part of the IWW show of solidarity with the workers.

Colin came for dinner more often than ever since her father's death, and as the weeks progressed, Ravelli continued to visit on Sundays and dine with them as well. Eleanor's mother seemed especially proud to have an important figure in the union dining at their humble home. Colin said Dante would have been just as pleased to eat in a cave, if he enjoyed the company.

Ravelli came more often, and Eleanor tried her best to avoid him. She ate as quickly as possible, then retreated to the back porch trying to read, though for some reason she was unable to concentrate. She avoided speaking to him unless absolutely necessary. She certainly did not dislike him. She still distrusted his repeated promises of victory.

And her guilt at having run away after the shooting of Modestino plagued her. Ravelli would despise her.

But much as she fought her emotions, she admired him more and more. She finally had to admit she desired his approval. She wished she could overcome feeling so small and shriveled, hovering in the shadow of his presence when he approached her.

When he arrived this Sunday with Colin, they stormed through the door. Ravelli thrust a bottle of wine into her mother's hands. "Would you open this please, Mrs. O'Bannion?"

He and Colin swooped down into the parlor, turning to her mother and Eleanor.

Dante pounded his arm on the sofa. "Well, the police and the O'Brien detectives have won. Cutherton has not been indicted. They got him an attorney from Weidmann's Mill. And Dyer, who was also at the shooting? He wasn't indicted either, even though he was a former policeman in Newark, fired for drinking. But, of course, this did not get taken into account in our great justice system. Six pickets testified both of them appeared drunk, that Cutherton pulled his gun out, acting wildly, and shot. And he's been let go go!"

Colin jumped up from the sofa, rushed towards the kitchen, plopped down at the table, stared in anger at the cutlery. "It's not a great secret that the manufacturers have the support of the police, with Chief Bimson patroling around in National Silk's car, for God's sake." He thrust his fingers through his hair. "God knows how many other ways they've been bought off. I can't take it any more, I tell you! The injustice. I can't take it!"

Elizabeth quickly handed each of them a large glass of wine, darted to the oven to check the chicken, rushed it to the table.

Ravelli drank his wine in a few gulps. "Worse than that, the manufacturers have the support of the courts. Tell me, is it a coincidence the Passaic County grand juries that indicted the pickets as well as our IWW speakers refused to indict Cutherton and Dyer? The judges are appointed, and you know who controls them. The manufacturers, of course."

"This will only make the strikers fight harder." Colin made a fist, punched his thigh. "Let them try all they can, they won't break the strike! The assaults on the pickets are getting worse and worse. And it all goes back to Mayor McBride. Everybody knows he's backed by the mill owners. And how about that commission he set up?"

He rose from his chair, pointed his finger at Ravelli, attacked the air. "The silk manufacturers got the stronger representation. But that's all right. It's all right. The strike will not be broken. We'll win in the end."

Eleanor listened carefully as they vented their anger, mashing the potatoes more and more aggressively, finally plopping them on the table.

As usual, Colin and Dante's conversation about the strike continued to dominate the meal and afterwards. Dante mentioned in passing that food in the pantry set up by the IWW had diminished to a frighteningly low level. How could they be so passionate about the rightness of a strike that now began to endanger the lives of thousands of men, women, children? But Eleanor forced control, kept her mouth shut.

Dante poured the last of the wine and raised his glass. "Modestino, his death must not be in vain."

Her throat constricted. She excused herself, darted from the table to the back porch, enveloped in the silence of the Sunday evening. Normally when she sat here, the vision of her father lunging to his death came back to her. It was one of her treasured memories. But now once again her heart flooded with guilt at her cowardice at the shooting. The vision of Modestino's child, his fingers crimson from touching his dying father, obsessed her.

She gazed at the tranquility of the river, letting its comfort sink into her. The much-needed spring rains had finally arrived. The garbage had washed away at last. The air smelled pure and fresh. She eyed the cluster of mills across this stretch of the river, parallel to it, mammoth rectangles of stone, their windows hundreds of black mouths, voiceless now with the strike.

She realized Dante stood above her.

"The water is so peaceful, isn't it?"

She did not answer.

"Would it be all right if I sit down?"

"I--suppose."

"I'm sorry. I think I must have upset you speaking of Modestino. Such a tragedy."

"I'm all right."

"I spoke with Mrs.Modestino, you know. Fortunately she has her relatives to comfort her at this sad time."

"I'm glad."

"You know, before her husband was shot she was look-ing from her window. And she saw a young girl standing nearby, not with the group, just a few feet away. She heard the shot, and when she saw the horror on that girl's face, she knew it was her husband or child who had been shot."

"Did she?" She hardly heard her voice.

"Yes, she did. She said she remembered this girl, a beau-tiful girl, because she was so admiring of her hair that flowed down her back. Sienna."

"Sienna?"

"In Italian it means red. No. More copper." He sat down next to her, covered her hand with his. "Like yours."

Words strangled in her throat.

"I think I might know this girl."

She forced herself to spring from the chair. "You think I'll deny it, don't you? Well, I won't!"

He stood slowly, faced her. She felt him studying her, could not defeat his knowing look. She bowed her head, cov-ered her face with her hands.

"It was horrible. The blood. The baby. Soaked in it. And what did I do? I ran."

She buried her face on his shoulder, tears wetting his shirt. The warmth of him felt strange and comforting. He encircled her in his arms.

What was wrong with her? This was the man who was destroying their lives with false hope. She tried to push him away.

He held her tighter.

"Is that what you wanted to hear? What a coward I am? Not strong, perfect, like you? You would have run to help her, I know it. I don't know why I get so afraid." She caught her breath. "I'm so tired of it, being afraid. Of so many things, but always hiding it. Hiding it."

"Listen to me. You think I am not afraid at times? I hide it myself. Please hear me. You've had your own worst punishment. It is time to stop your suffering and get on with life. There is no time for suffering. There is too much work to be done now."

She sighed with relief. He did not condemn her. She let his strength enfold her.

"I'm so ashamed."

"Do not live with shame. Or guilt. It accomplishes nothing."

Her thoughts darted to her father, of her constant fear while he was alive. Was that when she learned to live with shame and guilt? Did she believe it would end when he died?

"I'll tell you something. When I was your age, I surely might have run away. We grow. We become stronger."

He held her until she calmed down. She had never been held this way by a man. By anyone. So much of her life centered around learning to conceal hurt, deny emotion.

She sat down again, wiped her wet lids on her sleeve. "I don't want my mother to see me yet. She'll know I've been crying."

"She'll notice, even if you stay out here a time. Your eyes are very red. And mothers know such things. She can know. She will not condemn you either."

She avoided his look, straightened her dress, tried to study the worn flowers scattered on it. "I'm glad you aren't thinking I'm a bad person, Dante. Somehow, that's important to me."

"Ah, finally I am Dante instead of Mr.Ravelli. Things are improving around here." She laughed in spite of herself.

"And never would I think of you as a bad person."

She met his look. What did he think as he searched her face?

"Look at you," he said. "How you struggle to survive every day.The stick you have become. Don't speak to me of shame or fear. When I look at you, I see a girl who has great courage."

He sat next to her, kissed her on the cheek. The touch of his lips made her flesh feel sacred.

"Why don't we go inside? You know tomorrow is Flag Day. I still have to meet tonight with the Strike Committee about our plans."

They went back inside. She watched his every gesture as he spoke with Colin about tactics for Flag Day. He did not look at her again, except to say his goodbyes. But still, something had passed between them.

Dante ached, body and soul. And he must still write to his parents in Italy when he returned to his flat. His whole life of dedication to the cause of the workers emanated from the memory of his parents' lives. He remembered his childhood, mostly as scorching sun hovering over Sicily, leaving parched crops in spring and summer. Then when winter arrived useless deluges battered those same fields, flooding their land. When unification brought water control, they were overjoyed. Until they learned only the wealthy north would benefit.

In the 80s came the relentless depression. Wheat became dust. Then the government decided to increase taxes on grain and salt, invaluable in a land needing salt to preserve food. That year he and his parents lived mostly on roots and grass.

And while the peasants nearly starved, the landowners, the *latifondi*, confiscated almost ninety per cent of southern

Italy's land. He changed after that, convinced that organizing workers and using violence if necessary was the only way to defeat the capitalists who preyed upon the poor and weak.

He begged his parents to come with him to America, start a new life. But they would not leave their heritage, their land, though it constantly betrayed them.

He left Italy brokenhearted at leaving them but idealistic concerning his future.

The misty rain felt refreshing against his skin. If only it would help him clear his mind. The strike had lasted nearly three months now. After hundreds of hours of negotiations with the Strike Committee and the mill owners, there was still no end in sight.

He grabbed a Chesterfield from the packet of cigarettes in his pocket, his one indulgence. His hands shook as he lighted it. He thought of Eleanor, remembering the time he sat with her in the sleet and snow, her prediction of a long strike. He envisioned her eyes. Gray steel, yet so full of sorrow. And tonight. The memory of holding her, feeling her bones jutting from the flesh of her back, the touch of her hollow cheek upon his lips.

He stood in the darkness, repulsed at himself for the desire awakened in him in those moments for a girl easily half his age. He had not been with a woman for a long time. That must surely be part of it. He understood desire. It had no part in his work in Paterson. He must prepare himself for the violence that might come soon. He would be ready. He brushed the memory of her aside, along with so many others haunting him.

It would pass.

Eleanor tossed and turned most of the night. Morning came too quickly. She vowed to forget the incident with Dante. All her efforts must be on survival, and right now she needed to get through Flag Day.

The manufacturers still tried to belittle the IWW as Communist radicals. Bimson, the chief of police, constantly tried to force 'those dirty Commies,' as he called them, out of Paterson. Elizabeth Gurley Flynn, Carlo Tresca, Big Bill Haywood and Dante Ravelli had to move their meetings to nearby Haledon. But the more Bimson ranted against them, the more the strikers became grateful for the IWW's unconditional support. Every Sunday cries for justice echoed so loud in Haledon the strikers hoped they surely resounded to Paterson.

Eleanor and Elizabeth walked toward Lafferty's, the focus of the strikers today, noticing the manufacturers' attempt to appeal to the workers' sense of patriotism and the American Dream. Huge flags flapped in the breeze at Dexter Lambert, Frankes, Barbour Flax Spinning, Passaic Rolling Mills, Lafferty's, Hamilton and Booth, Bamford's Ribbon and the rest of the strip of silk and ribbon mills. Members of the IWW Strike Committee stood in the middle of Market Street, shouting their disgust at the mill owners trying to make the workers think they must choose between the flag of socialist revolution or the flag of America. Eleanor could not help but be impressed, though, seeing the giant cotton flag of the manufacturers hanging across Market Street, its slogan emblazoned across it:

"We live under the flag,

We work under the flag,

And we will defend this flag!"

She smiled at her mother. "For once the workers agree with something the manufacturers say."

Her mother nodded.

Eleanor noted Dante and other members of the Strike Committee beginning to distribute flyers. Her mother grabbed one from an IWW member.

Important! Come to Turn Hall at 8 p.m. tonight,

May 18, for the latest information on the strike! IMPORTANT!

That evening she and her mother arrived at Turn Hall a few minutes after 8 p.m., tried to push their way as best they could through the noisy crowd to hear the speakers. She especially wanted to hear Elizabeth Gurley Flynn, who had already begun to speak. She stood on the platform in a dark blue dress, a white collar accenting her pale skin and raven hair, moving her arms about with each phrase she spoke. Eleanor quickly forgot her legendary beauty, realizing her real power lay in her voice and in the force of character behind it. No wonder Chief Bimson and the manufacturers feared her.

"The IWW has done what no other institution in this city can do!" Flynn shouted over the crowd. "It has brought together men and women of all nationalities united in one goal--freedom from the oppression the manufacturers have made you live under! But that is over. Over!

"The employers are trying to frighten the businesses now to get them in sympathy with them, to get them to fear their businesses are menaced by the strikers, to turn businesses against us. Do you know 25,000 workers produce four million dollars for the mill owners? The bosses, a few hundred men at most, get three million dollars back. And how do the employers spend the three million? Do they spend it in Paterson and Paterson businesses? Does the Silk Association have its banquets here? No. They dine at the Waldorf-Astoria in New York City. Have their spacious offices here? No. Their address is 354 Fourth Avenue, New York City. Do the wives and daughters buy their gowns, silk or otherwise, their furs or jewels or automobiles in Paterson? Do they attend the opera in Paterson?"

She moved backwards towards the members of the committee, including Dante, who focused their attention on her.

"Whenever were Caruso and Tetrazini in Paterson, though there are thousands of their countrymen who would go without food to hear them once. Do the employers build their homes, attend church or send their children to school here? How many grocery, clothing, shoe, dry good or drug stores, meat markets, coal dealers or doctors and dentists could exist if they depended on the mill owners for patronage?

"We address these plain words to the businessmen of Paterson. The manufacturers and stockholders are not your customers. The workers are!"

She paused and the crowd broke into a roar. Haywood, Tresca and Dante, behind Flynn, linked hands and raised their arms above their heads. Seeing such anger sketched on Dante's face jolted Eleanor when she remembered how gently he spoke to her a few nights before.

Flynn stepped forward again.

"We must remain strong! The symbol of the red flag is not one to fear or hate. It--"

She was startled when a thick-set man with scruffy hair, one Eleanor recognized as a dyers' helper she often saw on the picket line, suddenly jumped on the platform. "Here's the red flag!"

He thrust his arm above his head, splayed his fingers, stained blood red from years of working with dyes at the mills.

The strikers stared in silence.

Flynn stood frozen.

A group of workers spontaneously began a line. Quickly the rest of the strikers including Eleanor and her mother, fell in behind them.

They marched around Turn Hall and out into the street, pounding the air with their fists crying, "Justice! Solidarity!"

The next day she rushed to the First Ward Branch of the public library, waited in line to read the Call and its comments about Flag Day.

"With flags flying and the city decked out in gala garb, the great silk mills reopened their doors and the ending of the gigantic labor wars was beautifully planned.

The factory workers were going to forgive their erring workmen. Mayor McBride and the police saw the end of trouble approaching. The ministers who had urged the workers to return understood that their exhortations were to be obeyed. It was a very successful end of the strike, marred by one thing--none of the workers went back."

She left the library with a smile on her face, decided to walk down to the IWW food pantry on the corner of Prospect and Ellison. She and her mother needed food assistance at this point. She refused to be stubborn in accepting help when it came to her mother's welfare.

The line of strikers waiting for food meandered around the corner to Market Street. After an hour or so of waiting, one of the IWW volunteers emerged.

"We have no food left for today. Maybe by tomorrow. Come back tomorrow."

Her stomach grumbled. Four months had passed. Food supplies were nearly diminished.

The strike showed not one sign of ending.

Charles Lafferty stared out his bedroom window at the garden in full bloom at his father's home on Silk Road. He had put on his old cotton shirt, pants, and galoshes, knowing the garden would still have spots of mud here and there from yesterday's rain. Normally he would have smiled at the thought of a whole summer ahead of him, watching the changing spectrum of color in the garden.

He had returned from Princeton three weeks ago with a degree in business as his father had desired. But he spent as much time as possible taking courses in botany, more and more interested in the concept of integrating nature into an architectural structure, popularized by the work of Mr. Frederick Law Olmstead. Based on his reading, he planned to make changes in their garden and landscape, but that was before he learned of the strike. He had understood little about his father's mill, except that it dominated the silk and dye mill district and provided the luxury he bathed in on Silk Road. He realized his father kept him unaware concerning its running. He had, in truth, been disinterested himself.

Until now.

Charles Lafferty kept track of the strike these three weeks since his return through the Call. At first he thought the newspaper might be biased towards the workers, until he compared its reporting to the New York Times. He read and reread them, not wanting to believe their content. As the weeks progressed and both newspapers reported the same facts he realized they must be true.

He sat in his room, his leather chair facing the garden, eager to get out and enjoy nature, yet compelled once again to read statistics given in an article in today's paper on wages his father paid workers. *Girl, 16 years old, employed at Lafferty's Silk Mill 32 weeks, average wage per week $1.85; woman employed at broadsilk, 2 looms, 40 weeks, average per week $7.17; male weaver 1 loom, 10 weeks, $10.59....*

He flung the paper down on the escritoire. The walking around money he carried in his wallet probably represented a month's wages for most of his father's workers.

His thoughts turned to his sister, Mary. She often spoke to him of injustices at their father's mill. He refused to believe her. Mary had always been at odds with her father because she felt he was insensitive towards their mother. But Charles's feelings were more complex. He knew he was a disappointment to his father. George Lafferty's dream was to have Charles take over the mill after he died, but Charles had no interest in it. He tried to alleviate his guilt at having disappointed his father by being as supportive and agreeable to him as he could.

Now these daily revelations in the newspapers soured his stomach. He realized he looked the other way too often, avoiding the truth about his father.

He went downstairs and found George Lafferty in his giant cavern of an office, ledgers and files surrounding him as usual, twirling his handlebar moustache, concentrating fully on his profit and loss ledger, its gold edges catching the glint of the sun as he turned its pages.

His father frowned at him. "Dressed for the garden, I see. I don't know what satisfaction you get puttering around out there. We've got the gardener and God knows, I pay him enough to do that sort of work."

Charles shrugged. "Father, you know I--"

"I'm sorry, Charles. Of course, if you enjoy that sort of thing." He rested his elbow on the desk and squeezed his fingers on his temples. "I'm just so sick and tired of this strike."

Charles stood above his father at his desk. "If you're so sick and tired of it, what must the workers feel?"

The crows' feet around his father's eyes slashed deeper across his skin as he squinted at his son. "There's no need for you to be concerned about these things. Eventually they'll lose. It's inevitable. We've still got plenty of excess yardage in Pennsylvania, and they never counted on that." He gestured to the ledger. "Our losses aren't half as bad as they expected. The plants out there are humming. The workers aren't so damned militant as those IWW scum."

"Perhaps I'd become more militant, too, if I worked for you for $1.85 a week."

His father's face reddened. He turned to a pile of recent newspapers on the floor, lashing his arm at them. "Pro-Communist rags. They don't give the whole picture."

"All of them? The New York Times?" Charles folded his arms across his chest, faced his father squarely. "Mary was right about you. All along."

His father closed his ledger slowly.

"I don't want her name mentioned in this house. You know that."

"You needn'tworryonthatscore. If thoseworkers don'tgeta decent settlement, I'm moving out. Perhaps I can find work apprenticing in landscape architecture. It's what I've wanted all along."

His father's face crumbled. "Moving out? Don't say such a thing, Charles. Look." He gestured around the room at the burgundy leather chair, the mahogany table inlaid with walnut, the Meissen propped in the teakwood cabinet, the velvet drapes trimmed with gold braid. "All of this. Everything I've done has been for you. You're all I have left now. I--"

"I couldn't enjoy it, father, not now. Not when I know of the pain that paid for it."

He turned, nearly ran from the room, his mind in shreds, his breath stifled as he passed the furnishings supplied by the sweat of the mill workers, besieged on every side by monuments of their suffering.

He finally slowed down as he entered the garden, knowing it would help him gain his equilibrium, as it always did.

Blessed Saturday. Eleanor slept until ll a.m. before going to meet Margaret Sanger, awell-known advocate ofbirthcontrolwhohad come to Paterson to help with the strike. The Strike Committee selected her to be in charge of sending the workers' children to sympathetic New York City families during the strike. Parents rebelled at first but relented when the IWW food store could no longer accomodate all the strikers, and their children began to suffer from lack of food. The Committee also reasoned sending them away would draw attention to their plight and more donations from the wealthy might be made to help them. Eleanor and other volunteers spent two hours helping eighty-five wide-eyed children to the trolleys that would take them to waiting families, mostly in New York City while weeping parents watched their children disappear into the horizon.

The growing inability of the IWW to feed thousands of strikers worsened each day. Eleanor and her mother could no longer rely on the IWW, now rationing insufficient food to each worker. They also decided that Colin must stop sacrificing his own small amounts of donated food for them.

The mill owners must give in.

They must.

The swelter of coming summer loomed early over Paterson. But today a cool breeze embraced her. The sun's energy comforted her, though she walked slower to conserve her strength. She turned up Fair Street, to Ryle Avenue, to Silk Road, stopping in front of the iron gate of the Lafferty estate, her favorite, watching the light explore the great house, its windows gleaming.

To Eleanor, the grounds were what gave the house its beauty. Bleeding hearts still dangled, aligned with hundreds of roses that would soon bloom in pinks and creams, flanking sections of the path's border. As summer progressed, they would be replaced by iris, peonies, black-eyed susans, sunflowers, so many others. She knew where and when every flower, shrub and tree would bloom from years of admiring the garden.

She imagined Mary Lafferty sitting in the dining room, having her breakfast of eggs, bacon, toast, waffles, and coffee served on porcelain plates. It seemed incomprehensible to her she would be at the strike meeting talking about women's freedom if she lived in this paradise.

"The flowers are lovely, aren't they?"

She startled, peering at the far side of the garden where the voice emerged. There was a man there in a cotton shirt, pants stained at the knees, in galoshes, carrying a trowel, the soil residue on it indicating he must have been digging in the garden.

She turned to run.

"Please. Miss! Don't run away. I'm so happy you're enjoying the garden."

She turned, watched him brush his forehead with the back of his free hand, leaving a smudge of soil.

"It's a lot of work, but worth it, I think."

She studied him. His short, brown hair crowned a plain face dominated by a nose too large for it and ears that stuck out like teacup handles. But when her eyes met his she saw their clear blueness. And he stood tall.

Then he smiled, and somehow his features softened.

"It's a wonderful time of year, isn't it?" he said.

"It is. I love to come here and look at the garden. It's my favorite by far of all of them on Silk Road. I hope it's all right."

"Why, of course. That is quite a compliment. I thank you."

"I've watched it change since the beginning of spring. It's planned just right, with one kind of plant dying off, then others coming into bloom to make up for it. You should have divided your iris, though. You won't get half the bloom you did last year."

He raised his brow, blinked.

She blushed. "I love flowers. I can't imagine being happier than when I'm around them. I get books about them from the library. It's free. Even the mill workers can go there.

And I can read. I'm not an ignorant girl, you know." It seemed essential he know that. "I paint them too. From the pictures in the books."

"They must be lovely, I'm sure. Won't you let me give you a bouquet?" He smiled. "As you can see, there are more than enough. And I don't think many people notice them as much as you do."

"I wouldn't want you to get in trouble. I'm one of the strikers from the mill. I'm sure you guessed. If Mr. Lafferty ever found out--"

"Let me worry about that. Wait here, won't you?"

He removed a small scissor from his pocket, cut her a variety of roses, large-budded salmon pinks, snow whites, blood fuschias, wrapping them with a handkerchief from his pocket.

She waited for him to return, the blazing sun causing dizziness that began to overpower her. If only she'd at least sipped some tea before leaving home. She swayed, clutching the iron gate separating her from him.

As he approached with her flowers, saw her condition, he quickly unlatched the gate, grasped her arm.

"Are you all right? Here. Sit down."

He guided her to the stone step next to the carriageway. She didn't know if her face reddened now more from the heat or embarrassment.

She hesitated, but as the street began to spin, she plopped onto the stone.

"Put your head down, between your legs."

Her eyes widened. "Pardon me?"

"Please trust me. It will help you bring blood to your brain."

She did as he asked, her copper hair cascading over her head in all directions.

"Young lady, when was the last time you ate?"

She did not answer.

"Stay right here. Don't go. Do you promise?"

She bobbed her head, knowing she would not be able to go anywhere until she mustered strength.

He returned a few minutes later with a paper bag filled with food and a piece of bread and jam. She snatched it from his hands, cramming it into her mouth.

She saw shock in his eyes, did not care.

He touched her arm lightly. "I hope that helps. Eat a little slower, if you can. You don't want to choke."

She ignored his advice, brushed her lips with her fingertips when she finished, licked them thoroughly.

"I want you to take that bag of food."

The bread and jam strengthened her. She sat a few moments, rose to leave as soon as she felt able, fearing Lafferty would see them from his window, run out, take the food.

"Thank you so much. For this."

She clutched the food, her arm cemented to the bag as she walked away.

"Dear girl, be brave. I pray this terrible strike will be over soon."

When she approached Ryle Avenue, she turned to see him still standing, watching her. He waved goodbye from the distance.

She carried the heavy bag as best she could, along with the bouquet. When she arrived home, her mother dashed to the bag of food.

Eleanor unwrapped the flowers, noticed the handkerchief that protected them, surprised at its fine creamy silk fabric. It must be one of Lafferty's castoffs. Or maybe he paid his gardener more than she realized. She placed the flowers in one of her mother's pots, admiring their color.

"It's God watching over us. I know it." Her mother smiled at the loaf of bread, potatoes, onions, apples, carrots, bananas as she unpacked them. "A miracle is what it is." She turned to Eleanor. "We must share some of this. It wouldn't be right to keep it all for ourselves, with all that are near starving."

"I don't see that we have to." She calculated the food could last at least a week or more if they stretched it. One whole week at least of not worrying about their next meal. "Don't you realize we don't have anybody, except ourselves? Nobody would care about sharing with us. You know they wouldn't."

"Of course they would." Her mother tapped the bag. "Someone did. And look how many times Colin's shared his food with us."

"Of course we'll share with him."

"And what about Mrs. Rooney?"

"She never shared any food with us, did she?"

"But how could she with no husband and three children to feed?"

"I won't let you make me feel guilty. I won't."

She plopped down until her mother called her to the table. They did not speak for a time. When she finished pouting,

finally dared to look at her mother, she could see she had been crying. Memories of the winter they'd survived, the absence of any reason to live except for her mother, pierced her.

"I was thinking," she said slowly, "about that poor girl that was injured the day I went to Lafferty's to apply for work. She never did come back, you know, with the strike. At least I never saw her on the picket lines, if she is back. If only she hadn't turned to smile at me, maybe to speak to me, she might not have--"

"Now don't go and blame yourself for that."

"But she never would have fallen." She rose slowly from the cot. "I'll bring her a few slices of bread. And an apple."

"You can't let this strike harden your heart, Eleanor. The Lord will see us through."

Eleanor held her tongue. She hated her mother's religious beliefs. But she never contradicted her, knowing she needed their comfort to survive.

"After church tomorrow I'll visit her, bring some food. But only the bread. And the apple."

Sunday they attended mass at St. Joseph's, their usual practice. Father Garrity's sermon seemed principally to say that the more one suffered on earth, the greater the reward in heaven. As usual her hands clenched when he spoke. But then she would look at her mother's face emanating such bliss. She studied her in silence, knelt with her at the railing during Communion, took the wafer into her mouth, and felt nothing.

She remembered the name and address of the injured girl, Catherine Devlin, from the ribbon weavers' conversations about her. She lived in a third-floor tenement next to Herlihy's Dry goods, not far from Eleanor's own River Street apartment. As she approached her tenement, she realized the clapboard building looked much like hers--three stories high, porches jutting from the back of each apartment, the Passaic River below running parallel to them, rills of water unleashed by the spring rains.

She climbed the squeaky steps and knocked on Catherine's door. No one answered. The weekly strikers' meeting in Haledon was a few hours away. Perhaps Catherine felt well enough to attend it and left early. Eleanor opened the screen door.

"Miss Devlin?"

No one responded. She entered, decided to leave the food. Her receiving it mattered more than knowing who brought it. She placed it on the kitchen table, glanced into the makeshift bedroom.

Catherine Devlin, nearly nude, lay on the floor, lines of blood trailing down her thighs.

"Miss Devlin!"

Eleanor ran to the bedroom, hovered over her. Clots of blood clung to her inner thighs, a large gob of flesh protruded from her vagina. The girl turned to her, her face sweaty, bloodless.

Eleanor knelt down, clasped her hand. "Don't be afraid. I'll get help."

She began to rise, but the dazed girl squeezed her arm, her cold fingers startling her.

"No--hospital."

But she must get her to the hospital somehow, yet didn't want to frighten her. "All right. But I have to get you help. I promise I'll be back. Are you well enough I can leave you?"

She nodded slightly, closed her eyes.

Eleanor darted down the stairs, her mind a jumble. She was certain the girl had no money to pay, but she must risk getting her to the hospital. She ran by instinct, headed towards St. Joseph's Hospital on Market Street.

But as she approached the IWW headquarters on Prospect, an idea struck her.

Dante.

He would surely know what to do. He knew everything.

She ran inside. Children like miniature cadavers sat on benches against the walls, the next group ready to take the trolley to New York City to their substitute families. A full-faced woman with lucid blue eyes directed some of the workers. She walked quickly towards Eleanor.

"Don't I know you? I'm Margaret Sanger. Are you here to help? Yes, I remember now, you helped us recently, didn't you? I--"

"I'm looking for Dante Ravelli. Is he around? I'm sorry. It's an emergency."

"Dante? He hasn't arrived yet. But--"

She did not wait for a full reply, turned to run towards her only alternative, St. Joseph's.

Outside the doorway in front of her stood Dante.

She sprang at him before he could enter the door. "Dante! You must help me. Now!"

"Will you slow down a minute?" His fingers seemed to penetrate her bones as he grasped her shoulders.

"I can't! There's a girl. She's bleeding. Down below." She felt herself blushing. "It won't stop. I don't know what to do. I'm sure she can't pay, but I'm going to the hospital to--"

"A girl? Where?"

"River Street, the tenement. Next to Herlihy's. The girl who fell on the machine. The day you were at Lafferty's. Please. I don't know what to do."

"Listen to me. Listen carefully. Go back to her. Do you understand? I'll get help. Next to the dry goods store? Herlihy's? Watch for me."

He pushed her away, began to run, turned to her as he ran. "I'll find help. Go on. Get back to her. Tell her."

He disappeared around the corner, the opposite direction from the hospital.

Had she made a mistake by trusting him? Should she have tried to get help at St. Joseph's? Her mistake could cause the girl to bleed to death. She ran back to the tenement, trying to vanquish her fear.

Catherine Devlin lay in the same position. She opened her eyes when she saw Eleanor again, did not move otherwise, her skin like chalk. Tears trickled down her face.

Eleanor kneeled, wiped them with the skirt of her dress. "I found someone. You'll get help now. You'll be all right."

She found a pan, filled it with warm water, applied a wet cloth to the girl's face, washed the blood from her thighs as best she could. The gelatinous mass still lay half embedded in her vagina. Then she saw it. What looked like a quarter-inch round piece of twig jutting from her opening.

The room began to sway.

She forced herself to examine it more closely. She must not panic, must remove it. But what if it broke off and a piece remained inside her, which would be worse?

Her breath came heavy. Where was Dante? He would know what to do.

Perhaps he couldn't get help.

If only she had gone to the hospital.

Minutes passed. The clock at City Hall tolled two. She half decided to run to the hospital. Then again, he might come with help. She paced the room back and forth, back and forth.

Catherine Devlin lay, eyes closed, motionless.

A carriage clattered below. She ran to the back porch of the apartment. Dante climbed out with a well-dressed woman carrying a satchel.

"Up here, Dante!"

She ran inside, quickly threw a blanket from a cot over the girl's lower body.

Eleanor recognized Mary Lafferty from the strike meeting as soon as she entered the room, efficiently attired in a white blouse with mutton sleeves and a stylish long skirt. Eleanor winced at the thought of the blood that would most likely splatter over it, though Mary Laffery didn't seem concerned.

She plopped down her satchel, lifted the blanket covering the girl, frowned, sighed deeply, turned to Eleanor.

"My dear, I'm here to help you. Don't be afraid any longer." She turned to Dante and Eleanor. "Can you find a pot and boil some water?"

Dante found a pot. He filled it, slammed it on the stove.

"I must remove what's inside, in there." She pointed to Catherine Devlin's vagina. "Everything must come out. Everything. Otherwise she could get a serious infection. If you could assist me, I would be grateful. If not--"

Eleanor swallowed hard. "I'll try."

She eyed Dante, noting his rage as he glared at the water beginning to boil. At the desperation of Catherine Devlin's condition? At Catherine herself? At the stupidity of a code that says a man must not look at a naked woman in such a condition? He placed the pot on the floor where the girl lay, avoided looking at her, his face a mask of fury as he went to the next room.

"I'm here if you need me, Mary. Call if you have to lift her to her cot"

"We can't move her yet. Eleanor, can you try to hold her--lower part--open as wide as you can?"

Eleanor blushed but did as she was told.

Mary examined Catherine Devlin. She slowly began to try to remove the twig in one piece. By then the girl lay unconscious.

Finally Mary extracted the embedded twig whole, along with the clotted mass, placed a long piece of metal in a bowl of aseptic solution, and pressed it gently into the girl's vagina, scraping away any residue still in the uterus.

Eleanor covered her with a blanket; she still remained unconscious. Dante helped lift her to the cot, then retreated to the kitchen chair, trying to control his temper.

Mary turned to Eleanor. "She wasn't aware, a blessing. I had to do it. We don't want septicemia to set in. I just hope she didn't perforate her uterus with that stick. She'll have to be watched closely."

Dante lunged from the kitchen, grasped the stick, smashed it across his knee, then helped Eleanor wrap the large gelatinous clots lying in a pot on the floor, placing them in newspaper and then a paper bag.

He stood above the girl on the cot. "And so we have another person to add to the statistics. Another woman who risks her life to abort an unwanted child."

Mary clenched her mouth, and the comment dissipated into emptiness.

After a time, Catherine Devlin opened her eyes, attempted a smile.

Mary held her hand. "The pain will eventually subside, dear. You were very brave. I think you're thoroughly clean in there now, but if it still pains you after a few days, you must get in touch with me at the Women's Alliance. Immediately. Perhaps Eleanor can stop in and contact me if I'm needed."

"Of course." Eleanor gently soothed the girl's forehead. "You'll be just fine. I'll stop and see you every day. I'll bring you more food, see if you're all right." She remembered from conversations with the women at the mill Catherine Devlin lived with two other girls. "No one has to know the circumstances. We put--everything--in this bag. I'll get rid of it. You can say you feel like the influenza's coming on and stay in bed a few days."

Mary cleansed her instruments and placed them in her satchel.

"I need to make a few more house visits. I usually do at the end of the day but might as well now since the carriage is out." She touched Eleanor on the arm. "You were wonderful, you know. So level headed. Have you ever thought of working at the Alliance? I can use a girl who doesn't faint at the sight of blood."

"The mill is all I know."

"But it doesn't have to be, does it?" She grasped her satchel, snapped it closed. "Think about it, won't you? You'll see Eleanor gets home all right, Dante?"

"Of course."

She whisked out the door before any one could thank her properly.

Eleanor looked in Dante's direction but did not meet his eyes. "I'll stay a while. I think I should." She sat next to Catherine on

the cot. "I may be here a long time. Until I feel she's all right. You should go. You have the meeting in Haledon soon."

"I'll wait for you."

He went to the next room, sat on the sofa, elbows on his knees, fingers steepled on his chin, staring at the floor.

She stayed by Catherine quite a time, her heart throbbing so hard she thought it would crack her ribs, hoping Dante would get tired and leave, then praying he would stay, fearing the emotions surging through her. He did not move from the sofa the whole time, sat studying the flaking plaster on the ceiling, the discolored walls, the cracked glass on one of the windows. She knew he must know by now Catherine finally slept peacefully, that she was stalling. She realized he would remain until they had to leave. Together.

She slowly lifted the bag holding the bloated lump of fetus, clots, twig, which must be gone when her roommates arrived.

Dante rose, stood by the cot, studying her. Always observing. If only she could read his thoughts.

"Why don't you let me take care of that?"

"I'll do it. It's all right."

She turned to Catherine who had awakened. "I'll help you. I promise."

"Yes," she managed, closed her eyes again.

She left with Dante, her body and soul raw with desire and confusion.

She held the bag tightly, trying not to imagine its contents. Without a word to each other they knew its destination. Halfway there Dante took it from her. They did not speak, walked past the mills adjacent to the river, sparkling and churning, past the mute tenements, peeling gray boxes lining the other side of the river's edge, then across the West Broadway bridge, abandoned now, most of the strikers in Haledon at the weekly Sunday meeting.

They stood at the end of the bridge, studying areas of strongest current. She found the embankment leading to the path she knew so well. The steep decline looked daunting. Dante went slowly at first, then held her hand, helped her maneuver her way down.

The water ran forcefully, its current catching the sun's light, glittering with streaks of gold. It finally disappeared amidst the underbrush of bushes ripe with red berries, thriving amidst Queen Anne's lace dotting the ground. They walked past large boulders that stood like sentinals for thousands of years, mute witnesses to time's passing. A few starlings swooped across the water, landed on the bushes, picked at the berries. She watched them devour the fruit.

Dante held her arm. "It's time."

She could not unclench her arm from the bag. He pried it from her, tossed it into the water.

The current baptized it, carrying it along on its journey. "It's for the best, Eleanor. I believe that."

"What's so sad is that I believe it too."

"It was a terrible thing you had to do, I know."

"I don't know what I would have done if you weren't there. At the headquarters."

"You were very courageous, helping Mary as you did."

"I was terrified."

"But you overcame it. I don't know how you have survived these past weeks with the strike. Now this. I don't."

They leaned closer to the water's edge, mesmerized by the bag, watched it carried by the current, sinking and rising, and finally rising no more.

They did not speak for a time.

"The strike will be over soon," he finally said.

"That's hard to believe."

"It will. One way or another. We can't hold out any longer, you see. We can't." He faced her, placed his hand on the hollow of her cheek. "The workers will starve if we don't." He half smiled in bitterness. "You were right all along. You knew it would be a hard battle. You are wiser than I am."

She saw sorrow lay deep in the shadow of his eyes.

"Dante, you did your best. Nobody could have done better. All the workers feel that way. And nobody could care about us more than you do."

She embraced him, her heart in shards at the thought of his pain at their defeat, knowing whether they won or lost, when the strike was over, he would leave.

"It isn't important I was right."

She continued to hold him hard, did not care how bold he might think her. He did not push her away.

"I need you, Dante. I do. I can't go on like this. Not anymore. I'm not the strong girl you think I am. I'm weak, and tired, and-"

"Stop it." His eyes misted. "Stop--" He kissed her. She felt the wonder of his flesh on hers, their hearts pounding against each other. She knew in these moments her heart would always be embedded with his, no matter where this love led her. She trembled, confused. How could she ever show him the depth of her love?

He loosened his hold on her, began to turn away. She grasped his arm, tugged it, forced him to face her again.

"How old are you?" he said.

She did not answer

"How old?"

"Almost eighteen."

"My God." He pressed his hand against his forehead. "Do you realize I'm over twice your age?"

She flung her arms around him again. "What does that matter?"

His face turned rigid. He pushed her away.

"Dante, what does it matter if I'm younger? I love you. And don't tell me I'm too young to know what it means to love someone."

He frowned. "Love is one thing. Desire is another."

"Is that all we feel for each other? Desire?"

He reached out for her, sheltering her in his arms. "How beautiful you are. Do you know that?"

"Skin and bones. That's what I am. Not pretty enough for you to care for me. I know that."

"The skin. And bones. The most beautiful part of all. A badge of honor."

His face stiffened again. He dropped his arms, began to move toward the path.

She watched him walk away. Her body without his touch felt like a puppet's with the strings cut.

"Come," he said. "I'll help you. We have to go. Now."

"I want to make love with you, Dante. I do. I don't care."

He walked back to her, stood struggling for breath, a single vein throbbing hard along his neck.

"I said we have to go."

She walked with leaden steps as he led her to the embankment, helped her up, her arms limp as water.

The street lay deserted when they reached the bridge.

"I'd better try to get to Haledon. The meeting. It must be three already, and I'm scheduled to speak. They'll wonder."

"I--don't think I can go today."

"Of course. I'll walk you part of the way. It's better you go home. Your mother can fill you in on what happens. Are you sure you're all right?"

"Yes. Really."

"Well, then, good."

They separated at Ryle Avenue, each lost in contemplation.

She bowed her head as she walked, reliving her declaration of love. Shame quickly replaced her joy. She was defiled. How could she ever could possess the love of a man like Dante?

She trudged towards the tenement, her defeat from near starvation trivial, bereft of hope, vanquished by love.

Catherine Devlin sat propped up on her cot. Bridget and Jeannie, her two other roommates, had long since left to go to the picket lines, half believing her story about influenza, wondering why she half-heartedly entered into the strike, only now and then going to the picket lines.

After they left she straightened up. Even in the shambles of the rooms with their rattling windows and chipped walls, she tried to maintain a semblance of order. Saturdays, until her malaise set in, she always polished the floor, washed and starched her dresses, shined her shoes in readiness for the next week's work. She knew she was plain, but she did not have to be slovenly.

Many of her beliefs came to her from her mother who had been a housekeeper at Catholina Lambert's mansion at Garrett Mountain before she died too soon of consumption. Her mother considered her a perfect daughter, a good girl.

And what would her mother have thought of her now?

She would have disowned her. She had committed the most heinous of crimes according to the Catholic church. But she could hardly keep herself, let alone a child. Who would take care of it? Who would have paid its doctor bills if it got sick? She had struggled with her dilemma for weeks as she lay on this cot, long after she should have returned to Lafferty's, immobilized at the thought of a child growing within her. She told no one.

They would want to know about the father.

She heard footsteps on the stairs. It must be Eleanor. She visited often, though she rarely brought food now. Her roommates told her unabashedly they got food money by selling their favors and she did not condemn them. They had no choice. She wondered if Eleanor did the same. Her story of a gardener who gave her food just didn't ring true. She did not believe in the goodness of people.

Eleanor's steps slowed as she entered the room, her smile painted on. "I'm afraid I don't have any food to share. I wish I did."

"It's all right. Tell me the news."

"We had a meeting last night. The owners called in the AFL, trying their best to separate us from the IWW, but it didn't work. Did they think we'd forget the AFL was in cahoots with Lafferty when he wanted to introduce the four-loom system four years back?" She cinched her arms across her chest. "The AFL. All they care about is helping the top dollar men anyway. The pawns of the bosses."

"Who spoke?"

"John Golden. I suppose they think winning us over is pretty important to bring in the head of the AFL. He went on and on, said if we end the strike there'd most likely be a general increase over the top notch wages before the strike. Not a word about those at the lower end. We got no place. Fast."

"When will it end? When?"

"I only wish I knew. And the worst part is the IWW said this problem of lower tier wages had to be solved. It would decide the future of the strike."

"Tell me all they said, every last word."

"That was most of it. Bill Haywood there, Elizabeth Flynn, Carlo Tresca, Dante Ravelli." She tightened her arms harder across her chest. "They came in the back, at the beginning of Golden's talk. Hundreds of us made an aisle for them to pass. It was a sight."

Catherine frowned. "I don't like the IWW. They have too much power. Things'll explode if it keeps up, I can feel it."

"You're wrong. They care about the workers, I can see that now. And they don't want violence, unless there's no other way." Eleanor rose. "I'll put some water on for tea if you like."

"Please. The only one worth anything is Dante Ravelli. He's a good man. He came to visit me."

Eleanor stood frozen.

"Did he?"

"Yes. He was so kind, said he knew how hard it must of been for me, what happened." She flushed. "And he mentioned you."

"He did?"

"Said you most likely saved my life, that you had such courage.

Said I could of bled to death if it wasn't for you."

Eleanor certainly did not see herself as courageous, but rather the opposite. But she felt so proud Dante saw her that way.

Catherine frowned. "I try so hard not to think about that day." Eleanor thrust the kettle on the stove. "Then don't."

"What?"

"Don't think about it," she said in a hard voice. Then she recollected herself. "It's often the easiest way to deal with pain."

The picket line thinned out drastically in the weeks that followed. Many single men left Paterson, hoping to find work elsewhere and knowing if they left, more food would be available for their parents and siblings. The IWW accepted their decision, though Elizabeth Gurley Flynn argued the men's presence was needed to show the mill owners their power and unity.

There were only a dozen on the picket line when Eleanor and her mother arrived. She did not see one dyer. Mill owners could easily find others to fill dyers' positions. Had fear finally made them give in?

Word passed quickly along the line the manufacturers laid down an ultimatum: return by July 7 or not at all. Eleanor realized now why the line became scant. Those going back last would be regarded as troublemakers, not rehired.

By mid-July over nine hundred workers had returned to Weidmann's and National Silk's mill, practically filling the building. They arrived, heads bowed, walking bones, having received no concessions.

The first real heat of summer bore down on Eleanor as she walked to Catherine's to give her the results of the union meeting the night before. She found Catherine bending over her sink scrubbing out some small clothes. She gave Catherine a wan smile. "I'm glad you're up and about."

"Something happened, I can tell."

"There's been a change," Eleanor said. "The broad silk weavers went back. We had a meeting of the ribbon weavers last night, over 2000 of us there, at least. They gave reports on how strikers are back. Hundreds from the beginning of July. We saw how small the picket lines got but we didn't want to believe it. Dexter and Lambert, Frank and Dugan,

Graef Hat Band are all working at full capacity again. We heard a speaker from Smith and Kaufman in New York, a big ribbon shop there. He said they had to give up the demand for an eight-hour day when they struck, finally settled for nine hours. After we heard him, we had to think, decide what to do."

She covered her face with her hands, her fingers now like spindles.

"There's no choice anymore. The owners know we're near starvation." She dropped her hands into her lap. "A nine-hour day, and it's to be decided on a shop-by-shop basis."

"But what about stickin' together? I thought--"

"It all broke apart. All of it. It's the hunger that defeated us. The hunger."

She sipped at the tea Catherine poured, smiled in mockery. "And shall we have some crumpets and jam and bacon and eggs with this?"

"And so it's over? After all this? And we're goin' back."

"There's no word yet on the weavers. But we can't live on tea. The IWW did all they could, but they couldn't pull food out of a hat, could they? And the papers didn't help, saying how we were going back before most of us did."

"I thought the people in New York were givin' some food. I read it in the *Call*."

"That's just it. When they read we were going back, they thought it was over and stopped giving."

"We have to accept it. What else can we do?"

"And Dante--" Eleanor caught herself. "All the IWW. "How they tried so hard to help us. Now it's all over but the vote. Hardly anything gained. What they must be feeling now. If only I could--"

She could not continue. "Could what?"

"I--don't know."

"Well, at least it's near ended now."

Yes, near ended.

Dante would leave.

A heavy, slack-jawed man, a messenger from the IWW, approached them, along with other dots of strikers, the next day at the picket line.

"Go home, folks. Come back tonight. Eight o'clock at the armory. A final settlement's been offered."

A final settlement. Had the weavers, the last holdout, given in?

Silence penetrated the air that night at the armory. The heat of the evening lay heavy, the air motionless. Fatigue and hunger had taken its toll. Many strikers huddled together on the floor, clinging to each other. Bones jutted from their flesh, their faces pallid, expressionless. Women sat on the floor or stood wide-eyed, staring at air, dreaming of their children, taken from them to homes where they still remained.

The IWW leadership entered. The workers helped each other rise, stood stooped and solemn.

A few showed glints of hope in their eyes. Perhaps change occurred. Possibly some concessions had been given during this last round of negotiations.

Eleanor was oblivious to Haywood, Tresca and Flynn, and focused on Dante walking to the platform. Dark circles were smeared under his eyes, his clothes hung loosely. He looked haunted.

The usual call to order did not sound. The quietude from despair brought its own silence.

"I must first tell you the good news." Dante's voice sounded hoarse, but he continued. "We have gained an important victory for the weavers. The manufacturers have agreed there will be no four- loom assignments!"

Applause sounded sporadically in areas of the armory, mostly from the weavers.

"But, we must face facts. The manufacturers' strategy of holding out until we nearly starve has worked. The excess goods they stored from previous years have saved them. We did not realize they had stocked such great accumulations of surplus goods, and the commission houses where they're stored unloaded them during the strike. At great profit. Ironically, the strike has been a blessing to the owners, allowing them to use up these excess inventories."

He paused, took a deep breath, studied the audience huddled in the oppressive heat of a mournful day.

"We must be realistic now. As you know, the owners transferred their business to Pennsylvania when the strike began, where the mills are now humming. The workers in Pennsylvania have let us down. If they had struck in sympathy, we would have won, no doubt about it. But they did not."

He moved forward onto the edge of the platform, swayed somewhat, caught himself, began again.

"What has proved most decisive on the part of our Committee in making our recommendations to you is the fact that the manufacturers' businesses are going full swing in Pennsylvania."

He hesitated. Here and there members of the crowd mumbled.

"We can no longer encourage their use of Pennsylvania to run their mills. You see the implication of that, I'm sure."

He raised his arm slowly, as though lifting lead.

"With the strength each and every one of you has shown, you can always hold your head high, as will your children, your grandchildren who will always remember your courage. You have lived through a great historic moment. You fought for justice for all men, not only for yourselves. And to fight for justice is never the wrong choice. Never!

"But to watch you weakening every day, after five months, with no relief in sight, cannot continue."

He lowered his arms slowly.

"The IWW unanimously recommends that you return to work."

Flynn, Tresca and Haywood walked quickly toward him to the front of the platform. Tresca grasped his left hand, Flynn his right, and they all lifted their arms high into the air.

The weavers applauded. The rest of the workers remained mute. No miracle in negotiations occurred after all. Months of pay lost, never to be regained. Hunger won.

And would the owners take them back? Their jobs might be lost to workers in Pennsylvania. The most outspoken of them might be blacklisted.

Had the strike destroyed Silk City?

Eleanor felt Dante would surely not leave without saying goodbye. Every day she hoped he would visit, then prayed he wouldn't for it meant he still remained in Paterson.

Colin dropped by more often since her father's death. She noticed how he doted upon her mother. She often wondered how Colin, a man with such a gentle heart, could have been her father's friend. She realized as she grew older it was their shared bond. Ireland. Not the romantic image of Galway Bay at twilight, swards green as emeralds, tiny cottages covered in snow in winter--but the hope for rebellion, for independence from the British.

Even as a little girl she saw the difference between the two men. Her father never made a request of her mother, always a demand. And Elizabeth would rush to fill it. Colin always said "Please" or "Thank you" even for the smallest act, like handing him a cup of tea. Through the years her father became fat and slovenly, his mane of hair hanging over his collar like clumped coal, his eyes snaked with veins. Then came the violence. But Colin remained handsome in a rugged way, his black hair always trimmed, his gray eyes clear as light.

Autumn arrived. Still Dante had not visited, though she had seen him from afar at IWW headquarters. She knew from Colin he did not plan to leave Paterson just yet, that he waited for another assignment. And the longer he lingered the more she dreamed he might stay, her knowledge of his presence postponing her grief.

The autumn breeze felt cool as she walked to the mill, grateful she had not been let go. Trees bragged with orange and magenta leaves. Mums showed off tiny umbrellas of white and gold along the gardens of Silk Road. She would sometimes hear snatches of the conversations of the wives of the mill owners as they strutted down the road--talk of trips to Newport or Europe, their husbands' new carriages or cars, the newest fashions in France, their gratitude that "the awful strike" had ended.

She passed, invisible.

Work at Lafferty's drone don as usual. She sighed. Checkingthewarp threads in the design of her silk ribbons had become almost automatic. She could now create a silk ribbon from start to finish on her own.

She peeked at Angus Clegg scrutinizing her from across the room, biting the edge of his lower lip, his thick thumbs stuck into the edges of his pockets. He put his index finger in his ear, scraped at it, rubbed the wax on his trousers as he approached her.

She said nothing, increased her speed.

"You caught on just fine," he said.

"Thank you." She turned away from the stench of him. "Sir."

He bent his head closer. His breath smelled sour, like her father's after a night of drinking. "You know I could get you a raise."

She thought what she could do with more money. A soft chair for her mother, more comfortable for the hip she knew ached her incessantly. Or replacement of the cracked panes on the windows before winter. Or repair of chipped plaster hanging from the ceiling in the kitchen. Or paint to brighten the walls.

"A raise?"

She noted his brows rise at the excitement in her voice. She immediately regretted her show of emotion.

"You know you're the prettiest girl in this place now that you got a little weight back. You know that?"

Her stomach curdled. She saw from the corner of her eyes the other girls watched.

He put his club of a hand on her shoulder. "If you was nicer to me I could fix it so's you'd get that raise. Nobody else need know."

"Let me alone."

He stepped back, his face reddened. Then bent forward and whispered in her ear. "You'll be sorry for that. I could fire you right now." He squeezed his index finger and thumb to his chin. "You want that?"

Her hands trembled.

"Didn't I ask you a question?"

"Yes, I know. I'm--sorry."

"Well, I won't fire you. You're too pretty. You'll come round to my ways. If you want to work here." He smiled at her through teeth stained from tobacco, turned away, moved toward the girls. "Get back to work."

Nora approached her, pretending to examine her work, bent close.

"Watch out for him, Eleanor. He's a filthy pig and mean as they come. Don't ever get caught alone with him. Never."

"He can't hurt me. I'll go to the union."

"The union? And what has the union done for us? Do you see us workin' for a fair salary? Do you see any chairs set up so's we can sit while we eat?" She spoke lower, tugged at her faded sweater. "No, you can't count on the union, we all learned that. Just stay away from him's all you can do."

"Are you two talkin'? You know that ain't allowed."

Clegg pulled a stubby pencil and small pad from his pocket, scribbled on it. "That talk'll cost you in your salary."

Nora scampered back to her loom. Both began work immediately.

Amidst the whirring of the machine, Eleanor contemplated the possibility he could fire her even though her work had been superior.

Nora was right. She would never allow herself to be alone with him.

All would be fine.

Dante Ravelli sealed the letter he had written to his mother and father in Italy. He sometimes felt lately his only comfort lay in the happiness he knew they experienced receiving his letters.

He had been saved as a child by the Coppino law, radical at the time, making free formal education compulsary for all Italian children between six and nine. His mother pounced on that law and broke a centuries-old tradition of the woman staying in the house when, for the years he attended school, she took his place in the fields. After he finished school, he continued to love reading, learning.

She had been well-educated in Ravenna. She named him Dante because of her love for the great Alighieri. He envisioned her reading to him during childhood, her calloused hands holding a story book, now and then pushing back a strand of her raven hair, her gentle smile. He vowed as he grew older to try to be the embodiment of her hopes and dreams.

And so he came to America fighting to attain a happiness that always remained out of reach. His education had not wiped out the memory of his suffering and that of his family. He had to constantly control the rage within him, his desire to destroy the forces denying justice to the voiceless.

He finished packing. A few shirts, his second pair of trousers, underwear, the books he could not live without: *Das Capital*, *The Divine Comedy*, *Hamlet*, Shakespeare's *Sonnets*, *I Promessi Sposi*, the poetry of Keats, Shelley, Wordsworth.

He hardly left his room since the end of the strike, except now and then for food, or to go to headquarters. He thought of the workers in the bleak buildings he'd entered last winter, surrounded by the flawless beauty of silk they created. He knew even the concession to the weavers would not last. They would most likely be running four looms before the year was out. The workers of Pennsylvania were malleable. If it became the norm there, the Paterson workers would have to succumb sooner or later or lose their jobs.

And then there was Eleanor. He thought of his studies, all of the writers and thinkers he'd read. If only they could serve him now, but they left him defenseless against the emotions that gripped him when he thought of her. He sat, battered by the memory of her suffering, covered his face with his hands, hoping to obliterate the vision of her copper hair turned dull, her gleaming skin pallid, her body transformed into a shadow. Of the thousands of workers he failed, it was her image that possessed him most.

He punched his cot. What had gone wrong? Should they have ended it sooner, eased the suffering, when they discovered the great cache of silk stored in Pennsylvania? Or should they have been more vigilant with food, not offering as much in the beginning? Perhaps Elizabeth Flynn had been right. They should have kept the young men in Paterson projecting a greater show of unity. Perhaps violence--.

He rose from his cot, paced the floor, frightened at the appeal violence had for him.

He started at the knock on the door. It was Colin, with a large bag and a bottle of wine. They had become so close during the strike, yet Dante had avoided him since his self-imposed exile in his room. Embarrassment flooded him.

Colin eyed the packed suitcase. "You weren't leavin' now? Without a goodbye?"

"Well, I--. Of course not."

"But I'm sure we need to say it soon. I think, with a glass of wine and some good food."

He began to walk to the kitchen area for some glasses. "I could use a glass."

"The truth is, I thought we'd go over to Elizabeth's. Have a good dinner as well. We haven't seen you at all, and now's more the reason, with you goin' soon."

"I--don't think I can. I'm meeting a few people tonight."

"And who might they be?"

"Well, Tresca and Flynn." Dante busied himself in the small cupboard, though the glasses were right in front of him. "I wanted to have a drink with them. I'm off to Colorado. Tomorrow."

He felt Colin's penetrating look. "It's no good, Dante."

"No good? I don't know what you mean."

"A man like you, he'd need a pretty serious reason to bite the hand that fed him. Elizabeth's been awful kind to you, all the meals she made. And shared. Gladly. You'd never be so thankless not to say goodbye the proper way. Unless you had good reason."

His jaw tightened, but he did not respond.

"Don't you think I can tell? It's Eleanor, isn't it? Oh, I don't blame you for it. And I don't blame her for feelin' like she does. It's written all over her face. It happens."

"Nothing has happened. I can assure you of that."

"I know, I didn't mean that." Colin sat on the kitchen chair. "But that makes it worse, doesn't it?" He slumped forward as he sat. "The mind. It's never free of it."

"It's just that I think it best I leave without seeing her. It may be pity I feel, more than anything else. She's been through so much."

"Oh, is it pity now?"

"Colin, I'm old enough to be her father, do you realize that? And there is pity in it. I keep seeing her working in those mills the rest of her life, when there's so much more. And the strike, it took so much out of her."

"Well, you go on and think your way out of it. Maybe it will help."

"I know I'm hesitating to say one goodbye. Perhaps I don't want to understand why."

"All I know is they're owed a goodbye. It's only right."

Dante slumped onto the cot. He stared at his shoes, not thinking, not feeling anything but a dark confusion.

Colin settled on the cot beside him.

"I know what you feel," Colin said. "The strike. The cost. But you did your best. We'll go on. And Eleanor. And--well, I know what it is to care for a woman so much you can't stand the thought of the day without her in it. I know. And it's a hopeless thing." He rubbed his thighs back and forth with the palms of his hands. "A hopeless thing."

"She's so young. It's foolish on my part. It's something I'll get over as will she. Time will do its job. It's been very lonely here, I'm sure that's part of it."

"But it's only right you face her. She's owed it. It would break her heart if you went and didn't see her. And you don't want to do that, I know." He sighed. "There's been too many broken hearts around here."

Dante slowly came out of the depression enveloping him, became aware of what Colin was saying. But he'd never seen Colin with a woman, except--

"Elizabeth?"

Colin sighed. "I love her more than anything in the world. Except for Eleanor. You see, Eleanor is my child."

Dante scrutinized him, his black hair a contrast to Eleanor's auburn. Then he focused on his eyes. The clear, gray eyes.

"I never told it to any man," Colin said. "But I trust you. Elizabeth, she made me swear Eleanor would never know."

"But why not?"

"She still thinks it's a grave sin she committed. Even after the confessional she still holds it in her. The church, you know, it was always her comfort, especially with the likes of Michael and the drink. Oh, don't get me wrong. He was a great man to fight for the rights of the workers. He was. When we fell in love, when I asked her to tell him, to leave him, she wouldn't hear of it. The church, you see. Divorce bein' a mortal sin and all that malarky."

"You were in love from the beginning?"

"From the minute I saw her on the ship. But she was so in love with Michael then. He never showed his true self in the early days, even went to church with her in the beginning. Him, who hated the guts of the priests more even than I do, but he was a saint in those days, for her. And me? I could never be anything I wasn't. I hate the church--dear God, the pain religion causes in this world. But he gradually showed his true colors. Crazy as it sounds, I can understand his churchgoin' now. He wanted her so. I could understand it."

"And after you both fell in love?"

"In truth, most of it's been pain. It was terrible how we loved each other so. And Elizabeth, she suffered so bad for what she did. Maybe I should of pretended to her I believed, like Michael did. What difference would it of been? But I just couldn't do it."

"We can't be what we aren't. Your character is your fate."

"One of your fancy writers said that, no doubt."

Dante smiled. "I'm afraid so."

"Well, he surely hit the nail on the head, didn't he?"

Dante reached for the bottle, began to unstop it.

Colin covered his hand. "We won't have enough for Elizabeth and Eleanor now, will we, if we open it here."

"I don't know how to do this."

"You'll find a way. I can't have my girl broken-hearted knowin' you went off without a word of goodbye. She means too much to me."

Dante handed the wine to Colin, donned his jacket, grabbed the bag of groceries from the table.

"Let's go then."

Eleanor sat on the back porch, looking across the river at the mills. The rectangular brick buildings dominating the water's edge from the West Broadway bridge to the Broadway bridge nearly half a mile away pulsed with activity. Smoke puffing from their stacks floated across the sky in gray cotton ribbons. The hum of the looms filled the air. Yellow light glowed from the windows, reflecting onto the water in hundreds of squares of shimmering glass.

She closed her eyes and listened to the voice of the river beneath the mill sounds, drawing comfort and strength from its eternal presence.

She began to shiver. Soon the cold would prevent her from sitting on the porch. Every opening of the door would release precious heat. She absorbed the miracle of the night one last time before going into the apartment to face another evening of agony, thinking about Dante.

Footsteps sounded below. She moved to the railing, saw Colin. With Dante.

She half stumbled back to the chair.

She heard them ascending the stairs, sat in silence, listening to their muffled voices greeting her mother. She must go in, face him. She forced herself to stand, though she felt disconnected from the floor, and entered the living room.

Colin and Dante greeted her warmly. She did not trust herself to more than glance at him. Colin handed a bottle of wine and a bag of food to Elizabeth.

Her mother searched it. "Beef? It's been donkey's years since we've had that. I'll make some steak. That would be nice." She plunged her hand further in the bag. "What in the world is this?"

She pulled out a small, black cardboard box with tiny round glass on one of its ends. She turned it, exposing a winding key on its side.

"A camera," Colin said. "A Brownie they call it. I took a few pictures with it, of the Falls. There's some left. We can take some, see if it works inside." Colin turned to Dante. "I'll send you a few." He laughed. "That is, if you and I don't break the camera. And if such a contraption really works, which I doubt. Though one of the weavers brought in pictures he took with it, and they looked so real."

Her mother examined it as though it were an insect under a microscope. "I saw them in the Sears Catalogue. A dollar each they are. And you went and spent that much for it?"

"We have to keep up with new inventions. Progress they call it, for want of a better word."

Her mother frowned. "Well, it was too much money." But already she began straightening her dress, pushing back wisps of hair dangling from her temples, readying for the photo.

Colin rubbed his stomach. "Let's eat first. I can't speak for Dante here, but I'm starved."

Dante said nothing.

Eleanor went to work with her mother in the kitchen. Dante and Colin joined them and sat at the kitchen table.

Colin yawned. "I'm weary as hell. Weary as hell. Still not back to my routine after two months. Just can't sleep."

"Such a long fight. Who would have ever thought it would take so much out of us, that it would last so long? I've seen such courage here in Paterson. No matter where I go, I'll never forget Paterson."

Eleanor stared at her carrots and potatoes. He was leaving. This might be the last time she saw him, and she couldn't even bring herself to look at him. While Dante, Colin, and her mother savored their food, she swallowed a boulder with every bite.

Her mother got the kettle going for tea. "And what's next for you now, Dante?"

"I'm assigned to Colorado. Ludlow. The coal miner's strike."

"Colorado's a lucky place to have you come." Colin said. You'll set those miners on fire with your words, like you did us."

"When do--" Eleanor's throat felt dry as dust. "When do you leave?"

"Tomorrow morning."

He gulped another sip of wine. She watched the bright light over the table fall upon his face, his dark, unflinching eyes.

Colin lighted his pipe, began puffing. "Well, you've given your all here. Every worker in Paterson knows that. We wish you well. And, in time, I think there could be changes because of the strike. It made the mill owners think, it did. Maybe more than you know."

Their talk turned to the mills. She heard the ticking of their clock in the background, and the one at City Hall tolled each hour. Finally it struck twelve.

"I suppose I should be going." Dante folded his hands on the table. "Although it saddens me. More than I can say."

Colin jumped up. "It'll not be before we have some pictures taken. Get right under the light. Elizabeth, bring that other lamp over too. We'll make it bright as can be. Try it anyway. Let's take Eleanor first. She's the prettiest here and we know she won't break the camera, like I might."

Dante and her mother laughed dutifully. Eleanor swallowed hard.

She submitted, unable to say a word of protest, sat at the table, bathed in the brightness of the light.

Colin held the camera steady, clamped his left eye, and stared down at the device. "And won't you even smile a bit now?"

She stared into the camera. Her mother, behind Colin, stuck out her tongue and waved her hands. "Can't you give us a smile, dear?"

Dante stood motionless.

"Smile, darlin'. Come on now. Smile. I'm ready to press the button."

Her face felt hard as glue, her lips paralyzed. She stared straight into the camera.

Colin finally gave up coaxing, snapped the photo, turned the winding key.

They took turns taking the remaining pictures. Her mother took one of Colin and Dante. Eleanor snapped another of them with Elizabeth, hoping her trembling hands were not too apparent.

"Why don't we have one with Eleanor and Dante? Let's see how many's left." Colin examined the film in the camera, frowned. "Ah, I was a fool to take those pictures of the Falls. They're all used up."

He gingerly placed the camera on the table.

She watched Dante walk towards the cot and his jacket.

"I--wish you'd stay longer in Paterson." She sounded almost inaudible "We--need you here."

He slowly shook his head. "I must go where I'm assigned."

She envisioned the sterile life before her, the mill she would enter every morning for decades.

A life without Dante.

The room closed in on her. She ran to the porch.

She heard his steps on the floor of the porch, felt his shadow fall upon her. She began to tremble. She pressed her arms across her chest trying to stamp out her shivering.

He sat next to her. "You love this place, don't you? So calm and peaceful. The water."

"Yes."

"Your tea will get cold if you don't go back in."

"I don't want it."

She forced herself to look at him. The light of the moon reflected on his skin. She must memorize every aspect of him, the kindness in his eyes, the dark hair crowning his head. Every look, gesture, word spoken. For the rest of her life she would live this night over and over, remembering this grief from loving.

"I don't want you to go." Her voice sounded thin as tinsel. "I don't know how I'll manage if you go. I'm afraid. Of how I feel. And I've never been afraid like this."

"You'll be all right. You're very strong, you know. It is for the best."

She heard words of comfort but studied his face, sketched in sorrow. He did not believe his own words, she could see it.

She grasped one last straw. "The workers need you here. Why, you could--"

"I have to move on. You know this. It is what I do."

She faced him squarely. "I love you. You must know it."

"You think that, but you're so young. And love is a very complicated thing. You haven't met many men yet, I think."

"Why do you always bring up my age? I'm not the girl I was before the strike. I'm not young anymore. The strike made me old. You made me old." Her eyes widened. "I could go with you."

"You aren't thinking straight."

"But I am! We could be like Elizabeth Flynn and Carlo Tresca. I could help you."

"And your mother?"

She hesitated. "But she would understand."

"You could never live with yourself if you left her alone, never know peace with worry about her."

She did not answer, looked up into the black sky, the only light here and there the winking of a star.

He smiled at her. "Do you know how many men will be in love with you over the next few years? More than I can count."

"But I don't want them."

"How do you know? You haven't met them. You'll find someone else."

Her face soured with anger. "How do you know what I'll find? You're afraid, aren't you? Of what you feel. Because it doesn't make sense you could love me, someone who isn't educated like you."

"Eleanor, no. You don't have to be well educated to have great intelligence. And you do."

"Stop trying to make me feel better. It only hurts more when you say things like that because they aren't enough to make you love me."

"I don't want to hurt you. I've damaged you enough with the strike."

"No. Never."

She took him into her arms.

He did not stop her.

"I'll always love you," she whispered.

She studied the flesh of his mouth near hers, felt his hands caressing her hair. And she knew.

"You love me." Her throat felt threadbare, spent by yearning.

He did not speak.

They held each other. For a fleeting moment she dreamed she was free of the torment she lived with every day. She had never been violated. Her heart was pure. She was worthy of him.

She began to cry.

"Is this what I make you do? Cry." His voice sounded broken as splintered glass.

"I'm crying from happiness. Because I finally know. You do love me." She cradled her head against his chest. "Nothing greater or more wonderful than right now will ever happen to me."

Suddenly the realization of his leaving struck her full force, knowing now she was powerless to make him stay. "How will I ever live without you? How will I ever go on? I can't."

"You will," he said. "Because you must."

Elizabeth and Colin sat at the kitchen table, now and then studying the door to the porch.

Elizabeth had known for months Eleanor loved Dante, although she never spoke of it. How well she understood her feelings for Dante, longed for her to speak of them. But Eleanor would never open herself to someone else. She clung to her self-sufficiency, though appearance covered a frightened girl. Did it go back to Michael? Had his violence forced Eleanor to develop her hard shell, to learn to hide her fear?

She prayed every night to the Virgin Mary that Eleanor not commit the mortal sin she had with Colin. She knew God forgave her, but a spot still festered in her soul for succumbing to passion. To sin. She knew Eleanor had a right to know Colin was her father, not the drunken scum Michael had eventually become. Yet, she could not say the words to Eleanor that would reveal she was born of sin.

She rubbed sweat from her forehead with the back of her hand, wishing the act could wipe away the conflict boiling within her.

She watched Colin sucking his pipe, then frowning at the table as she poured yet another cup of tea. Did she dare ask him what he knew of Eleanor and Dante?

"I don't like what's goin' on, Elizabeth," he said, reading her mind. "Not one bit."

"And there's nothing we can do. He'll leave." She set the kettle down, pressed her fingers to her forehead. She could feel yet another headache coming on. "If only we could save her the hurt."

"It's easier said than done."

"Don't you think I know that?"

"Of course. But some things could be different, better for her."

"And how could that be? Can we take away the suffering she's got to know?"

"Alas, no. What I mean is, well, it's been quite a few months now that Michael is gone, and I think you've mourned enough."

"What is it you're saying?"

He squirmed in his chair, nervous as a truant schoolboy. "What I think is, well, I thought we could get married."

"Married? Why, I can't do that. It's not been a year--"

He threw his pipe into the ash tray. "It's not been a year, I knew that's what you'd say. But we're not gettin' any younger. There's not a thing to stop us now. And if I'm sworn by your foolishness not to tell Eleanor I'm her father, well, at least I can be a father to her. Not to mention what I told you a thousand times before, how I love you dearly. And always will."

"What would people say? To marry so soon after Michael's death."

"Who cares? I've not brought this up without thought. And if you won't marry me and let me be at least Eleanor's stepfather, I'm goin' back to Ireland. I'm sick at heart that you still think you're a sinner, even when you look at the daughter we created, so beautiful and strong. One we should be proud of. Together. Sick at heart every day I have to wear this mask." He recovered his pipe from the ash tray. "And to tell the truth, it's an important time in Ireland now. I miss it. And maybe I should be a part of it."

He took a puff on his pipe, placed it back on the ash tray, grasped his arms around his stomach.

"How can I stay here when every day all I see in you is guilt. You have to decide."

"Can't you give me time to think about it?"

"You've had over seventeen years. If that's not enough, I don't know what is. It's best you say it now if the answer's no and be done with it."

She scrutinized his face, saw the desperation of a man who deserved more than he got.

"I might as well be dead in the grave without you," she said. "That I know. I'll marry you. I will."

He reached across the table, enclosed his hands around hers. "We'll be so happy, you'll see. And Eleanor will have a father. At last."

"You have to keep your promise she never knows. What we did."

"I swore it, didn't I?"

"And you won't press me for an exact date now."

"I won't bring it up until you do. Within a reasonable time."

"I'll tell Eleanor when I think it's the proper time. It will be a shock to her when she finds out I have plans to marry. I don't know what she'll think if we got married before the year's up."

He laughed. "And how much does Eleanor care about appearance? But we'll do it your way if that's how you want it."

"It is."

The door from the porch rattled. Elizabeth wrestled her hands from Colin's.

Dante entered, his face ashen.

"Thank you so much, both of you, for your kindness to me." He embraced Elizabeth, shook Colin's hand. "I'll write."

And then he disappeared into the night.

Cold set in that evening, but Eleanor remained on the porch until early morning. Even after Colin left, Elizabeth knew not to approach her.

Whatever their goodbyes, they had been said, in the darkness.

* * *

Eleanor lay on her cot, studying rust stains shaped like pieces of a jig saw puzzle and holes from chunks of plaster dotting the ceiling. She curled her body, clenched her arms, buried her head in her chest, felt like a branch hacked from its life-giving tree.

Her mother's pot clunked on the stove as she prepared breakfast. The looms at Lafferty's were already clattering waiting her arrival.

"Aren't you up yet?" Her mother's soothing voice greeted her. "It's five-thirty. You'll be late and you know how Lafferty'll feel about that. It's lucky you still have a job, all they let go for being active in the strike."

"I'm not going."

"Not going to work?" Her mother sat on the edge of the cot, scrutinized her. "You're not sick, are you?"

She lay unmoving, tasting her misery. "Yes."

"Well, you'd better stay in bed then." She felt her forehead. "Though you don't seem to have a fever."

Her mother left her on her cot most of the day while she worked on picking. Neither one ate breakfast.

Colin came by that evening, saw her condition, frowned at her mother and sat next to her on the cot.

"You've got to try to get up, Eleanor. You're stronger than you think. Your mother's worried about you."

She did not answer, continued to furrow her head into her chest.

"You know Lafferty won't be happy with you out. You can't afford to lose your job." He bent down, whispered in her ear. "You and your mother can't live only on her piece work. You know that. She needs you. She does."

She opened her eyes, glanced across the room at her mother whose wide eyes were filled with silent tears. She remembered Dante's words about her.

She sat up. The pain was still there, but it was no worse than when she was lying down. And would probably be no worse if she ate.

"Was it soup you were making? I'll have some. With tea."

Colin helped her walk to the kitchen. Her mother already had the soup on the table when they sat down.

Days droned on. Winter arrived. Flurries dusted branches of trees in patterns of white lace. Cold pummeled Paterson, freezing the pipes of the tenement. Colin skidded his way to their apartment, tried to help, could do little. Eleanor cringed each morning at the thought of walking to Lafferty's but survived the trips to and from the mill, walking slowly, avoiding branches glazed with ice snapped to the ground.

Her mother bundled up as best she could when delivering the bolts of silk picking with her wagon, refusing to stop for freezing weather. One day in January Eleanor arrived home, found her lying down, covered with blankets above her chin, her face flushed. The next day she remained in bed, complaining of aches and fever she said would surely pass, insisting Eleanor go to work. She did, but spent a great part of the day worrying about her mother.

When she arrived home that evening, Colin, huffing and puffing, had just finished chopping ice from the steps.

"Come inside," he said. "Your mother's not good."

Her mother lay on her cot, eyes closed, her face wet with perspiration. Eleanor laid a gentle hand on her forehead.

"She's got a terrible fever," he said. "We'll have to get her to the Alliance to take a look at her."

Her mother, tried to rise, fell back on the cot. "No. No Alliance. I'll be all right."

They bundled her up amidst her protests, treading the icy streets, staggering like toddlers.

"Just go slow, Elizabeth," Colin said. "And stop your stubbornness. Mary Lafferty'll fix you up, blessed woman that she is."

They finally reached the clinic after much slipping and sliding. The first floor facade bulged with gray cobblestones and large windows, their frames peeling. Inside cots lay side by side across the room, forming five long aisles. Every one was filled, many by children covered with worn blankets. At the back a large screen separated a small area from the rest of the floor. An aide and a nurse fluttered back and forth. Moans and cries filled the air.

On the immediate left they entered a tiny makeshift office, sat her mother down, loosened her scarf, unbuttoned her coat. Then Eleanor found Mary Lafferty behind a screen, tending a child who appeared almost lifeless. Mary motioned her away, pointed towards the office, approached them a few minutes later.

Elizabeth breathed with Mary's stethoscope on her chest. Mary took her temperature.

"Well, it looks like you've gone and done it, Elizabeth." She clicked her tongue against her teeth. "Pneumonia. I can give you some medicine that will help you out." She sighed. "You should stay here, but I'm afraid there isn't a single bed to offer you right now."

"Please, can't you find room?" Eleanor grasped her arm. "We can't go back in this freezing cold."

Mary's face seemed to touch the floor. "I promise you, there isn't a spare cot to be had, my dear. I wish there were."

Colin stepped in. "We'll have to make the best of it. If you could give her the medicine, Mary. She'll have that. I'd be most obliged."

Eleanor's anger flared like wildfire. "This is terrible. That people have to be turned away. I don't blame you, doctor. But it's not right."

"Of course it's not right. I could fill a hospital twice this size with ease. But here we are."

She went to a shelf in her office, wrote something on the labels of two medicine bottles, handed them to Eleanor.

"Two pills every six hours, and two tablespoons of this syrup every hour. Without fail." She studied Eleanor. "You know, we can always use extra help here. Always. I believe I mentioned that to you once before. I'm quite desperate now." She stretched her arms out. "As you can see."

"You know I have a job at the mill as a ribbon weaver."

"And you should be proud of that. But I do keep hoping you'll think about it. I can't seem to keep aides. They break down constantly and cry their hearts out with all they see here. I need someone strong."

She wondered what Mary Lafferty would think about her strength if she knew that each night she lay thinking of Dante, feeling her body and bones would dissolve aching for him, her hand covering her mouth to stifle the sound so her mother wouldn't hear her crying.

"I'll think about it."

She returned to the work at hand, preparing her mother for her dreaded trip home. Colin tightened Elizabeth's scarf and tried to button her coat but his hands trembled so much Eleanor had to do it.

She forced a smile. "Well, then, we'll get you home. Get you better. That's all there is to it."

"All I am is a burden to you" her mother said. "I hate it."

Eleanor cringed at the rattle in her mother's voice.

As they neared the door, a man entered. He wore a gray wool coat and hat, both trimmed with fur. His leather boots gleamed, and soft woolen trousers neatly edged them. Despite her worries, his clothing caught Eleanor's attention. She so seldom saw well-dressed men. But when he removed his fur hat exposing his ears, her mind jolted with recognition.

"The gardener!"

She hadn't realized she'd spoken aloud until he gave her a puzzled look.

"Don't you remember me?" she said. "The food you gave me? At Lafferty's home on Silk Road?" She pulled her skull cap off, her hair tumbling down in a cascade of spun copper. "I gained my weight back, maybe that's it. But I'll never forget you. Never. We had next to nothing, and you gave us food."

He stared at her, speechless.

"Mother, Colin, this is the gardener who gave me food that time, during the strike."

Mary laughed aloud. "Oh, my, Charles. You know you're never going to live this down." She swooped down on them. "May I introduce you to my brother, Charles."

Brother? Eleanor shook her head, then frowned. "You should have told me your father was Mr. Lafferty. You made a fool out of me."

"Please, Miss O'Bannion, forgive me," he said. "But I feared you wouldn't accept the food had you known. And I felt you needed it so very much."

"You were right about that. But I hate the thought of it. That we lived off the food of your father. I would have starved first, and that's the truth."

Colin stepped in. "Now, Eleanor, don't be like that. This man did us a good turn. Be grateful for it. And, remember, he may have saved your mother's life as well."

Elizabeth tried to thank him, could not speak.

"I'm glad you're here, Charles," Mary said. "Eleanor's mother is unwell. Pneumonia. There's not a bed here for her, and they've got to walk home."

"You can't mean you two have to walk this poor woman home when she's so ill? In this weather? I have my carriage and driver outside. Please allow me to take you home."

Eleanor's temper immediately calmed. Submission seemed a small price for her mother's life.

Charles helped her mother out into the carriage and covered her with a blanket. Eleanor sat next to her mother and placed an arm around her, warming them both. Charles and Colin settled on the seat opposite.

The carriage crept along over cobblestones crusted with ice. The horses hooves clicked, their instincts slowing them as they crept along. Eleanor huddled next to her mother, their breaths puffs of frost, even inside the carriage.

Now and then she studied Charles as they rode. His hat seemed useless, did nothing to cover his large ears, red as raspberries. But she noted a gentleness in his soft eyes. He must be so unlike his father. But then so was Mary.

He caught her looking at him and smiled. She lowered her eyes.

The trip which would have taken ten minutes in good weather lasted nearly an hour. Her mother could hardly walk when they arrived. Colin tried to lift her, could not.

"My cursed back." He rubbed his back through his coat with his thumbs.

Before they could decide their next move, Charles alighted from the carriage, lifted her mother, slowly began to carry her up the stairs. Eleanor slipped past him and opened the door as he carried her through.

She pulled back the curtain dividing the area where her mother slept. He carried her to it, laid her down gently. He helped remove her coat and replace it with blankets. She found a spoon, gave her mother the medicines as Colin comforted her on the cot.

When she felt certain her mother slept, she turned to Charles. She had caught his look of shock when he first viewed their apartment, but his face was now well under control. She watched him twirling his hat, uncertain whether to remove his coat. Courtesy dictated she offer him some tea but the thought of their chipped cups and saucers, the worn and faded roses on them, stopped her.

Colin eyed her with a puzzled expression.

"Would you like some tea?" he said. "It seems Eleanor's worry about her mother has made her forget her manners."

"I don't mind if I do. If it's not too much trouble."

He placed his hat and coat on the chair in the living room. As he walked past her cot, he paused to study the flowers pinned to her wall. He scrutinized the white blooms on the lilies, the wild violets in shades of magenta, the orange-fleshed poppies pierced with color, so many others. She watched him mouth the names of some of the Latin labels she marked on them.

He turned to her. His eyes were filled with tears.

"I hope you haven't gone and done it," she said. "Got yourself the start of a cold. Because of us."

He wiped his eyes with his handkerchief, placed it neatly in his pocket, cleared his throat.

"Oh, I don't think so." He gestured to her paintings. "I'm just-- amazed at what you've accomplished in such a--difficult---situation. They're exquisite. You've captured the soul of the flowers. And I must say, I know a great deal about flowers. Gardening and landscape architecture are my passions."

"Landscape architecture? What is that exactly?"

"Well, it's trying to plan the grounds of a house so the flowers and trees bring out its beauty."

"That doesn't make sense. Flowers and trees would always outshine the house, don't you think?"

"I never thought of it that way. Perhaps you're right."

"Did you really like my flower paintings? I take books out of the library, draw and paint from them. I have my own library card. Even a mill girl can have one, you know. I've learned a lot about flowers. You'd be surprised. I love them more than I can say." She felt incapable of stopping herself from speaking of her passion. "Colin gets me the dye from leftovers at the mill. I love to work with the different colors, try to match them as close as I can to the pictures." She stepped closer to him. "About the dye. I never took any from Lafferty's. Never."

"Would it matter? You've created such beauty. And that's what counts, isn't it?"

While Elizabeth slept they had tea. Charles asked if it wouldn't be too much trouble if he brought a cup to his driver. When he returned, they made small talk for a time. He said he planned to move out of his home on Silk Road but his father's illness had prevented it. He seemed surprised they were unaware his father had a heart attack, that his father rarely visited the workers.

Eleanor asked if he'd ever divided the iris she'd told him about, and that started a long talk about his garden. She never knew how exciting it was until now to converse with someone who shared her passion, who gave genuine, intelligent attention to her questions. Later as he prepared to leave he said he hoped her mother would improve, that he would send his father's personal physician to check on her.

"I must thank you again for the tea and bread and jam. I can spot home-made jam anywhere, and it's a credit to your mother to have made some so delicious. Please tell her I said so when she improves. And she will, I assure you."

Colin shook his hand. Charles turned to Eleanor.

"I hope I'll see you again, Miss O'Bannion. In any case, keep up with your painting and study of flowers. You have a wonderful gift for it. I say that sincerely."

She blushed, despite herself. "I can't thank you enough for bringing us home in your carriage. It's twice now you've helped me."

"It was my pleasure, I assure you. And I do hope I see you again, Miss O'Bannion," he repeated.

She thought of his first reaction to the apartment, of the way he had focused on her flowers. The distrust she carried from childhood emerged. Perhaps he was trying to bury his shock and disgust. She had enjoyed their conversation, but had he? Could he? They were from such different worlds.

"Oh, I don't imagine so," she said. "Goodbye."

He stood lamely at the door, twirling his hat once again before he put it on, his ears protruding.

She closed the door quickly to preserve the warmth, left him standing in the raw cold.

Eleanor listened to her mother's lungs wheezing. She wanted to stay home yet knew they needed the money her job provided, especially as Elizabeth couldn't manage her piecework. And she knew Lafferty frowned upon absences. She finally decided she would stay home and take her chances with punishment when Colin stepped in and offered to stay with Elizabeth. He could better afford loss of a few days. His excellence at his craft and the scarcity of good loom fixers gave him a great advantage.

Five o'clock in the morning he knocked at their door, ready to spend the day making sure Elizabeth received her medicines, keeping the fire going in the stove.

When Eleanor returned from the mill that evening he served a soup he had concocted. It tasted like a salt lick, but she ate it, smiled and smacked her lips.

Most of the night her mother remained intermittently feverish, then chilled. Eleanor kept vigil over her, dragging the kitchen chair to her cot, waking her at appropriate times to administer medicines, wiping the sweat from her face, listening to her sluggish breathing. She held her hand, felt the crinkling skin beginning to cover it, tried to banish the thought of her mother aging.

If only Dante were here. He would put his arm around her and she would draw strength from him. Perhaps he thought of her this moment in that forsaken place in Colorado, felt her love transcending the distance between them.

Reality returned. Her heart began to pound when she saw beads of perspiration gleaming on her mother's forehead. She wiped them away, discarded her phlegm as she spit out, nursed her through the night.

Colin showed up the next day and she returned to work. The hours crawled at the mill, her thoughts constantly on her mother rather than the warp and weft she wove. By now she felt she knew the ribbon looms by heart and did not have to rivet her attention on the process, so it was with half an eye that she watched the silk from one of the beams feeding through the gravure printing press. She knew how important it was to watch the reed, which resembled a comb, moving along with over two hundred and fifty warp ends per inch. Nora warned her she must monitor its progress constantly especially since Lafferty had been experimenting with difficult cotton wefts in the warp-faced ribbons where filling would be invisible. The comb seemed to be running smooth, had been all morning.

Her thoughts turned to her mother's medicine. She hadn't remembered to check how much was left. It might run out today and Mary had said it must be administered on schedule. Colin would have to go to the Women's Alliance for more, perhaps before she got home. If he did, her mother would be left alone. Her heart thumped faster as she pictured her alone, possibly choking on the relentless phlegm stuck in her lungs.

The silk thread snapped as it went through the gravure and fell limp. Eleanor stared at it a moment before she realized what it meant. The machine would have to be completely reset. She pushed the pedal that shunted the drive belt onto the idler pulley, immediately stopping the loom's whir.

Angus Clegg stomped across the room, shaking his shovel of a hand at her. "What's goin' on? I thought you knew this job. More time and money lost by you. Again."

"I'm sorry, Mr. Clegg. I'm sorry."

"And what good does that do? I could see you makin' a mistake here and there as you learned, but you know this job by now. And Lafferty's big on tryin' these cotton wefts. You know that."

"I'm sorry, Mr. Clegg."

He stood near her. "I can't always look the other way with your mistakes. Unless I get somethin' out of it. If you get my drift."

She stared at the broken threads dangling from the machine and felt helpless.

"Once more and you're fired," he said. "Untangle this mess. Reset the loom."

She immediately began to dismantle the loom, the fragmented threads, reset it.

She thought of Clegg's words over and over as she walked home. She sighed, grateful he gave her one more chance. But when that chance was gone, what was she to do?

Colin greeted her with a smile. She took heart immediately and pushed past him to the bedroom.

Her mother breathed comfortably as she slept.

"You'll never guess," he said. "First thing this mornin' Lafferty's doctor showed up. Gave her more pills, medicine, a needle. Said he thought for sure she's past the crisis but to finish up all the medicine. Said she was awful lucky she had the medicine she did in her."

Charles Lafferty had said he would send their doctor, but Eleanor thought that was just politeness. Why would a rich man like that care about her mother?

"He was nice as pie," Colin said. "Said he'd be back next week. To call him here at this number if needed. Anytime at all." Colin gave her a small piece of paper.

Her joy at her mother's recovery began to fade. "I'll--I'll have to figure out how I can pay him."

"I asked him about that--and you know I'd of paid if you and your pride would let me. It seems Charles Lafferty paid him and we don't owe a penny."

"Lafferty paid? I don't like it."

"I'm a bit shocked myself. I suppose we should just accept it. Maybe someday we can do him an act of kindness. Though I don't know what we could ever give a Lafferty they don't have."

That was the problem. Eleanor did. She thought of Clegg offering her favors and expecting favors in return. What was Lafferty's kindness but a more sophisticated form of the same transaction?

She shook her head. "We can't accept him back."

"It's the way it went. That's all. Can't we just be glad of his help?

For your mother's sake."

Eleanor nodded, but she still didn't like where this could lead.

Her mother awoke, smiled, and ate a soft-boiled egg. Eleanor savored the moment.

Her life line had returned.

She studied her mother's expert hands, picking silk tapestry. It had been a month since her illness and she was finally strong enough to start piece work again. Colin took over her ritual of taking her wagon, somewhat unstable but adequate, to pick up and deliver silk from Dexter Lambert's mill, dragging it along, carrying it to her apartment. Time and again he offered to do the chore permanently, but her mother's stubborn streak prevailed. Once she felt completely recovered, she would be at it again.

Her mother's illness had diverted Eleanor's mind from Dante. Now that the crisis was past, despair clouded over her again. She waited for Colin to mention he'd received a letter. He never did. Every day she walked to work as in despair. Weekends dragged. She tried to work on her flower paintings, read, take walks, but no matter what she did, her thoughts always returned to Dante. When she painted, she realized she'd never asked him about his favorite flower. When she read, she wondered if he knew Edith Wharton's books. Walking gave her some release, until she passed the bench where they spoke, or stopped in front of Turn Hall, remembering his speeches to the workers. He was always present in his absence.

Each day she tried to concentrate on good parts of her life. Such as Catherine Devlin. Eleanor continued to visit and slowly began to feel comfortable with Catherine as she had with no one else, even asking Catherine home for dinner. For the first time in her adult life she had a friend she trusted. She sometimes thought to ask Catherine about the father of the child but she never did. This baffled her. Catherine's appearance did not lend itself to a man paying much attention to her, though Eleanor berated herself for such thoughts. Their conversation centered mostly around the mill. Eleanor encouraged her. Catherine said she had great plans for her life, told her she felt certain she would not always be a soaker.

One Saturday evening when Catherine was there for dinner, she tapped on her teacup for attention.

"I have bad news, and good news," she said. "Bad because I'll miss you both. But good because it will be a change for me. Plus extra money. I'm goin' to apply for work at the Women's Alliance on Saturdays."

Eleanor's mother smiled. "That's very selfless of you, Catherine."

"Well, the truth is, it's not, really. Besides the money, well, I would like to get married someday. To the right person, of course." She bathed her tea bag in its cup, laughed. "Even I'd look good to a man if he was sickly and needed me."

"You shouldn't say such things about yourself," her mother said. "You're a fine girl."

"If you don't mind me saying so," Eleanor said, "I think it's a big mistake. Why, with all the hard work you put in all week soaking, you need the weekend for rest."

Eleanor could not bring herself to say she would miss their Saturday meetings.

"I'll still have Sundays."

"It's something you might think about, Eleanor. It would do you good to get out among people more." Her mother stared at her tea as she spoke. "You spend too much time with your thoughts."

"I don't need to be with people. I have enough to keep me busy. My painting. And reading."

"If you say so. But it's just that Mary Lafferty was so good to me when I was sick. And I heard her say how capable she thought you would be for the work there."

Eleanor did feel a sense of gratitude to Mary Lafferty. She knew Mary's kindness had no ulterior motive. And her failure to emerge from her despair over Dante continued. She had to admit it. Her mother's suggestion made sense.

"Maybe I will try it. The extra money wouldn't hurt."

"I'm goin' over from here," Catherine said. "Why don't you come?"

"I will."

Dr. Mary Lafferty sat down for a few minutes rest, unlaced the ties of her high shoes. The pain from her corns throbbed. She kneaded her toes back and forth, vowing once again she must get to a doctor. She had so little time. The Women's Alliance and the Suffrage League filled her days. She fell into reverie, thinking of the march last year when she strode down Fifth Avenue with twenty thousand other suffragettes showing the country women would no longer sit back and accept this as a man's world. She remembered her years in England studying medicine and discovering others who felt as she did. She would never forget the day she met Christabel and Sylvia Pankhurst, or Alice Paul, who immediately became a close American friend.

She dearly missed Alice. She remembered her climbing the roof of St. Andrew's Hall in Glasgow, freezing rain pelting down on her, attempting to draw attention to their cause at a cabinet minister's meeting. She didn't budge from that spot the whole night. And dear Marion Dunlop, still in England, who sat next to her during their hunger strike when they were imprisoned and finally force fed, their jaws opened with metal clamps, food pumped into them by rubber tubes forced down their throats.

She would have stayed in England had Christabel not become, to Mary's way of thinking, too obsessed with authoritarian centralization. To Mary the whole meaning of the movement lay in democracy and equality. Christabel's autocratic style went against that very goal. The final split came when Christabel denounced any link between suffrage and labor.

Mary couldn't understand Christabel's thinking. When she returned to Paterson and saw firsthand the lives of women at the mills, she became completely convinced suffrage and labor rights were intertwined. After she finished her medical studies in England, she returned permanently to Paterson amidst the usual labor conflicts and decided to dedicate her life to the city's poor.

She sighed and retied her shoes. She had to admit there were moments when she wondered if she had made the right decision. She sometimes grew sick and tired of all the poor who would not help themselves, who turned to drink, content to work in the mills until they died rather than try to better themselves. She understood the roadblocks to their advancement. But, still, so many of them accepted defeat.

She supposed that was why she was drawn to Eleanor O'Bannion. She sensed this girl struggled with life every day yet possessed a hunger for learning and improving herself.

And then she thought of Charles.

In the past month or so he stopped by too often and asked with a studied casualness what Mary knew of Eleanor. She teased him, asking if he hoped Eleanor would come down with an illness and be brought to the Alliance so he might see her again. His blush indicated she was right sensing his attraction to her the day he drove her, Colin and Elizabeth home.

She was taken aback, for just as she thought about Eleanor she appeared outside the window, along with the girl who aborted her child. Eleanor's hair blew in the frigid breeze, her coat with its upturned collar inadequate against such an abnormally cold day, her hands stuffed into her coat. The other's plain face bulged from her thick, woolen cap drawn around her ears protecting her head like armor.

She expected they would pass by, but they turned in at the entrance way. She went to greet them.

"I do hope one of you girls isn't feeling poorly. Or not your mother again, Eleanor."

They set her straight about the purpose of their visit. It seemed they wanted work.

"I'd expect to be paid as much as I make at the mill," Eleanor said. "I'm paid more than a soaker."

"And why shouldn't you both be paid a decent wage?" Mary said. "The reason women have been treated so unjustly is because they give too much of their time volunteering, when they should be accepting the same wages as men receive for their work."

The girls' eyes widened, either from the promise of wages or the promise of new ideas or both.

"Well, if you agree then," Eleanor said, "I suppose we could both start next Saturday."

"I'd be glad of it. And if you work out, why, I'll be glad to give you raises. I need good help."

The shock on their faces was all she had hoped to see. If there were ambitious women here she could help advance themselves, then maybe she had done the right thing coming to Paterson.

Eleanor knew Mary Lafferty appreciated her work. Catherine looked askance at certain jobs, like cleaning the bedpans or washing soiled sheets. But Eleanor changed bedpans almost immediately when summoned, washed soiled blankets until her knuckles reddened, took temperatures without fail at prescribed times, changed blood-encrusted dressings with complete concentration. She never complained and completed her tasks with vigor. Mary doubtless thought she was a paragon. In fact, her busyness saved her from thought.

One Saturday parents carried in a little girl who somehow fell off the fire escape of one of the tenements on Ellison Street. Mary dressed her wounds, splintered her broken arm and told her parents the child would need to stay a few days but would be all right.

Eleanor fluffed the flabby pillow of the child's cot as best she could, tucked in her blanket. The parents sat with eyes stamped on the child. She knew she should have approached them, comforted them.

She turned away, an empty vessel.

She began cutting needed bandages, each measurement of gauze, each snip of her scissors diverting her from the thought of the approach of another night of aloneness, when memory, her constant companion, would leave her sleepless.

As winter moved into spring, Eleanor came to admire Mary Lafferty more and more. She even began to consider Mary's ideas on suffrage, though she did not mention this to her. She knew Mary overworked herself so she volunteered to work Easter Sunday when she knew Mary would most likely have little to no help. She would still have the evening for dinner with Elizabeth, Colin, and Catherine, whom she invited knowing she'd be alone.

Although unwilling to admit it, she began to look forward to her days at the Alliance, even Easter Sunday. Besides the nurse, Lucy Pennington--a wiry-haired widow with two children who stomped more often than walked--she and Mary were kept busy much of the day. She thought Mary looked more wan than usual lately, though she attempted to disguise her fatigue with a forced smile now and then.

"I'm so grateful you came in today, Eleanor," Mary said. "I do think Catherine could have come in, even for a few hours. I do wish she would be more dependable. Like you."

"I really don't mind. Truthfully, Easter is just another day to me."

"I'm planning to have dinner with Charles. The holidays aren't a very joyful time for us, really, being estranged from our father, you know. Charles is finally moving out next month, regardless of my father's health. Of course, father has Dr. Belli from St. Joseph's if needed and a nurse there all the time. And he is impossible to live with. But, still, he is my father and I worry about him alone in that huge house."

"I understand. But you must know I don't like him very much."

"Of course. You know, Eleanor," she added, changing the subject, "I do believe I was right about you having a calling for nursing now that I've seen you here."

"I just work as best I can."

"I hope you realize what an extremely intelligent girl you are."

"I do, thank you."

Mary smiled.

"But I don't want to be a nurse."

"Well, then, what do you want?"

What she wanted was to feel pure, to have Dante return and claim her as his own, as elusive to her as putting out her hand and touching a star.

"I--couldn't say. I don't really care."

Mary brushed her arm gently. "It's because of the strike, the horror. If only you had a cause to believe in--suffrage, for example. It can give you strength seeing women working together, supporting each other."

"I have been thinking about women's rights. How a man can take terrible advantage of a helpless woman." She blushed. "But right now all I can manage is to try to get through each day. For my mother."

"Well, all I ask is that you think about it. It's a lot more than most of these women who come in here do. I must say at times I get so discouraged by them. With the poor in general. They succumb to the same patterns. For heaven's sake, can't they see they can do more with their lives?" She grasped Eleanor's arm more tightly. "Remember, you have your whole life ahead of you. There's so much you can do with it."

The thought of a life ahead of her, a life without Dante, was nearly more than she could bear.

"I don't want to talk about this any more," Eleanor said. "If you don't mind, I have to bathe the patients."

She approached Mrs. Green, an arthritic woman recovering from pneumonia, who would be released in a day or two. She smiled at Eleanor as she bathed her, water seeping through the furrows of wrinkles sketching her face and gnarled hands. Eleanor tried to smile at her, but her lips felt wooden. Someday she would be this old. Decades, half a century or more, without Dante.

When she finished, she glanced into the makeshift office, noticed Charles Lafferty talking to Mary. He must be picking her up for dinner, though earlier than Eleanor would have expected. No, something was amiss. Mary looked stricken. He placed his arms around her. They embraced a time.

Then Mary broke away, wiped her eyes, threw her shoulders back. She approached Eleanor with her usual air of self-sufficiency.

"My father's had a serious heart attack," she said. "I need to leave immediately. Would you mind very much staying longer than you were supposed to, just until Dr. Belli arrives from St. Joseph's to cover sooner for me? Charles has spoken with him already. I wouldn't want Lucy to be left completely alone." She turned briskly. "I'm in quite a fix."

The bells of St. John's tolled five. Her mother and Colin would wonder what became of her. And her bones ached. But she admired Mary too much to say no.

"Of course I'll stay."

She sensed Charles standing in the doorway, watching her as he held Mary's coat, slipped it on. She caught his eye. He took a step towards her, about to speak.

"Hurry, Charles." Mary sped towards the door.

He waved goodbye to her, his words unspoken.

The next Saturday, Mary said her father had been hospitalized at St. Joseph's with a second more serious heart attack. She offered little other information and Eleanor did not ask. She didn't see Charles Lafferty again until one day in early summer he appeared at the Alliance on a Sunday--now she worked the full weekend--and approached her as she tidied up to leave.

She neither greeted him nor turned away.

"Don't you ever stop working, Miss O'Bannion?"

She scrutinized the mass of patients as she spoke. "I was just thinking about that. About work."

"In what way, may I ask?"

"Oh, that I need to work. Not only for the money, though that helps, of course. Just as much to pass the days, I suppose."

"I can assure you there are ways to pass your days more enjoyable than work."

She looked at him squarely. His clothes helped make up for his plain physical appearance. But then, how handsome Dante would look in calfskin pants and a silk shirt like the one he wore.

"I wonder if I might be so bold--" His ears flamed red at his stumbling. "Miss O'Bannion, may I introduce you to some of life's enjoyments?"

She raised her eyebrows but smiled inwardly. "I beg your pardon?"

The red now spread over his entire face. "No, I didn't--I wouldn't- -It's just--I would be so grateful if you would accompany me, well, perhaps to a film sometime?"

"Me?"

Eleanor loved to read about film stars, Mary Pickford and Francis X. Bushman and Lillian Gish being her favorites. She often received gifts of *Photoplay* from Colin who knew her love for them. She sometimes even posed in front of her mirror, trying to style her hair in the manner of her favorites. Being reminded of Mary Pickford carried her to a momentary reverie, and she dreamed of the glamour of a movie star's life.

"Miss O'Bannion?"

She snapped out of her fantasy. Charles Lafferty was still blushing. "I assure you, I have nothing but honorable intentions. We could arrange a chaperone if you like. I feel certain we could have an enjoyable--"

"I haven't seen many films, you know," she said. "But I do love to read about the stars."

He relaxed to such an extent she thought he might collapse. "Would you go with me then?"

She frowned. Even if his intentions were honorable--and she was by no means sure of that--the thought of her employer's son feeling pity for a mill worker disturbed her.

"I don't think so. No."

His face deflated. "I hope I haven't offended you in asking."

"No, not at all. I would just prefer--"

"Not at all, I understand. I'll--just go and wait for Mary then, if you'll excuse me."

He walked toward Mary's office. Eleanor noticed Mary had watched their conversation. Mary now approached her while Charles waited in the office.

"Eleanor, I'm leaving now. You've been here since eight this morning. Lucy's here, so don't stay much longer, will you? I need you too much to risk your getting an illness from overworking yourself."

"I'm fine. I'll leave soon."

"I hope you weren't offended by Charles' offer. About the film. He'd mentioned it so many times to me and was so hesitant. I'm afraid I kept encouraging him. You work so hard, and he's seen that as well, and admires you so. You might have enjoyed going out. But, of course, I respect your decision."

She felt a fool. Perhaps his offer really had been a kind gesture, one Mary sanctioned. Though she hated to admit it, Mary's example showed that not all wealthy people are unkind and uncaring. For an instant she thought to say she changed her mind, would tell Charles she would love to go. But her pride would not let her. He was still a mill owner's son.

"Well, goodbye, Miss O'Bannion."

A pasted smiled could not mask the look of hurt in Charles' eyes when he approached, then left with Mary.

She walked home, listened to the silence of the night, her sense of loneliness strangling her.

Colin and her mother did not seem as surprised as she expected about Charles Lafferty's offer.

"Why, you should have gone," her mother said. "It was a kindness on his part and Mary meant well. Her brother can't be such a bad person, the way he treated me when I was sick."

"And Mary's a saint," Colin said. "She'd never do a thing but good for you. You must know that. I think her brother's a decent man, or she never would of let him ask."

She ate her soup and tea quickly, left the table for the porch. Knowing her mother and Colin approved of Charles convinced her she should have accepted his offer. Her head began to throb.

She had missed her chance.

* * *

Sweat drenched her dress, soaking its front, creeping down her back as she stood by her loom. No overhead fan circulated the stale air. Windows stayed tightly sealed throughout the year. Finally, the work bell clanged, signaling the end of the day. The girls shut down their machines and scurried down the stairs, disappearing in seconds. As usual, she waited at their bottom for Catherine to walk part of the way home with her. Minutes passed; she did not arrive.

As she stared up the stairs, Angus Clegg came into view. His heavy tread assaulted the floor as he strode towards her, panting. He scrutinized her, dug into his ear with his thick index finger, wiped it on his pants.

"Not gone yet? All the other girls are out of here as soon as that bell clangs. I don't blame them. The heat."

She noticed his shirt stuck to the layers of fat on his chest.

Suddenly she remembered Nora's warning to never be alone with him.

"I'm waiting for Catherine," she said quickly. "We walk home together. She'll be here any minute."

"Catherine's not in today. At least I didn't see her at the tubs."

"I'll be going then."

She turned to leave.

In an instant he lunged toward her, blocked the door, grasped her shoulders.

"Ever wonder what it would be like to be with a man?" His voice sounding almost friendly. "I bet you wonder all the time, a beauty like you."

She struggled to wrench his hands from her. He scarcely moved. The more she fought, the more his grip tightened.

"Now, now, don't fight so hard. Don't you know how much I've been wantin' to kiss you all this time? And you know you owe me. Did I report all the yardage you lost the times you broke the machine down? No. Least, I made it a lot less than it was."

He clenched her shoulders.

She kicked him hard. "Let me go!"

He laughed. "I like a woman who's a devil. I do."

He plunged his face within inches of hers. His breath set her stomach churning. He kissed her, bruising her lips as she fought him. Then one of his hands cupped her breast. Her heart pumped harder.

Think. She must think. She would not submit to this beast. How could she break free?

His grip tightened. He removed his hand from her breast, lifted her skirt, began to rub her inner thigh.

Her heart banged harder against her breast. Memories of her father welled up inside her, tried to drag her down.

He pressed her tightly against the wall, continued to move his hand up and down her inner thigh. He bowed his head, cradled it in her neck. She felt his hair, wet, greasy on her cheek.

The darkness had a name now: fear. A fear so powerful it left no room for her. Fear of her mother finding out, fear of her father, all the fear she carried within her constantly, always threatening to break out.

He began to kiss her neck, his breath heavy, mesmerized by passion. He moved his hand higher, rubbed his fingers on her private place. He jolted his head, looked straight at her, then closed his eyes.

She could not fight the fear, could not stop it. But she could use it.

She grasped his hair, yanked back his head, pressed her lips to the side of his face. Her tongue felt the saltiness of his slack jowl.

She bit, deep and hard.

He howled. Blood gushed down his face; she felt it trickling down her chin. She clenched her teeth around the pulp of his jowl in her mouth, reveling at the sound of his wailing.

He loosened his grip on her, and she shoved him away. She glared at him for a moment, blood running down his shirt, a trembling hand pressed to his face. Then she spat the pulp of his flesh onto the floor and ran for her life. Down the stairs, gagging, spewing saliva and blood, over and over.

After she ran a block, she turned to see if he followed. The street was empty. She lifted her petticoat, cleaned her mouth and face of blood as best she could, then tucked it back under her dress. She still tasted the blood of him, saw it splattered onto her dress.

She prayed her mother would not be home when she arrived.

For once her prayers were answered. Elizabeth had not yet returned. She vomited into the sink. Slime and food lay in the drain. She pressed it down with her fingers, then rinsed her mouth, spitting until the pink water ran clear. Then she removed her dress, scrubbed it and her petticoat, washing away all evidence of what she had done.

The sun's rays pricked her skin when she went to the porch, yet she welcomed the heat, burning away the past hour. She closed her eyes, reliving the horror. She had been propelled by dark a force. Had she momentarily lost her mind?

Yet, she felt no remorse for her act, only a great sense of justice. After a time she began to breathe slower. She had fought back. She could fight back. She snuggled against the back of the chair, no longer a defenseless little girl.

Elizabeth awakened her.

"For heaven's sake, why did you ever sit out here in the heat of the sun on such a day?" Her mother felt her burned cheeks with the back of her hand. "Though the good Lord knows it's not much better inside."

Her mother didn't notice anything different, except the wet dress and petticoat on the clothes line. She explained that it had been spotted with dye someone dropped after slipping and falling at the mill.

For the rest of the evening, she listened to her mother's small talk, trying to act her usual self. She was surprised how easy it was to keep the changes in her bottled up. All was well until the knock sounded at the door.

"Police. Open up."

An officer with a pock-marked face stood at the screen.

Her mother gave her an alarmed glance, then let the officer in. "What is it? Has Colin--"

"We have reason to believe this young lady, Miss Eleanor O'Bannion, I take it," he gestured to her, "brutally attacked her employer today, ma'am."

Elizabeth grasped the back of the kitchen chair.

Eleanor stepped forward. "I'm Eleanor O'Bannion."

"We need to take you to the station, young lady, ask you a few questions."

She never thought Clegg would involve the police, though she should have remembered that the Paterson police aligned with management during the strike. Still, he must know she would give her side of the story, and she couldn't imagine any explanation Clegg would give superior to hers.

"Eleanor?" her mother said, nearly breathless.

"It's all right, mother."

She knew the truth, and would speak it.

She had never been in the police station on Main Street, a structure of cobblestones, cement oozing from between them, resting in gray stiffness for almost a century. Copper lanterns long since turned green decked each side of its oak door. The officer led her to a large, empty room the color of putty, bare walled except for a few photos of criminals and a tack board with messages.

The officer who brought her in pulled out a small, slightly tattered notebook, and she finally learned Clegg's side of the story. Clegg claimed she went berserk when he told her she would be fired for her poor work record. He reported her most recent error, could give witnesses she damaged very expensive ribbons. He said she lunged like a crazy woman, screamed she needed the job, that she would kill him for firing her. Before he knew it, she grasped him and gouged his face.

For the first time, she felt doubt. It was not true, but it was a story that could be believed. And if it was her word against his--a mill worker against management--she knew which way the courts would go.

But all she had to fall back on now was the truth.

As she explained her side of the story, the officer folded his arms tightly. He scrutinized her as she spoke, then unfolded them, wrote down the information she gave.

When they led her back to the anteroom, she found her mother and Colin waiting. She insisted they leave to spare them seeing her brought to the holding cell at the back of the building.

Moonlight fell through the window, obscured now and then by clouds scurrying across the sky. Someone cried now and then in another cell. She slumped onto her cot, squeezed her hands to try to stop their shaking. She would be imprisoned for years if found guilty.

But surely Colin would write Dante and he would return and rescue her. He always knew what should be done. Or if she did go to prison, he would surely come to her. She relived both scenarios over and over, until finally she fell asleep around four in the morning.

At nine o'clock the officer who had interviewed her appeared at her cell, unlocked it, motioned to the hallway. "You can go, young lady. Bail's been met."

She felt touched by Colin's gesture of putting up all of his savings to bail her out. "Is Mr.McCarthy here?"

"Nobody by that name. The fellow who paid, he came and went a while back."

"Who was it?"

He flipped through his record book, found the information. "Charles Lafferty."

Charles?

As soon as she left, she went to his home to thank him, but his servant said he had left on a trip.

Colin and her mother, of course, believed it was his affection that led him to post bail. But she had her doubts. She could not ignore her station in life and his. And her experiences did not allow her to believe in kindness.

Perhaps Mary had suggested it to him.

But when she thanked her, Mary stood open mouth, said she knew nothing of it. Nothing at all.

The trial approached. Colin wanted the union involved, felt the situation really represented a larger issue, the bosses against the workers. Eleanor refused. Even if she hadn't felt this was her fight, she was too uncertain of victory. She didn't want the union involved in another losing battle for her sake.

Catherine stayed with her constantly the days before the trial. She sat, stared at Eleanor and mumbled that all would be fine. Catherine appeared unstrung in other ways too-- weight loss, dark circles under her eyes. As the day of the trial grew nearer, Eleanor became the one comforting Catherine, constantly reminding her truth lay on her side.

A few days before the hearing she showed up, eyes bloodshot and puffed.

"You look awful." Eleanor motioned she sit down. "Why did you ever come over today? You should be resting."

"I--need to tell you something. I want to testify for you. I thought and thought of it, and I know it's the right thing to do."

Eleanor smiled. "You mean testify I have good character? You're very sweet, but I don't think that will help. Not now. I'll get through it the best I can, no matter what--"

"It's not your character."

"Then what?"

Catherine's chest heaved up and down. She seemed almost terrified. What was--?

Suddenly, everything made sense. She should have guessed earlier.

"It was Clegg, wasn't it?" Eleanor said softly. "He was the father."

Catherine slumped into a chair. "He raped me. After work, just like he tried with you. I couldn't tell. The bosses, they'd side with him, just like they're doin' with you now. Where would I go?" She began to cry. "I would of been black-listed. I couldn't fight him, like you did. I'm so ashamed, I'll always be sick about it. Always. But I should of spoke up. I will now."

"No. I won't let you. It would always be a black mark against you, just the way you said and it wouldn't help. They'd ask why you didn't tell. And how could you prove it was him? Mary would testify about the abortion, I know, but they'll say it could have been anybody. You could lose everything with trying to help me. What man will be interested in you if he hears it? And it would make no difference. You know that."

"But I have to tell. You can't go to prison for something he's guilty of. I know I can help you. Why would I lie about such a thing?"

"I won't allow it and that's all there is to it."

"Well, then I'll do it, no matter what you say."

She rose, slammed the door hard in Eleanor's face.

She thought long and hard about what to do about Catherine's revelations.

No matter how she reasoned, she came up with the same decision.

The ponderous granite facade of City Hall on Market Street projected strength and power. Eleanor hoped it would transfer to her. She looked up at its clock, its face gleaming below the ornate dome surrounded by Carrera angels. Two o'clock.

It was time.

She walked up the steps to the main entrance, rehearsing once again details of what she would say to the district attorney.

William Kiernan had a reputation in Paterson police politics that went back to the silk strike of 1902. And during the strike of 1912 he had prosecuted several cases on behalf of the silk manufacturers. He also had connections with the newspapers, wearing his friendships with the manufacturers like a cloak of gold.

Eleanor sat across from him, studying his red-veined face, pouches protruding under his eyes--most likely signs of late nights and parties, rather than sleeplessness over the fate of Paterson workers. He brushed his hand through the few strands of gray hair on his head. The stone of his sapphire ring became a rainbow as sunlight streamed through the window upon it. He unwrapped and clipped a cigar.

"Well, young lady, it seems we have a real impass here. I don't see why you needed to see me, to tell you the truth. I'm always willing to oblige where justice is concerned, but I do think all we have to say will be said in the court room."

"Please hear me out, sir," she said as meekly as she could. "I only want to save you and Mr. Clegg embarrassment."

"Embarrassment? I don't think you need to worry about that." He lit the cigar and drew it to life. "It's you who attacked him, isn't it?"

"I have quite a few witnesses gathered now who will be testifying to help me, against Mr. Clegg."

"Of course, your friends--or anyone with a grudge against management--will testify to your character. It won't make much of a difference, I'm afraid."

"It's not my character they'll be testifying about," she said. "It's his, sir. About the fact he either raped or attempted to rape them."

He took a long, hard puff on his cigar, exhaled a cloud of smoke. She could feel the power starting to shift her way.

"No woman in her right mind would admit such a thing in public" he said, offhand, "and you know it."

"You're mistaken, sir. I know girls from the mill who have been attacked by Mr. Clegg, who are willing to speak out in court about it, about him. They will take the stand and swear it. Under oath."

He flicked his ash into a tray, never taking his eyes from her. "I don't believe you."

She met his stare. "That's all right. It's the judge that has to believe me. And the newspapers." She allowed herself a slight smile. "You're a good prosecutor, but you can only work with what you're given. And Angus Clegg isn't worth the trouble, believe me."

She stood up straight.

"You tell him about our meeting. You tell him."

His face still remained placid. "I don't believe those women will testify, Miss O'Bannion. They would be too ashamed to say such a thing in public."

"With respect, Mr. Kiernan, you can't understand what they've suffered, the memory they have to live with. Every day. There comes a time when the need for justice overcomes shame. You'll see."

She went to the door, her steps deliberate. She slammed it, then sagged against it. She'd done it. She didn't think she could, but she'd done it.

But what if he called her bluff?

She suspected which girls had been molested, saw it in their stricken faces, the way they shriveled when Clegg approached. But the only one she knew would testify was Catherine. She told Catherine to ask the others to try to show up tomorrow for the trial. Just for moral support, she'd said. But she doubted they would do even that. Lost wages, retribution from Lafferty would not allow it.

If they did show up, she could give their names, point them out, call them to the stand. Being mostly believing Catholics, having to swear on the Bible would play upon their moral obligation to tell the truth. She could win if she used that tactic.

She couldn't. Their shame and fear of reprisal hung too heavily in the equation. Many had beaus or husbands who would never look at them in the same way again. How could she destroy their lives to save hers?

If they chose not to appear as part of her plan, not to speak up, she would face the consequences, alone.

She looked across the courtroom. Every girl who worked on her floor ribbon weaving and every soaker sat in the front rows. The rest of the room was packed to overflowing with broad silk weavers, loom fixers, dyers' helpers. It was Colin's work, it had to be. She approached each ribbon girl and soaker, thanked them for coming, her eyes filled with tears she fought to hold back.

From the corner of her eye she saw Kiernan and Clegg surveying her every movement, whispering. Clegg studied each of the girls in the front rows. He frowned, set his teeth hard on his underlip, made a fist, punched into his hand. Kiernan flew his hand to his shoulder, continued to whisper.

Eleanor's heart pounded against her ribs, but she tried to at least look calm. She peeked at Clegg again, memories flooding her. She raised her head higher as she stood before the judge, whose eyes drooped so low he appeared almost asleep.

Kiernan approached the bench.

"Your honor," he said. "Angus Clegg has reconsidered. He feels the defendant should not be punished for a momentary fit of crazed temper. He can not see her life spoiled forever because of one terrible mistake. She not only has herself to support but also her mother, as we understand it. And with that in mind, Mr. Clegg has decided to drop the charges against her."

Eleanor stood wide-eyed. Catherine and the workers ran to her, embraced her. The girls wept uncontrollably, not having the faintest idea how their presence had brought the victory.

"You won, dear girl! You won!" Colin embraced her, led her to Elizabeth who sat stunned on the bench. She held her mother so hard she could have broken her into pieces from loving her so.

At the door, Clegg turned. He watched the girls from the mill, particularly the O'Bannion bitch. He touched the bandage on his jowl, which constantly pulsated with pain, swirled his tongue around it, feeling the line of stitches closing the flesh. He would have a scar for the rest of his life because of her. People would stare, then pretend not to notice. For the rest of his life.

He focused on O'Bannion, the adoration in her eyes as she spoke to her mother and clasped her hands. He knew people saw him as a beast, a lummox. But he understood love, its power to shatter or heal, that the person loved can mean more than one's self.

And the O'Bannion bitch loved her mother.

Despite the pain in his face, he smiled. He'd get his revenge. Through the mother. His heart banged in his chest as he began to formulate his plan. But he must be patient, wait for his moment.

Then he would strike.

Elizabeth celebrated the victory with a roast beef which Colin bought. Colin dutifully carved the roast, wiped his forehead with the back of his hand after he finished. Abnormal heat of October wore through the apartment, humidity hung in the air like a wet sheet.

"I don't know how you can stand the heat of that stove," he said. "It can't be true it's the fall with this awful weather. You'd think Colorado would be better, but Dante says--"

"Serve the meat, will you?"

Elizabeth's eyes pierced him like stillettos.

His face reddened. But it was too late.

Eleanor had wondered why Dante never wrote him. She'd heard him promise to write, and he would never go back on his word. But she'd never guessed Colin would not have shared information with her. "You heard from Dante?" she said. "Why don't you share his letters? It's not because of me, is it? Of course, I won't forget him, but he's in the past. That doesn't mean I wouldn't like to know how he is."

She hoped she sounded believable.

"Well, I do have a letter from him." He glanced at her mother. "Fresh from yesterday's mail. I didn't hear from him for months, honest I didn't. And to tell the truth, I wasn't sure how you would take the letters."

"You're foolish to hide them from me. I know I'll never see him again. I'm all right."

"Well, in that case, after we eat I'll read it. If you think so, Elizabeth."

"There's no sense hiding them now, is there?"

The pace of dinner moved slowly for Eleanor. Finally Colin finished his coffee, took the letter from his pocket.

"Don't mind my bad readin' now."

She sat, breathless.

"Dear Colin,

I finally have a moment to write. We are still trying to encourage the strikers not to give in and continue to fight for an eight-hour day, safety regulations, the end of company scrip and the right to choose where they will live. Governor Ammons called out the National Guard to restore peace, which may have made the papers there. But what does the rest of the country know of all the men killed and maimed in mining accidents, over 400 in 1913 alone, men black with soot from coke ovens, living in dirt and filth. They are ripe for the union to help them. Since they have evicted the strikers from company homes, the tent colonies are all around. They have estimated at least 14,000 are on strike now. Colorado Coal Mining is at a standstill. We have been close to open warfare here with gunfire exchanged between the strikers and deputy sheriffs.

They killed several strikers, using a frightening vehicle they nicknamed the Death Special, much like an armored car with two machine guns. I can not believe that this is happening in this country.

I met John D. Rockefeller, Jr. He personally visited the mines, ate with the men and tried to be friendly. He wants to introduce a joint representation type plan which seems to make some sense, though I never thought I'd be agreeing with a Rockefeller idea. I know company officials are against it, but I must say the man seemed sincere enough, made a gesture of having me, along with other union organizers, circulate with the workers.

Yet, what good this is I do not know, since we union organizers are not recognized by the company.

I hope you, Elizabeth and Eleanor are well.

Best regards, Dante

P.S. Could you save newspaper clippings for me that have to do with the strike out here, and send them with your next letter?"

Eleanor fought to control herself. She expected to hear about the conflict in Colorado, realized the strike would be as long and hard as the one in Paterson. But why didn't he say more about her, acknowledge his feelings in a stronger way? Perhaps he reasoned her mother would hear the letter and frown upon it. Surely that was his reason.

He would write again, say something more meaningful about her then. She lived on that hope.

Colin folded the letter, stuffed it into his pocket. "It seems all I hear about these days is death." He wiped sweat from his temple again. "I'm off Tuesday, and so is the whole shop and that means you too, Eleanor. I got word before I came over. Lafferty died. They're givin' us a day off for the bastard's--excuse me, the man's-- funeral. As if any of us would go pay respects to the likes of him."

Eleanor's mother stopped clearing the dishes, stared in thought at the sink. After a few minutes she brought in the pie.

"Well, I for one, will certainly pay my respects," she said, "For Mary Lafferty's sake, and for her brother. Even though some of us--" her eyes darted to Eleanor--"have forgotten the man's kindness."

"I didn't forget, mother. I tried to see him the same day I was released from jail. But he was away."

"One time. One time you went. It's been weeks now, hasn't it? It isn't right, Eleanor, and you know it. Sometimes I wonder if you remember anything I taught you about the way to act when others are kind to you."

Eleanor hung her head. She hated when her mother was right, which was more often than not.

"I'll thank him when he's back. He must be now, with his father's death, when I see him again at the Alliance."

"And why wouldn't you be going with me to the wake to pay your respects?"

Once again, her mother's words rang true. She was about to reply when Colin banged the table with his fist.

"Well, I'll not set my foot at a wake for that scum."

"And need I remind you that you may owe Mary my life, Colin McCarthy? And Charles Lafferty, bringing me home like that?"

He frowned. "Aye, you're right. I don't know how I could of ever thought not to go."

And so it was agreed. They would all attend the wake of the man who nearly killed them during the strike.

* * *

The Lafferty estate, one of the largest on Silk Road, stood back a few hundred feet from the street, its lawn dotted with smatterings of hemlocks and maples, now almost bare, fallen leaves forming gold and red rings around their trunks. Hundreds of yellow and white mums still garnished either side of the cobblestone path leading to the house. Eleanor smiled. It was a well-planned garden to still have some color so late in the season.

As they walked towards the gate they passed myriads of automobiles lining the street along the Lafferty property. Colin could not resist the temptation to examine a few, bending to study a leather interior, peering at the shiny gadgets that miraculously made it run. Many gleaming carriages also lined the street, the horses lazily waiting their owners' return.

Eleanor still felt confused about her presence here. George Lafferty refused to meet any of the demands of the workers during the strike, drove them to near starvation, and probably made a profit from the excesses of silk stored in Pennsylvania.

Yet, here she stood.

A hundred or so workers gathered around the great wrought iron gates, curiousity seekers who came to view the opulence, female workers to study the women mourners' fashionable clothing. Joe Collucci, one of the workers at Weidemann's Dye Works, called out to them.

Colin acknowledged him with a wave of his hand.

"Is good to see the sights." Joe stared at the iron filligree of the fence, fingered it. "Never see such richness. I wonder now. Maybe it was this I pay for? With money from my fair share of earnings? What do you think?"

"I'm disgusted to say it could surely be," Colin said. "But we still can't give up hope. I have some plans to tell you soon that might change things for the better."

"I never give up hope." He smiled again. "We are here to see the cars, to see the rich go in with their rich clothes. And to dream. Same as you."

"Truth is," Colin said, "we came to pay our respects--to Mary and Charles Lafferty, not to himself."

Collucci laughed, as did some of the other men and women listening nearby. "That will be the day, huh? When we give them respect."

Eleanor's mother stepped forward.

"We have. Mary saved my life, Joe Collucci, at the Alliance. And her brother, he brought me home in the freezing cold. He's helped out my daughter as well. And so we're paying respect for their sake. And come to think of it," Elizabeth turned to the crowd, "I can't speak for the men, but I could name a lot of women here I think should be grateful for all Mary Lafferty did for them, knowing they couldn't afford the hospital." She raised her arm, pointed her finger at the group. "And that's not to mention your children she's nursed back to health. And didn't ask one single dime for it if you couldn't pay."

The crowd became silent. More than a few men and women shuffled their feet, stared at the ground.

"If you'd step aside," her mother said, "we'd like to get through, please."

They began the walk up the path. Soon they heard the sound of shoes clicking on the stone path behind them. Eleanor turned. Most of the members of Lafferty's, others from nearby mills, walked slowly behind them.

But the feeling certainly wasn't unanimous. Shouts bellowed from the street below. "I never thought I'd see the day our own, one of our union leaders, no less, would pay respect to a man who treated us like shit!"

Eleanor peeked at Colin, red faced, hands clenched as they walked the path, Elizabeth on one arm, she on the other. She sighed with relief knowing he would not fight here. Not with them at his side.

A large wreath with a black crepe bow adorned the oak door. The knocker sounded like an explosion when Eleanor rapped on it. The maid led them to the large room where Lafferty's body lay. As she followed, Eleanor tried to take in as much as she could. She eyed a mahogany grandfather clock carved around its door with cherubs, glanced at portraits in oil of somber-looking people on the walls, especially two hanging separate from the others. One must be Lafferty's deceased wife, and the other was Charles. She did not see a portrait of Mary.

Once inside the room, she could not help but stare. It was larger than their whole apartment, decorated with velvet curtains and burgundy flocked wallpaper. The casket sat at the far side of the room, encircled by autumn flowers overflowing into the room. Women in silk moire, men in gray or black frock coats sat in chairs or stood conversing quietly.

They joined the line waiting to offer condolences to Mary and Charles.

When they finally approached the coffin, Eleanor and her mother kneeled on the kneeler. Colin stood behind.

Behind them the crowd, which had been talking in hushed tones, grew absolutely still. Her mother remained oblivious, moving her lips in prayer.

Eleanor studied Lafferty's once somewhat handsome face, now porcine and waxed. His bloated hands were folded, and a giant emerald shone on his now very dead finger. Part of her felt the urge to spit in his face. She thought of Dante, what he would think seeing her now. Then she thought of Charles' and Mary's kindness and kept control.

She continued to stare at the body while her mother prayed. She thought of the suffering that could have been prevented if only the rich would share their wealth more equitably with those who produced it. But change would come. She heard recently that Denham and Whatley was allowing some of their workers buy their own looms. Colin said he heard some weavers from Lafferty's were thinking of leaving to work at Denham and Whatley on commission weaving.

She could not control a tiny smile as she viewed Lafferty's corpse. He would turn somersaults in his grave if that happened at his mill.

She wondered who would run it now, what its future would be, what would happen with her job.

Elizabeth rose from the velvet cushioned kneeler, made the sign of the cross. Then they turned to Mary and Charles, their faces sunken by sorrow. Even though Mary was estranged from Lafferty, he was still her father.

And Charles Lafferty. She stood, shamefaced at not having thanked him for putting up her bail.

Mary's eyes filled when she saw them. "I thank you so much for coming."

Her mother reached for Mary's hand. "I can't tell you how sorry I am you and your brother have to go through this pain, Mary. Had he been sick long?"

"He's had a bad heart for years. Then he had a stroke. He seemed to have improved, and then, this. It's still a shock."

Mary's hand felt weak when she took Eleanor's.

"I know it took a great deal for you to come tonight, Eleanor." She turned to Colin. "All of you. My father was not the man he should have been with the workers."

Eleanor faced her squarely. "It was for you and Charles we came."

"I know that. And it means a great deal to us, doesn't it, Charles?"

She turned to her brother who, having finished speaking with other visitors, gave his complete attention to Eleanor.

"It does. It certainly does."

She felt the trembling of his hand as he shook hers, his eyes a study in gratitude, then anticipation, although she had no idea what he expected her to say.

She cleared her throat.

"I'm--ashamed--I haven't thanked you in person for putting up my bail, Mr. Lafferty. I did go to your home and the servant said you were away."

"Of course, I understand. Won't you please call me Charles."

"Charles then."

He continued holding her hand as she spoke. "There's no need to apologize at all,--Eleanor? I assure you it was only fair and just you receive all the help possible. I'm so glad things turned out all right in the end."

He continued to hold her hand. She gulped. What must the workers think of her holding hands with a Lafferty? Yet, she did not pull away. The least she could do would be to let him hold her hand in thanks for putting up her bail.

"I'm very sorry for your loss," she said. "Truthfully, he wasn't a man I could admire, but he was still your father. And you have my sympathy."

Still he held her hand.

"I see there are so many others waiting to offer their sympathy," she said. "I think I better move on."

"Your flowers," he said quickly. "Are you still painting them?"

"My flowers? Oh, yes."

The line of viewers watched, waited.

"I should move on."

"I'll never forget your coming tonight." His voiced sounded thin as paper. "You'll never know how much it means to me." He looked down at the carpet for refuge, as though he might hide under it.

She pulled her hand slightly. He finally released it.

Colin stood behind her. She heard his offer of sympathy and the line began to move.

As she turned to find a seat, Charles said, "I hope so much I'll see you again."

She did not respond and he finally turned full attention to the others in line, as did Mary.

Eleanor searched the room, saw her mother gesturing, pointing to two seats reserved for her and Colin. She sat down, began to squirm.

"Can't we go now?"

"We need to wait for Colin and should stay at least half an hour. It's the right thing to do."

"Half an hour?"

She sighed. She tried to keep busy watching various people kneel at the coffin, studied their clothing, the room, the flowers. She found herself observing Charles Lafferty more often than not. Almost every time she did, he glanced at her as well.

She had to bolt.

"I'll be outside when you're ready."

She darted from the stuffiness of the room, waited for Elizabeth and Colin in the cool night air.

The crowd began to disperse by the time they left the Lafferty mansion. They stood a few moments on the street, inhaling the crisp air, listening to the last cries of cicadas before cold weather set it. Work did not exist in these moments of tranquility as they walked home, clinging to each other.

Eleanor had her loom set for a floral pattern, one of her favorites, in moire velour, twenty-four ribbons woven in individual sections, one shuttle for each width of fabric. The weaving was nearly done, but she could hardly focus on setting up the next process, mechanical crushing to create a watered effect.

The news Catherine gave that Clegg would return to work in a week unnerved her. She stared at the myriad silk ribbons lying in the bins--satin bayard, satin beauvoirs, tinsel and roman belts, gros grain, taffeta, moire velour. A few months back they were merely skeins of silk and meant nothing to her. Now each possessed a beauty created by her. She swelled with pride as she studied them. But she knew she could never remain once Clegg returned. And she felt certain every mill owner in Paterson would give excuses not to hire her, whether they believed Clegg or not. When she told Stephen Kosinski, in charge now, of her decision to leave, he did not discourage her. She would have to try to find work in the mills of Passaic.

She ached to the bone as she walked the streets of Paterson. She loved their every nook and cranny. The secret place on the Passaic River's bank where she found refuge, the First Ward Branch of the library, Lefkowitz' Grocery where she sometimes bought a penny candy, Turn Hall, where

Dante's ghost still spoke to her each time she passed, and, above all, the Great Falls.

She sat on her usual bench near the Falls, listening to their roar, shuffled away dry leaves as they dropped upon her shoes. She studied the half denuded trees forming webs against the pewter sky, dotted here and there by blankets of clouds. She buttoned her sweater, walked home with head bowed, thinking how lost she would be when she left Paterson.

Eleanor noticed Mary looked tired and drawn when she returned to the Alliance the following Saturday. But despite the weariness, there was a jauntiness in her step when she called Mrs. Pennington, Catherine and her together.

"I have some good news," she said. "The bread company on Matlock is moving to New York City, and I've decided to buy the building. We'll easily have five or six times the room we have here. Just think of how many more patients we can take in."

Eleanor guessed Mary's father left her some money that she would use for the clinic. It seemed fair. Earnings from the sweat of the workers' brows would now benefit them.

"I've called you over to thank you as well," Mary said. "Your work has been wonderful. Especially yours, Eleanor, even giving up your Sundays to care for the patients."

Eleanor had to admit the money allowed her to buy extras. She recently bought her mother a copy of *Great Expectations* for her birthday. They took turns reading a chapter aloud each evening. And blessed work filled in the days she waited to hear Dante's next letter.

"Anyway, I'd like to offer you all full-time positions at the new Alliance. I'd be so glad if you'd accept."

The wrinkles in Lucy Pennington's face crinkled around her eyes as she smiled. "I'd be glad of it."

"I'll pay you girls two dollars more a week than you make at the mill. You too, Lucy. You deserve it."

Catherine's eyes widened. "I'd be happy to work full time."

Mary turned to Eleanor. "What do you think? I know you've got a good job, one you should be proud of, but I'm offering you a better salary. And I do believe nursing is your calling. You don't think so, I know, but I can sense such things."

Eleanor did not immediately speak. She knew she should be grateful to receive such an exceptional offer. And in a short time she would be unemployed. But the idea of working full time at the Alliance seemed daunting. The work she did at the mills was mechanical. It didn't demand that she feel anything. Her work at the Alliance on weekends had begun to affect her. Saturday and Sunday nights she often relived the day, trying to erase not only the visions of torment of those she nursed but also the triumph of those who left well, returning to lives full of love she would never know.

Yet, did she have a choice? She had little chance getting a job as a ribbon weaver at another mill, doubted she would even be hired as a soaker. And she possessed one certainty. She could not bear to leave the city she loved.

"Can I think about it?" Her voice sounded flat.

"You don't seem as enthusiastic as I thought you would," Mary said. "I know it can be so frustrating working with the poor. At times I want to shake them, try to convince them they can rise above their situation." She frowned. "So I suppose I can understand your hesitancy. But I'll be losing such a wonderful nurse if you say no." She blushed. "Not to mention someone I would like to think of as a friend."

Hurt poured over Mary's face.

"What was I thinking? "Of course I accept. I'm just--in shock, I suppose."

"Well, I'm glad you're aboard," Mary beamed. "I need an excellent nurse like you. More than you imagine."

"I see you girls have heard the good news."

They turned to see Charles Lafferty dressed in a lamb gray frock coat, matching trousers, soft leather boots. He immediately focused on Eleanor and smiled.

Catherine approached him, treading air. "We can't believe it, sir. Dr. Lafferty is so generous. We'll work hard to deserve her trust."

"Oh, we owe it all to Charles, not me," Mary said. "He's the money behind this move."

Eleanor hid her surprise and managed a smile. "Why, that's very generous, Mr. Laf--Charles."

He beamed. "Thank you, Eleanor. Though it was the least I could do, given the way my father treated you."

Eleanor again swallowed her surprise. That was precisely what she was thinking.

Mary clapped her hands. "It's back to work we go, girls. There's so much to do."

Mary gestured to the seats near the door. Three people waited, one with eyes closed, hands clasped, resting her head against the wall. Another blew her nose in a gray handkerchief, breathing through her mouth. A third, in tears, crunched forward, held her wrist, tied with a makeshift bandage.

Eleanor turned to the new patients with the others.

"Miss O'Bannion? Eleanor."

He seemed bent on delaying her. She squirmed a bit, remembering how he held her hand at the wake. His manner made her think he must believe he spoke to the Virgin Mary. She cringed at the thought. She studied his hands while he indulged his habit of twirling his hat.

"I--don't suppose you could reconsider my offer, could you?"

"Not now, I don't think," she said. "Rumor has it you plan to take over the mill. I wouldn't feel right."

"I'm not running it yet, not really. I still have so much to learn. I have Stephen Kosinski helping me, he's been very patient. If it doesn't work out, well, I'll sell it. And then you needn't be upset seeing your employer any longer. Besides, Mary said she thought you might be working at the Alliance full time soon. So then it won't matter, will it?"

She smiled in spite of herself. "You certainly don't give up."

"Not on this. Please. Say yes."

"It's just that I don't want people to think I'd be seeing you because you're rich."

His laughter rumbled the room. He finally gained control.

"Well, I suppose it's as good a reason as any. And given the way I look, you probably wouldn't be seeing me if I were poor. A man knows such things."

"That's not the reason," she said quickly.

"Eleanor, there's a wonderful life outside of Lafferty's Weaving Mill and the Women's Alliance. All I want to do is show you some of it."

She frowned. "I don't know."

"I suppose you could lose some friends, if they see you with the mill owner. Is that it?"

"I don't have any friends. Except Catherine, the best friend anyone could have. And Mary. I think the world of her. I don't need any others."

"But there are so many good people. Anyway, I know the workers have no idea what kind of employer I'll be but I hope they haven't condemned me already. I won't be like my father. That's part of the reason I'm trying to take over the mill." He blushed. "To make amends."

She felt touched by his comment. And it was becoming clear that he was truly, honorably, interested in her. But why? It could not be loneliness. Many socialites would be throwing their daughters at him for his wealth. Perhaps his plainness made him shy with women. Maybe he thought a factory girl would not care about appearances, only money.

No. She remembered his reaction to her flower painting, her mother's illness, her conflict with Clegg, his putting up her bail.

"I--suppose--I could go."

"I'm so glad. Would Saturday night be all right? I'm sure Mary would let you off a few hours early. I could pick you up at, say, seven."

"All right." Her look darted to the clock. "I'd better get back to work. I've lost too much time already. I'm behind with bathing the patients. I don't like to let Mary down."

She went to the sink, retrieved the basin, soap, towels. When she turned to begin her chores, she noticed he was gone.

* * *

Charles Lafferty wondered why most people focus exclusively on spring and summer, forgetting the beauty of fall in the garden. The hibiscus nearly finished its bloom, the sedum turned blood red, burning bush blazed scarlet, raintree pods hung like golden lanterns, viburnum bragged red berries. He walked along, examining leaf textures, touching their distinctive surfaces--rue, lamb's ears, barberry, rosemary, many others.

He wished his mother could have seen the garden, the changes he'd made through the years, felt she would have approved. He missed her every day of his life. He thought of summers they explored the garden, studied botany, hoed and planted. His father watched from his study window, arms clenched around his waist. Now they both lay in the earth. He gardened alone.

What would she say regarding his decision to try to run the mill? He felt certain if she knew how his father treated the workers after her death she would want him to rectify those wrongs, run the mill fairly. If he could.

But his fears about running the mill seemed miniscule compared to the feelings enveloping him since speaking with Eleanor O'Bannion in his garden. He was haunted by the vision of her, sitting on the carriage stone, so isolated and sad. Surely because of the strike? He longed to console her. Later, he thought it was guilt at his father's treatment of her and the other workers that motivated him to offer food to her and her mother. But when he paid her bail, he knew he could no longer rationalize.

He was in love with her.

Only later when he saw her at the clinic after the strike, coloring improved, weight gained, did he realize her beauty. He lay in bed, obsessed by thoughts of her. When she turned down his invitation to the films, he lost sleep, could not eat. Seeing her at the wake was worse. He knew he looked a fool, but could not release her hand.

The globe of sun was already descending when he left the garden. This evening must be perfect. He could not win her by good looks and savoir faire, for he had neither. But he could give her something he sensed she rarely experienced.

Happiness.

Eleanor's mother surprised her with a collar and cuffs she embroidered with pink roses and green stems, made from silk strands Colin managed to salvage from the discards. She snapped them onto her dress; its appearance changed immediately.

She sensed her mother's excitement about the evening, though she now regretted agreeing to it. What would she say to such an educated man? She'd never had these feelings with Dante. If only he could see her, wearing her silk-embroidered collar and cuffs. She imagined him knocking at the door. They would walk near the river, hold hands. He would kiss her good night.

Her reverie abruptly ended when she heard Charles' footsteps on the stairs.

Her mother greeted him with a genuine smile. He handed Eleanor a bouquet of roses. Her mother took them promptly, began to search for a pitcher.

"How lovely your dress is," he said. Such a beautiful embroidered collar of roses."

Her mother beamed.

"My mother made it."

"I should have known. I walked to your place since we can take the trolley on Ellison more readily to get to Palisades Park."

"Palisades Park!"

She'd read of the amusement park, which was supposed to have surpassed even New York's Coney Island, but she never dreamed she'd visit it.

She saw his pleasure at her excitement over his choice.

"You won't believe how wonderful it is. At least I think so. You haven't been there, have you?"

"No, oh no."

"Ah. Good. And next week it closes for the season. So we're in luck."

A moment later, and her mother was waving to them from the top of the stairs. "You two have a wonderful time."

Eleanor felt a happy glow all the way there. Charles, too, seemed content to ride in silence, perhaps to keep from babbling. When they alighted from the trolley, she looked ahead and saw thousands of electric lights strung through the distant trees. To the south she saw what she read was the largest electric sign in the world, with thousands of incandescent lights spelling out "Palisades Amusement Park." The Call said it measured something like four hundred feet in length.

Here she stood, actually seeing it.

She remembered its importance to Mary who told her she had been to the Park for the largest outdoor meeting for women's rights ever held in New York or New Jersey. Women from both states met, having gathered signatures for petitions seeking a constitutional amendment to guarantee a woman's right to vote.

Noises from the crowd prevailed, pitchmen aglow with fervor hawking from booths. Aromas from popcorn and hot dogs permeated the air.

"Let's go over to the games and attractions," Charles said. "Shall we try to win something?"

He selected a game titled "The Disk Stein Board: A Game of Science and Skill." He gave the pitchman some change and he handed him six brass disks he must throw onto a table numbered with circles five to eight inches in diameter. The smaller the circle the disk fell within, the greater the prize.

Charles made a ringer at the second throw. She wondered if he'd played it before, knowing he could win to impress her.

"You did it! You won!"

He beamed. "And what have we won?"

"You circled eight, sir." The gap-toothed boy running the concession glanced around for the prize corresponding to eight. "A teapot." He plunged beneath the counter, brought out a box, showed Eleanor a teapot adorned with red roses and purple violets, entwined with green leaves.

She held it to her heart as though it were a piece of Limoges. "It's beautiful!"

"You'll have more than that before we leave," Charles said.

He kept his word. At the "Days of 49" dart game he accumulated twenty-seven points winning her a silver-plated spoon. At the "Cane Board" his ring hooked an ornately-carved walking stick she immediately decided to give to Colin. They moved to the "Shooting Gallery" and she watched Charles easily hit moving targets using a "genuine Smith and Wesson," as he described it.

After the concessions came the Wild West Show and Nebraska Bill, a husky fellow who commanded a band of Indians, cowboys, female riders, ponies, bucking broncos, even trick horses.

Later, they passed the Dancing Pavillion. She hoped he would not ask her to dance, did not want his physical closeness.

He did not ask.

It was all so astonishing and wonderful. She felt dizzy from excitement.

"Could we please sit for a while?" She needed to calm down, plus her new shoes began to pinch.

"Of course."

They found a bench, and she rested while Charles visited a concession, brought back two ice cream sundaes covered with caramel topping.

They sat enjoying their sundaes, watching people on the Great Ferris Wheel, resplendent with lights, circling nearly four hundred feet above the Hudson River.

"Would you want to go on?" he asked presently.

She laughed. "I don't think so. I just ate a giant sundae."

They sat a few more minutes, watching the crowd in, Eleanor realized, a companionable silence.

"May I show you my favorite ride," he said, "only if you're not too tired to walk."

"Of course."

They walked the midway, saw more attractions than they would ever possibly be able to visit. The "Big Scenic Roller Coaster" soared. As it dipped, she heard shrill screams. She feared this must be Charles' favorite. But they moved on. They approached "The World's Most Daring High Diver," "The Dirigible Balloon," "The Hippodrome Circus," "The High Diving Horse." He led her past them all, even beyond the great salt water swimming pool and its famous wave-making machine.

Finally they stopped. "There," he pointed, the light of happiness shining from him.

The carousel.

They moved closer. The horses galloped in stately movement, up and down, round and round, each ornately carved and painted with colorful flowers. White or black manes flowed behind them as they twirled around in harnesses of gold gilt.

She sensed him watching her study the painted flowers garnishing them.

"Yours are more beautiful," he whispered.

She looked up, drawn to the border of the carousel, a circle of incandescent lights illuminating embellished carved roses, interspersed with medallions surrounded by gold frames.

"It's so lovely. Can we go on?"

"If we hurry. It's just starting up."

He paid for two tickets, grabbed her hand, helped her jump on. She mounted a white horse decorated with pink and white flowers, surrounded by a gold-gilt harness. She clasped the pole, watched Charles mount a cream-colored horse directly across from her.

"We're lucky we made it. I guess it was meant to be."

Her heart pounded as her horse moved round the circle of incandescent lights. Music began. It filled the air like the scent of verbena:

> *Meet me tonight in Dreamland*
> *Under the silv'ry moon.*
> *Meet me tonight in Dreamland*
> *Where love's sweet roses bloom.*
> *There with the lovelight gleaming*
> *In your dear eyes of blue*
> *Meet me in Dreamland,*
> *Sweet, dreamy Dreamland,*
> *There let my dreams come true.*

She swayed with the music, her horse rising up and down, and looked around. Most of the people on the horses were adults. Some stood next to children, held them tightly on the horses. They were all smiling. She caressed her horse, and she smiled too.

The ride ended too soon. The music stopped and they alighted.

"We could go on again," Charles said.

"No, thank you," she said. "I think just once. I want to remember this one time, for now."

He smiled. "I think I understand."

An announcement blared, reminding visitors the park would close in half an hour. As they neared the exit, Eleanor spotted a sign, "Gypsy Fortune Teller," noticed a sagging-faced woman, plump as a stuffed goose, wearing a peasant-style dress, its gauze straining across her breasts, sitting outside a small tent.

"Oh, Charles, could we go in? Could we?"

"You don't believe in that silliness, do you?"

"Please. Could we?"

"Very well, if you'd like."

The woman rose, her earrings catching light from the string of bulbs above her. She waddled inside the tent, decorated with drawings of astrological signs and stars.

Eleanor sat across from her, Charles on her left.

The gypsy appeared mesmerized, studying her crystal ball. After a minute or so, she stared at Eleanor, knit her brow.

"I see you very unhappy. Very unhappy. You work too hard."

She hesitated, began again, stole a better look at Eleanor's hair in the light. "I see an older woman, a red-haired woman, around you."

Eleanor gasped. Charles sighed heavily.

The gypsy's gnarled fingers hovered above the crystal ball, circling it. "I see a change in your life."

Eleanor stared at Charles. He clenched his jaw.

"I see a man. A man so handsome, with dark hair. He will come into your life. Change it."

Her heart began to pound. "When will he come back?"

The gypsy moved closer to the crystal ball, studying the glass. She waited.

"Soon. Very soon."

"And he will change my life?"

"Yes. But he is troubled."

"About me?"

"Yes. But about other things too."

Of course! She knew Dante's concern about the injustice in the world.

The gypsy clasped her hands, her bracelets clinking as she pressed them to her chest. "I see sadness."

Eleanor held her breath. Charles' sighs became heavier.

"Is it--death?"

"No, not death. Worse than death."

"Worse than death? Does it have to do with the man? With the red-haired woman? With me?"

The gypsy's face darkened like smoke from soot. "I--can't--see anymore."

Eleanor seized her arm across the table. "But you can't just leave it like that."

Charles jumped up, threw coins onto the table.

"Eleanor, let's get out of here. Now." He led her from the tent, his face suffocating with anger. They did not speak for a time.

"Are you angry at me, Charles," she said at last.

He sighed. "No, not at you. At the gypsy." He took her by the hand. "Eleanor, you can't let what she said bother you. It was all sheer guesswork."

"But she knew so much--"

"Anyone could look at your hair and guess your mother was a redhead. And as to your working hard---well, look at your hands."

Eleanor glanced at her hands, clean but calloused, with short- trimmed nails.

"But the dark man, the sadness--"

"That, I believe, was for my sake. She realized I saw through her and wanted revenge. That was what angered me so, that she would frighten you to hurt me."

Did the gypsy's predictions mean nothing then?

"You won't let her foolishness upset you, will you?"

"What? No, of course not."

They said little more on the trolley trip back. She considered the evening. She would be cruel to upset Charles who tried so hard to show her a perfect time. And so much of it had been wonderful.

They finally arrived at the stop on the corner of Market and Matlock and soon faced each other at the top of the stairs by her door.

"I want you to know I've never had a better time, Charles," she said. "In my whole life. Especially the carousel."

"I'm so glad. Thank you so much for coming. You must know-- how much it meant to me." His face reddened. "I wonder if perhaps we could do it again. Of course, Palisades Park will be closed, but we could do other things I think you'd enjoy."

"We'll see."

"I'll say goodnight then."

She sensed he dared not kiss her.

And so, she kissed him lightly on the cheek.

Charles' persistence paid off. In months following, Eleanor spent a great deal of time with him and even came to look forward to the weekends. He took her to see "Tillie's Punctured Romance," and she laughed hysterically at the antics of Charlie Chaplin, Mabel Normand and Marie Dressler. She cried unabashedly at the sorrow of "Uncle Tom's Cabin," with Sam Lucas and Marie Eline and envied the beauty of Lillian Gish in "Home Sweet Home." The movie stars in her *Photoplays* became real to her, feeding her fantasy world even more.

Sometimes the films weren't easy to watch. So many of them centered upon love. While Mary Pickford, Clara Kimball Young, Lillian Gish and Alice Joyce bared their passion on the screen, she wallowed in memories of Dante that clung to her as tightly as her skin. Then guilt overtook her for thinking of him as she sat next to Charles in the darkened theatre.

But she kept her part of an unstated bargain with Charles by allowing him to continue worshipping her. After all, their relationship benefited them both. She knew her good fortune to be admired by someone of Charles' stature in Paterson and took advantage of it. And she knew he received enjoyment from her company as well.

The old Alliance's lease finally expired. They needed to move to Matlock Street within two weeks, hoping to escape the coming winter. The building Mary bought was the size of a field compared to their current cramped quarters. The sturdy pine structure also sat higher than the sidewalk, with the windows well above ground level. Passersby could not peer into them unless they climbed the cement stairs, an added benefit. Mary didn't have to install curtains to provide privacy and block the therapeutic sun.

Charles helped Mary supervise the transporting of patients, beds, furniture, cabinets, and equipment. Eleanor often wondered how he managed to spend so much time helping them given that he had the mill to oversee. He did have help from Stephen Kosinski. She never asked questions about the mill. He never spoke of it, even after she left to work full time at the Alliance.

Near the end of the move, Charles greeted her at the door of their new headquarters. She had just carried over a large box with medical instruments Mary did not trust to the movers. The temperature had begun to fall. She felt her face must be a block of ice, though she bundled up in her hat, scarf, coat.

"Why did you ever carry that box all the way?" Charles said. "You know I could have taken more in the carriage or car. What's to happen if you come down with a cold or flu or worse? You'll be no help to Mary then."

His constant worry about her often infuriated her, but she controlled herself, trying to accept his concern.

"I'll be fine."

She plopped the box into his outstretched hands, perhaps harder than she should have, then surveyed the giant room, beds in place. Patients transferred from the former Alliance dotted the room. She went to each one's bed, conversed a bit, satisfied they survived the move, lay in comfort.

She sensed Charles watching her, as usual. She knew--because her mother so often reminded her--that his constant concern was a sign of his regard. But to her it often felt proprietary, as if he had some personal right to her well being.

She finally removed her coat and scarf, indulging in the warmth of the room.

"Do you ever doubt you made the right move, Eleanor?" he said. "Coming here? Of course not. I could never have stayed at the mill with Clegg there. It's strange. Because of what--happened--I'm better off. Not only because of the extra money, but I do enjoy working with the patients more and more. As long as I don't let it all overwhelm me."

She moved towards the hallway leading to the office where Mary and the girls must be.

He followed her. "If you don't mind me saying it, that's something I need to learn."

"About being emotional? You don't seem to let your feelings get the best of you. At least most of the time."

"Is that how you see it?"

"Of course. Charles, you're rich. You say what you want and it's yours."

She turned from him but felt the pressure of his hand on her arm.

"And what if I were to say I don't have a perfect life. Because I don't have you."

When she turned to face him, he turned crimson.

"I'm sorry. I shouldn't have said that. Please, excuse me."

"No. It's all right. But what do you mean, you don't have me? We go to the films, don't we? And dinner? And have a good time."

He swallowed hard, his gulp seemed loud as cannon fire in the momentary silence.

"You must know these months have been the best of my life. Because I--" He caught his breath. "I'm in love with you."

"With *me?*"

"Eleanor, will you marry me?"

If the ceiling had crashed down on her, it would have jolted her less.

"Marry you?"

"Please say you will." He clasped her hand. "Or at least that you'll think about it."

His faced glowed, lips quivered. He moved closer, within inches of her.

"Won't you say something? Anything."

"But I didn't think it was like that with you." Her lie sounded feeble as she spoke it. "We've had such good times but--Charles, I don't love you."

"I know. I'm intelligent enough to realize that. But I think you could come to love me. I do. And I could give you such happiness. I know it. I realize my shortcomings. I'm not a handsome man--"

"Don't say things like that about yourself."

"I know my limitations."

"I don't know what to say."

"Don't say anything now. But remember, I promise I'll be so good to you. You'll want for nothing. Nothing. I'll try to be a good husband. And I'll take care of your mother. Whatever you'd like. She can even live with us on Silk Road, if you wish."

"On Silk Road? My mother? Me? Now I really don't know what to say."

"Think about it. That's all I ask. See what she says."

"But I--"

"And Colin as well."

"What they think has nothing to do with it. It's my decision, isn't it?"

"Of course. Of course."

She studied the passion sketched across his face, the look of longing she knew so well. Pity churned within her.

"I'll--think about it."

He unclasped her hand. His eyes misted. "It's all I ask. All I ask."

"I have to get back to work."

"Of course. Of course."

She scurried to the patients, busying herself. Her head pounded like a gong the rest of the afternoon.

Sunday evening she decided to bring up the topic of Charles' proposal to her mother and Colin. He came every Sunday now, and most evenings. She had little interest in his conversation lately. He shared news about a war that seemed imminent, something about an archduke killed by a serb for some political reason, and Germany and France started a war over it. Colin and Elizabeth feared for the allies, with more and more losses incurred. The war did not touch her, so she dismissed it.

Until he said if the United States became more involved, it could affect the mills. Then her ears perked up. Paterson's livelihood emanated from them. Elizabeth still worked at home as a picker and Colin said that due to the war the value of silk kept rising. He complained mill owners demanded unrealistic overtime to meet the increasing demand.

He removed his boots, sat on the couch wriggling his toes.

"I'm dog tired from all these extra hours. I tell you, I think I might make a break. It just might be the time."

"But the mill is all you know." Elizabeth looked troubled. "And isn't it a bit late to change now. If you don't mind me saying so."

"I could weave. It's how I started out, you know that. I might go over to Denham and Whatley, work there. In time I might start my own small shop, do commission work. I can always fix looms again if it didn't work out. I do like the idea of it, bein' my own boss. A lot of the men have left, started up shops. And with the wartime demand, the chance for high profit is very good."

Eleanor's attention was piqued. She thought of Charles' mill, wondered if he would be open to commission weaving.

Colin squeezed his toes a few more times, took the platter from Elizabeth, brought it to the dinner table. He held it to his nostrils, breathed deeply, smiled at her.

"This smells grand."

"And how does this commission weaving work exactly?" Eleanor said.

"Well, the owners of the mills purchase thrown silk and would hire me to prepare the warps, operate the looms to weave it. They would sell it directly for finishing. Or they might sell it to retailers.

A lot of family shops are being built up now, paid on commission. Denham and Whatley's tryin' it on twenty looms. I'd pay the boss each month for use of the loom until I own it. Then I'd really make money. I wouldn't get paid wages regular but I could work as many hours as I want so I'd still make good money, I know it. It'd be like I have a share in the business."

Eleanor plopped some mashed potatoes on her plate. "But what does it accomplish? I don't understand."

"Why, in time a man can have his own business if he works hard.

He's nobody's employee anymore."

Her curiosity worked overtime. "Do you think Charles would go for it? Do you know if he's trying it?"

"I don't think so. I would of heard. Don't forget, he doesn't know that much about the business. But Kosinski says he's a fast learner, seems to take to it. Though Kosinski told me Charles hasn't been at the mill much lately."

"I know." She thought of Charles, owner of one of the largest silk mills in Paterson, hauling boxes of supplies to the new Alliance these past weeks.

"Well, if Kosinski was to argue for it, I think he'd try it. Who's to say?"

"Colin, what do you really think of him? Charles, I mean."

"I like the man. Kosinski gives him good marks. Joe Briody, Tommy O'Malley, all the workers at the mill ten years or over, they got a raise. Two dollars more a month. All the others got a dollar-

-including the soakers, mind you. He said they should all share in higher profits he's making with the coming of war. I don't think the other mill owners are any too happy about it."

Her mother handed him the knife to carve the chicken. "Margie Kennedy told me he's hired a woman to clean up the place. And they don't stand for lunch anymore, like you did. They have benches now. All against one wall."

"I think the man's tryin' to show he's decent, and the workers know it." Colin sneaked a look at Eleanor. "And maybe he has other reasons."

Eleanor raised her brows at his inference. So it was that obvious. Well, she had to tell them sometime. Now was as good as any.

"He asked me to marry him."

Her mother dropped her fork. "What did you say?"

"I said he asked me to marry him."

"I mean, what did you say?"

"That I'd think about it. I don't think I will." She studied the corn bread, trying to decide if she should have a second piece.

Her mother retrieved her fork and pointed it at Eleanor. "One of the richest men in Paterson asks you to marry him and you don't think you will?"

"Now, Elizabeth," Colin said. "I'm sure she has her reasons."

Eleanor started. Did Colin realize how much she still loved Dante?

He took a sip of wine, looked directly into her eyes. "As far as I'm concerned there's only one question to be answered. Do you love him?"

She decided she would have some corn bread and placed a piece on her plate.

"Of course I don't. I told him that."

"And he still wants to marry you?"

She nodded.

"Well, the man's a fool. No marriage will work unless both people love each other."

"Colin, you romantic fool." Her mother made a sweeping gesture. "Look around you, Eleanor. Always a struggle, all your life. This is your chance. Charles is a good man and there's nobody else for you in Paterson. Was there anybody you could care for in the least at that God-forsaken mill? Do you want to spend your days nursing others at the Alliance? It's a noble thing, but I want you to have more. A husband. Children. Happiness."

Her mother made sense. She would never love another as she did Dante, but more and more he seemed lost to her. Colin never spoke of him, mentioned a letter.

"He is good and kind to me. And the money. I can't imagine what it would be like to have whatever I want."

She stared at the faded flower pattern on the tablecloth. Then it came to her.

If Dante knew she were marrying, he would never allow it. He'd come back. She envisioned the wreckage of her life restored to bliss. "I will marry him." She turned to her mother. "You'll never have to worry about money again. He said that."

"Goodness, don't do it for me. Besides, well, now's as good a time to tell you as any. I think the proper time's over with mourning. Colin's asked me to marry him, and I've said yes. So you see, you won't have to worry about me."

Colin choked on his wine.

She jumped from her chair, hugged her mother hard. "That's the best news ever." She turned to Colin. "I've been wondering when you would ask her. You took long enough, didn't you?"

Colin rolled his eyes.

"We'll make it a double wedding," Eleanor said. "Whatever date you decide. Won't it be wonderful?"

Conversation overflowed. They talked of the wedding, dresses, guests, who would be in the bridal party, so much else, while Colin sat puffing contentedly on his pipe. The evening passed quickly. It seemed hardly any time before Colin stood to leave.

"When you write to Dante next time," Eleanor said, "don't forget to tell him I'm getting married."

Colin seized her wrist. "Don't do this. Play with the man's feelings if you don't love him."

She refused to look at him, found refuge once again in the faded flowers in the tablecloth pattern. "I don't know what you mean."

"No man deserves the hurt Charles'll have if you use him to get to Dante. If I thought for one minute--"

"I thought you both want me to marry him."

"Not that way. Not if you have love for another man in your heart."

"I'm not marrying him to spite Dante. If that's what you think."

She could see by his look she fooled no one. Suddenly she reached out to him, clung to him. He rocked her back and forth, let her cry herself out.

"Darlin', his whole life is the movement. There's no woman he could care for more than that. You surely know it in your heart."

She pushed him away. "You're wrong! I know he loves me."

"Stop it, both of you, do you both hear me?" Her mother scurried to the stove. "I'll make more tea, and we'll calm down. Is that clear?"

Colin led her to a seat at the table. She suddenly felt small, shriveled, tried her best to sip tea, her mother's solution to everything, but her hands trembled too much.

"I'm sorry," she said. "I was foolish to act like that. It's just that I've held it in so long. I just need a rest. I'll be all right."

She took her tea, went to her daybed, laid down.

Colin left. Her mother did not read that night. Eleanor heard her tossing and turning in her bed.

She gulped her cold tea, listened to wind clatter at the windows.

What was Dante doing right that moment? Was it earlier or later in Colorado? He might be in his room, most likely reading. Now and then he might pause, think of her in his loneliness.

Soon he would return.

Calm enveloped her. She slept, enmeshed in rapturous dreams.

Spring arrived. Snow that had lain on roofs most of the winter and mounds piled at curbs began to disappear. Clumps of snow encrusted with gray ice turned to slush and began to give way to sprouts of green.

Germany and France mobilized. England committed to fight alongside France. Uppermost in the minds of the country was whether the United States would enter. Eleanor ignored the political situation. She felt grateful Dante's age made him ineligible to fight. Charles, as a mill owner supplying essential war materials--especially silk for parachutes--was also safe. So how could war hurt her?

She did not ask Colin if he wrote Dante. She knew he had. She simply waited for his response. She told Charles she would marry him, stalled on an exact date. She also continued to mold him to her every whim, knowing she crushed him when she showed the slightest unhappiness.

Another half an hour and her day at the Alliance would end. She made her usual last-minute rounds, folded towels for tomorrow, cleaned instruments, when she noticed an ashen-faced woman at the door, her dress soaked, holding her stomach.

"My water. It's broke."

Eleanor helped her to a chair and ran for Mary. They placed her on a bed at the end of the aisle, removed her filthy clothing, wiped her sweaty face.

Mary checked her stomach with a stethescope. "She's ready. Get hot water and towels."

Eleanor prepared to witness yet another delivery. Within minutes the baby's head emerged as the woman screamed, hair and face soaked with sweat. Mary clipped the umbilical cord. Eleanor dried the slippery baby--a girl--wrapped her in a blanket, handed her to her mother, who smiled through exhaustion at seeing her baby for the first time.

How wonderful it would be to have Dante's child.

She sensed Mary studying her as she began gathering soiled towels.

"The birth of a baby," Mary said. "Every time I see a newborn like that I'm overcome at the miracle of birth. It reminds me once again about how fulfilling my work is to me. How it saves me." She smiled at the newborn. "Such a joy. Don't you think?"

She nearly gave the easy answer. Her honesty and respect for Mary would not permit it. "How can you say that?"

"What do you mean?"

They walked from the bed, Eleanor's hands filled with bloody towels, instruments to be cleaned.

"That woman has nothing. What chance will that baby have? And where was her husband? She may have to make a go of it alone, bring that baby up by herself. Even if she does have a husband, what future will the baby have? The mills?" She threw the blood-soaked towels in the basin. "It would have been better if that child had never been born."

"Life's been too harsh on you, Eleanor. It's made you bitter. I hope life with Charles will help you overcome that. He's such a kind person. He'll help you see that life can be wonderful as well."

"I hope so. Understand, I'm not saying I don't admire you for your work. You're one of the few people I do admire."

"I'm honored to hear you say that. I feel quite the same about you, you know."

"About me? There's not very much for you to admire about me."

"No, you're wrong to think so little of yourself." She clasped her hand. "Look at you. You started with little more than that child has and rose to become a ribbon weaver. And your work at the Alliance is so meaningful. And you and Charles will have a wonderful life together, I'm sure. Isn't that worthy? We don't know where life will take us, do we? Perhaps this child's life will turn out well."

"You know how slim those chances are."

"For some reason that woman wanted that child. You could see it by the look in her eyes. And I feel quite sure Charles will want children." She smiled at the air. "It's in his nature to love and give."

Her face reddened. She thought of her secret shame. If Charles knew she was unclean, he would never want her as the mother of his child. What man would?

"Why, you're blushing. My dear, I hope I didn't embarrass you. It's just that I thought with you working so much around pregnant women and--. Well, let's just say I know you'll make Charles a wonderful wife."

"I hope so."

She rinsed the towels, hung them across the sink.

When she turned, she saw Charles approaching.

He held her hand, his face aglow. "How good it is to see you."

He kissed her on the cheek. "I thought perhaps you'd like to go to dinner tonight."

She sighed as loud as possible. "I'm so tired, I don't think so."

Colin was coming over, and it might just be the night he would bring a letter from Dante.

Charles embraced her, then held her from him, examining her face and form as though she were priceless porcelain. "You know, I'd be so happy if we could set a date for the wedding."

"You promised you wouldn't rush me."

"Certainly within the next few months?"

"I'm--perhaps. And don't ask me again. Please. I'll tell you the date as soon as I'm sure."

His face crumbled. "Sure? You don't mean you're not sure of whether you want to marry me?"

"Of course not. Sure of the date, I mean. I just don't know--if I want a winter or spring wedding."

"Of course."

It was so simple to lie, have him believe her. His weakness from loving.

He helped her don her coat and they left. In the carriage, he held her hand and rhapsodized about the wedding. Then discussion went in an unexpected direction.

"I've been wanting your opinion on something. Some of the mills are trying commission weaving--Colin might have told you about it."

"What? Oh, yes. He mentioned it the other night."

"Do you think it's something I should try? You know I value your opinion. After all, you have first-hand knowledge of the mills."

"I think it's a good idea. It gives the workers some sense of ownership. And it could be a boon to you, not having to be concerned about strikes all the time. With the possiblities of war, we'll need more production, and they'll work longer and harder if they get more out of it."

"Just what Kosinski thought."

"Why don't you try it on a limited basis? See how it works out."

They discussed its possibilities further, where it could be set up, how many looms should be involved in the beginning, costs, profit sharing. Charles seemed to value her opinions which she found rather pleasing. She promised she would ask Colin more about Denham and Whatley's, which was now running largely on added commission weaving.

The carriage arrived in front of the tenement. He prepared to enter for a cup of tea, visit her mother, but she stopped him.

"I do feel guilty not asking you in. But I feel so tired. And I think I'm coming down with something." She rubbed her nose. "I think I might be getting a cold."

"It's the Alliance, it's wearing you out. I don't understand why you constantly have to busy yourself with all the overtime, especially now that we'll be married soon. Perhaps the heating in that place isn't as adequate as it should be. I'll have a man over this week, check it out."

"Oh, stop worrying about me." She had visions of Mary, mouth open wide as a cave when an unnecessary heating repair man showed up. "A good night's sleep's all I need."

"If you say so." He kissed her tenderly. "I'll stop by tomorrow to see how you're feeling."

She devoured dinner, in between filling in Colin and her mother on Charles' plan for commission weaving.

"Why didn't you invite him in?" her mother said. "You know there's always room for one more for dinner. I'm surprised at your poor manners. I taught you better than that, or at least I thought I did."

Her sniffles excuse would never work on her mother. Even worse, she might believe it and cart her to bed.

"He's very busy with work and couldn't come up. At least that's what he said."

"And have you two come up with a wedding date yet? Elizabeth is as anxious as I am about it."

"I will. Soon."

Colin squirmed in his chair. "I got a letter from Dante today. Things are bad in Colorado."

Colin must have written him about her wedding. Was he returning? She felt as if her heart was being run through a mangle.

"How is he? I've been keeping up with what's happening out there."

"Have you now?"

"I can't seem to stay away from reading about major strikes," she lied. "I suppose it's because of Paterson."

"I'm glad of it. You should know about what's goin' on in the rest of the country." He removed the letter from his pocket. "When one man is not free, no man is free--I must of read that somewhere. And it's the truth. I blame the Rockefellers for the situation. If somebody like Helen Keller, a great woman, is against them, you know they're in the wrong. It seems she was a great supporter, so the paper says, but now, "a monster of capitalism," that's what she called John D. He gives to charity in the same breath he lets helpless workmen and their wives be shot. Upton Sinclair, he accused him of murder. You'll read it in the papers tonight, last page of the second section, of course."

Her mother looked confused. "Upton Sinclair?"

"A writer. Dante gave me one of his books to read," Eleanor said. "He admires him a lot."

"And have you read it?"

"Well, not yet." In truth, Eleanor much preferred reading romances. "Have you got the letter? What's happening?"

Colin took a century to unfold it.

"They had demonstrations outside Rockefeller's offices on Broadway, all the pickets in black armbands, with a delegation from Ludlow. They say he's so scared he wants to install barbed wire fences at his estate--Kycut, or some name like that. Has to be a fancy name, of course."

"Why don't you read the letter?"

"Now, give me a chance." He held it closer to his eyes.

"Dear Colin,

I have wanted to write you for months now, but have been busier than ever organizing the IWW here. The labor struggles get more intense each day. I don't know how much the papers report, but the miners have been evicted from their homes by Colorado Fuel and Iron, a Rockefeller subsidiary.

They were living in a tent colony with militia surrounding them. The women were so afraid of the militia they dug a large cave under one of the tents and it's there they put the children to sleep.

In April the militia set fire to the tent colony with kerosene. Two women, one pregnant, and thirteen children were smothered to death in the cave. And over thirty miners were killed in the battle that followed.

The pretext of the massacre was that "a fugitive from arrest" was in the colony. One woman, a lovely lady I have come to admire so much, Mrs. Petrucci, lost three children. No one has been arrested for their murder. Louis Tikas, a Greek unionizer, was shot in the back trying to rescue a child.

I am sick at heart at all the tragedy I have seen.

I was surprised to hear Eleanor is to be married, to Charles Lafferty. I met his father at negotiations and was not impressed with him at all. Of course, the son may be one of those rare capitalists willing to see the point of view of the workers. I know Eleanor would not consider marrying him unless he is. She may be a great influence on Charles by encouraging him to make a better life for his workers. She is one of the most courageous women I know, and I will never forget her. She is so fortunate to have a chance to help make a difference in the lives of so many. Please give her my best wishes.

Yours sincerely,

Dante

Colin pounded the table. "When will there be justice in this world? When?"

Elizabeth bowed her head. "Mary, mother of God, please help those who died and those left behind."

Eleanor hardly heard them. She was waiting for more of the post script.

Colin folded the letter and placed it in his pocket.

Her mother laid a hand on her arm. "It's for the best. You can see now, can't you? He won't be back."

"And surely you know how he admires you." Colin said. "Why, that shines right through. Right through."

Their searching look begged for response. She slumped in her chair, unable to speak. She was certain he loved her, so why must he focus on her role of bringing justice to the workers as Charles' wife? He said he would never forget her. But he didn't have the courage to claim her.

She bowed her head, struggled for breath. Her head began to pound. Then suddenly grew worse.

What was she going to do about Charles?

The lie Eleanor told about coming down with an illness became truth. Her limbs ached and her head pounded when she tried to sit up on her cot the next morning. Her mother made her stay in bed most of the day, filling her with homemade soup and tea with honey. And as she lay there, she vowed she would no longer let Dante possess her heart and soul. Let his idealism be the great love of his life, she would not care.

She wallowed in that state much of the day, driving away any memory that put him in a positive light. Her illness angered her as well. She wanted to get back to the Alliance with her patients and bathe in the balm of busyness.

Her mother placed her cool hand on her brow.

"You don't feel as feverish." She smiled. "It's for the best. You know that. But it's made you sick. The mind can do terrible things to the body."

"I think I can get back to the Alliance tomorrow."

"I'm glad." Her mother tucked the blanket around her. "Glad you're accepting things."

She turned to her pieces of picked fabric, folded them. "I need to get these over to Lafferty's."

Darkness had begun to smother the day. Eleanor knew her mother should have brought them sooner but wanted to make more soup, not leave until she felt somewhat better.

"They won't care if you bring it tomorrow. Charles is the boss, you know."

"I always bring it Fridays. I gave my word, and I'll keep it."

"If I marry Charles, you won't have to do that anymore."

"Actually, I'd rather." She gestured at the bundle of silk lying on the table. "It gives me something to fill the day. I need that. Before you know it I'll be a married woman, busy with my life with Colin. Maybe I'll give it up then."

Her mother put on her coat. When she bent down to kiss her goodbye, Eleanor pulled herself up from the cot, embraced her. She closed her eyes, inhaling the scent of Ivory Soap on her skin.

"I want you to be happy. More than anything."

She met the troubled look in her mother's eyes. "I will be. I know now I have to go on with my life."

"That's what I wanted to hear. It's so hard, life." She released her, faced her. "But it's wonderful too. Always remember that."

She grabbed the heavy bundle of silk fabric, just about managed to scoop it in her arms. "I won't be long. Try to drink more tea. And soup."

"I'll burst if I have one more drop."

She turned to her before she left. "Be strong. Whatever you do, never give in."

And then she left her, alone.

The time since the hearing had not gone well for Angus Clegg. He returned to Lafferty's Mill, hoping to take up his job. Instead Kosinski called him in, said he had instructions from Charles Lafferty to fire him. Well, he'd expected it. The publicity about the trial throughout New Jersey must have soured him, plus rumor had it he was sweet on Eleanor O'Bannion. He'd dropped the charges but he could see that didn't count for anything.

He decided to leave Paterson, applied for work in Passaic with its great woolen and textile mills. But there was nothing. He, a former supervisor, began asking for the most menial jobs, even soaking, but the answer was always the same. They would contact him if an opening became available. They never did. He finally realized he'd been blacklisted. His savings dwindled, not that there'd ever been much--he thought he would always have a secure job and drank so much of it away. And now, here he stood, nearly penniless.

Because of her.

He touched the scar that branded him, something he must have performed a hundred times a day, felt the flesh left from the attack by the bitch he so foolishly underestimated. The man he had been no longer existed. With no employment in sight, he was heading to the poorhouse.

Because of her.

He felt enough time passed for him never to be connected to his crime. He rehearsed it weeks on end, waiting where he stood now, studying the bitch's mother's movements. Soon she would leave the apartment with her silk picking, and he would get his revenge. If only he could rape her as well. But it would be too dangerous to risk the time.

He would never forget his first sexual pleasure, his awareness of its power. He was ten years old, lying on his cot in the cottage where he lived with his parents in Scotland. When he was almost asleep, he heard a muffled sound of pain and fear coming from the kitchen. He tip-toed to the kitchen door, opened it a crack.

His mother was pinned down on the table, her dress above her waist. His father, pants down, was thrusting himself into her. Her hand was cupped around her mouth trying to muffle the sound of her pain.

He wanted to run to her, defend her. His father was hurting her in a way he could not understand. Then he thought of the buckle of his father's belt he used so often to beat him. He did not move, watched wide-eyed, as his father thrust into her again and again.

Finally, he sneaked back to his room, saw a stiffness under his nightshirt. He rubbed himself there. The release exhilarated him in a way he never knew before. He walked to his bed in delicious exhaustion.

He often thought of that night when he later began sexual encounters women. The more he dominated, the more he enjoyed it.

Then everything fell apart. That stupid tart in Glasgow told her husband he attacked her, even though he threatened her with harm to her children. He could still see her husband, his giant hulk thumping across the yard, his milky skin. He tried to defend himself but was powerless against him. And so he did what he had to, pulled out his knife as they fought, stabbed him, watched him bleed to death.

He buried his body in the woods in back of his house. He wasn't foolish enough to doubt the police would suspect him. Before he knew it, he was on a ship bringing him to America, beginning a new life.

He had been all right until he wound up at Lafferty's. The powerlessness of the girls fed his need, until he was unable to control it. But all had still been safe.

Until Eleanor O'Bannion.

He stopped reliving the past. Now was time for sweet revenge.

For weeks, every Friday evening Eleanor's mother emerged from the tenement, pulling the cart with silk work she delivered to Lafferty's. But the clock at City Hall had already tolled seven. Would this be the day she didn't come, when he boiled with vengeance?

Finally, he heard the squeaky wheels on the makeshift wagon clacking. He drew a deep breath, donned his gloves. He waited until she passed, stepped out of the shadows, began to follow her.

He hung back until she made her usual turn into the alleyway between Lane and Matlock Streets, risking that stretch of darkness to save a few minutes. He grasped the knife from his pocket, held it hard. He could feel the blood throbbing through the veins of his head.

She turned, checking the piled silk, guiding her cart. As she faced forward again, she faced him for a split second.

Before she could even drop the handle to run, he grabbed her, covered her mouth, dashed her to the ground. Her head smashed against the stone. He lay above her, stabbed her through her coat. A crimson stain of blood soaked through the cloth.

He studied her face, mouth open as though about to speak, eyes full of fear. He wrenched the knife from her stomach. Droplets of blood fell upon the gray stone.

He searched her pockets, found her change purse, opened it awkwardly with gloves on, pocketed a few bills, hurled it to the ground.

He took one last look at her face. Pale, motionless, eyes glazed like marbles.

He was finished.

He removed his gloves, stuffed them into his pocket, ran through the alley. He gasped, slowed down. Then he turned right onto Lane Street one block, then down Albion. The street lay empty. He squeezed the money from her purse in his hand, more than enough for a celebratory drunk.

He walked across town to the farthest saloon from the site of his crime, O'Leary's on North Sixth. He sat down, pressed his hands against the bar to stop their trembling. Finally, he went to the bathroom and settled himself down.

He came back to the bar, celebrated by ordering a whisky, savoring every drop. He had not been able to afford whiskey for a long time. Confidence flowed through him again. It was time for him to leave Paterson for good and start over. He wasn't caught when he had killed before, he wouldn't be now.

He toasted his future with the whiskey bought for him by Eleanor O'Bannion's mother.

Eleanor sipped the soup her mother left her. Confusion was momentarily replacing the emptiness gnawing her over Dante's letter.

Her current worry lay with Charles. It seemed no one was going to stop her from marrying him, so should she stop herself? She'd ask her mother's advice. Why wasn't she back yet? She might have stopped at Lefkowitz's for groceries--but, no, he would be closed this time of night. Her mother's moral principles, driven into her by the priests and nuns from her childhood, were so often such a bother. She could easily have returned that piecework tomorrow instead of trudging over to the mill tonight.

She sighed. She loved her mother too much to upset her by arguing.

Someone was flying up the stairs, pounding at the door. Eleanor opened it to find Catherine, eyes red-rimmed.

"Eleanor, you have to come, your mother's been hurt bad. She was attacked."

"Attacked?"

Catherine grabbed her coat from the peg above her cot, dropped it around her. "You have to hurry. Hurry!"

Shock overtook her. Catherine lifted her arms, shoved them into her coat.

"It was a couple of boys found her. In the alley by DeFrancisco's. They come runnin' to the Alliance. Mary had her brought back."

"But she's all right? It isn't serious?"

"It's not good."

They ran through the streets, Eleanor's lungs exploding.

"Tell me. Everything," she managed between breaths.

"She hit her head, she got a bad wound. She's still conscious."

"Conscious?"

Catherine would not look at her. "Mary will tell you."

After a few minutes they reached the Alliance. Mary waited by the window.

Eleanor felt the strength of Catherine's arm supporting her as she climbed to the top of the stairs. Mary embraced her.

"I'll run for Colin." Catherine left in a whisk.

"My dear, it's very serious," Mary said, as they rushed to the bed where her mother lay. "It wasn't the fall to the ground, her hitting her head, that was the worst injury. Bad enough. But a knife wound."

"Knife wound?"

"It does not look hopeful. I'm so sorry."

She stumbled to the bed with Mary's help, her mind mangled by images of her mother thrown to the ground, stabbed and bleeding. No. Mary was wrong. She might be all right. Hadn't she tended so many supposedly hopeless patients and helped them heal? She could save her mother too. She would nurse her. A sense of comfort washed over her, sustained her.

Then she saw her mother lying on the bed, her face ashen.

"Mother."

She would surely open her eyes now, as soon as she heard her voice. She did not.

Eleanor bent down, kissed her on her cheek, held her limp hand. "Mother. Can you hear me?"

Elizabeth managed to half open her eyes. Surely a good sign.

"Colin."

Her voice sounded thin as thread. Eleanor moved her face closer to her mother's. "He's coming, mother. He's coming."

She struggled to inhale, grasped the air. "Your father."

Why did she think in what might be her last moments about her father, a monster?

"Mother. Don't think about him. Save your strength."

"Forgive me." Her voice trailed.

"Forgive you?"

She heard footsteps. Colin ran through the door with Father Garrity. She saw the valise he carried, implements for last rites.

"He's here. Colin's here."

She doubted her mother heard her. She held her wrist, still felt the faintest pulse.

Colin sat at the other side of the bed. "Elizabeth? I brought the priest. I knew you would want him." His hands trembled. He grasped her hand. "My love."

He spoke to her mother's ghost.

Father Garrity opened his valise and spread its contents on a wooden table next to the bed: two candlesticks, yellowed wax candles, fresh water, cotton, a wafer of bread. He touched his thumb to holy oil from a container, then he motioned to Eleanor to lift the blanket, drape it over the back of the iron footboard. He anointed her feet, each time emblazoning the sign of the cross into her mother's flesh.

"By this anointing and His loving mercy may the Lord forgive you whatever wrong you have done by the use of your eyes, nostrils, hands--"

She sat on the bed, half heard Father Garrity. The cold from her mother's hand rushed through her.

He inserted the wafer between Elizabeth's lips. "Body of Christ."

Her mother's pulse dwindled, then ceased.

She kissed her cheek, still smelling of Ivory Soap, ran her fingers through her burnished hair, held her one last time. Paralysis enveloped her. The vibrant woman she said goodbye to a few hours earlier lay dead in her arms.

Strong hands grasped her at the back of her shoulders, tried to pry her away. She could not fight them. They were too powerful and she felt numb. She placed the body back upon the bed.

She tried to stand, could not. The room swam around her. She felt those hands lifting her, propelling her to rise.

Through the blur she recognized Charles, crumbled into his arms.

PART II

The Marriage

Charles was a godsend after her mother's death. He purchased a plot for her in Holy Sepulcher Cemetery, surrounded by massive oaks. Eleanor felt great comfort knowing her mother lay nestled under their protection. She felt the strength of Charles's arm on one side, Colin's on the other during the funeral. The words the priest spoke meant little to her. She would never understand a God who brought such sorrow to one's life.

Sundays changed. Charles and Colin still came to dinner, but a pall hovered over the atmosphere. She forced herself to cook a meal, go through the steps to make them think she accepted her mother's death, and cried alone.

One Sunday about two months after her mother's death, Charles arrived with a bouquet of daisies. She placed them in a pitcher, used them as a centerpiece on the table.

He sniffed the air. "It smells wonderful in here."

"You say that every Sunday."

"And it's always quite true." He gestured to Colin, already at the table. "I see somebody else feels the same way."

Suddenly, regret overtook her at Charles's kindness. It was he, not Dante, at her side at her mother's funeral. It was he who was so constantly attentive and loving. Why couldn't she will herself to love him?

After dinner, they sat quietly for a time. The emptiness in the room came by stealth, then engulfed her, as it always did. Her mother's presence hovered in every nook and cranny of the apartment.

She looked at Colin, Charles, knew they felt it too.

She hit the table with her fist, eyes moistening. "Why did she resist? It was that stubborn streak of hers. Why did she have to fight for a few dollars in a coin purse?"

Charles seemed about to speak, then did not.

She wiped her wet eyes. "What is it?"

"Well, I hesitate because I don't want to open old wounds. But, you know, there's something that never made sense to me. Why would he take the time to open the coin purse, take the money out, and then throw it to the ground? And he wore gloves. It's as if he knew he would touch the purse, then discard it." He rested his elbows on the table. "He was wasting time. Precious time he was losing getting away. I would have thought he'd grab the purse and hightail it out of there. Take the money out later and throw it in the river or somewhere."

Colin frowned. "What is it you're coming at?" "I think he wanted it to look like robbery."

"But what else could it be? It had to be robbery. Mother followed that same path every week, and he must have known it."

"Of course, I'm sorry. I didn't mean to say anything to upset you, after all you've been through."

But Colin refused to let it drop. "What do you think happened then?"

"I'm not certain, of course. But also--this is hard to bring up--- well, it would have made more sense if he had--knocked her out, and robbed her. But to--stab her." He turned to Eleanor. "My dear, I'm so sorry to have to bring this up. You know the last thing I want is to upset you. I won't continue if--"

"No, I'm all right. I want to know. I have to know."

"Well, so would I. If it's all right with you, I'd like to hire a private investigator."

She could hardly catch her breath. "You think it was planned? To--kill her?"

"I'm not saying that. It's just that it doesn't make sense, the way she died. For a few dollars? Will you give me permission to pursue it?"

She sat speechless. Who could want to hurt her mother?

"Of course," she finally said. "I want the truth."

Colin nodded. "Call him tomorrow, then."

"I will."

They sat immersed in thought, stirring their tea until it seemed the porcelain on the cup wore away.

Eleanor knew Charles's offer to help sprang from genuine concern, not an attempt to win her admiration or rush her toward their wedding date. And this only increased her gratitude. His sense of fairness at the mill also impressed her. He would walk through fire if it gave her happiness.

Keeping busy with work at the Alliance helped relieve her sorrow, but she wondered if she could continue working where mortality lay raw every day. Her constant show of bravery left her exhausted. Perhaps Colin was right saying she returned to work too quickly but the alternative--sitting alone in the apartment surrounded by memories of her mother--was more than she could bear.

She looked at Charles, his wide smile a comfort, his soft blue eyes a study in adoration. Her sense of his plainness faded. He would never possess her heart and soul, as Dante did. She would fight the rest of her life against his memory. But she found herself actually liking him more and more. She also knew her mother wanted her to marry Charles. She began to realize that, although a future of complete happiness with Charles would be tenuous, the present was unbearable.

She touched his hand. "Charles, I want you to know I've made a decision about marrying you."

His spoon clattered when he placed it on his saucer.

She kept her hand on his. "If you still want to marry me, we'll set a date." She kissed his cheek. "And I'll try to be a good wife."

"This--this is--it's wonderful. We'll celebrate with a drink."

Colin brought a bottle of wine to the table. He smiled. "One thing I'm sure of is Charles will be a fine husband." "I know."

"Would it go against mother's memory not to wait a full year, do you think?"

"Not at all. She would want it. And so do I."

"April, I think. The gardens just coming into their spring glory. The last Sunday of next April, though it will be less than a year since mother's gone."

"She wouldn't care. You know that, dear girl. She'd be so glad of it. I'm so pleased, you bein' happy. What I wouldn't give if--" He stopped speaking, lost in thought.

"I know," Eleanor said. "She loved you so. Why, at the end, she asked for you."

"I'm comforted at it. Did she say anything else? Anything at all?"

"No." She could never break Colin's heart by telling him her mother's last words concerned her father.

Charles lifted his glass. "Let's drink to our happiness, shall we?"

They clinked glasses, toasting what they believed could only be a bright and shining future.

Charles favored a small church wedding, but Eleanor refused to be married within a church. The church had robbed her mother of so much happiness, she would have nothing to do with it. Still, she wanted a large affair and she felt her mother would want one as well. Nature was as close as she could get to spiritual belief, so she would be married at the back of Charles's property, an area she loved the first time he escorted her around his land. By April's end it would blossom in paths of cream and pink dogwoods, and the daffodils and hyacinths would surely be in full flower. Charles feared the weather. A day of showers and mud would surely spoil the occasion, but Eleanor remained convinced the day would be perfect.

Of course, Father Garrity objected to her decision not to be married in church. As Eleanor well knew, when Charles gave him a large donation to repair the church roof, he relented. A Mass would be said. She would receive Communion, a hollow gesture to her, but she felt Colin right that her mother would have wished it.

Colin would give her away, with only Mary as maid of honor. Catherine refused to be her bridesmaid. At first she said she couldn't afford the cost of a gown, but she still declined even when Eleanor offered to pay for it. She was hurt but had to accept her decision.

Eleanor invited a number of her co-workers from Lafferty's and former patients at the Alliance she'd become fond of. Charles's guest list included associates from the mill, friends of the family living on Silk Road, and several mill owners. Charles's best friend from Princeton, Michael Buchanan, would attend as best man. If Charles hesitated at the number and diversity of people invited, he did not show it.

Eleanor stood in the yard the morning before the wedding in the chill of cold, dank weather. She had been certain the sun would shine on her wedding day. Prospects dimmed. She hated to think Charles might be right.

When she saw the sky the evening before the wedding--clouds of fluffy pink trails--she knew the sun would shine the next day. The next morning it gasped through the clouds, in golden splendor by noon.

The morning of the wedding Mary arrived filled with excitement. "Well, you've done it. I never would have believed we'd have a glorious day like this. Somebody must be watching over you."

"I wish he could help with my nervousness."

"Oh, that's to be expected. It's a dream for most women, isn't it, to marry a man who absolutely adores you? I envy you."

"I'll do all I can to live up to that love. You know that."

Mary faced her squarely. "You know I love my brother more than anything else on the face of this earth. And I want him to be happy."

"So do I."

"I know he isn't tall, dark, and handsome. Not like Dante Ravelli. But Charles is so good and kind. That's what's important in the end. You'll realize that some day. And he loves you so."

"Dante's in the past."

"I know how much you cared for him. I could see it every time you looked his way, at the strike meetings."

"That's finished," Eleanor said, but her voice sounded weak, even to her own ears.

Colin arrived and they left, her mood more somber than she wished. Why did Mary have to bring back thoughts of Dante on her wedding day?

She walked down the path to Charles. Colin beamed as he held her arm, looking like a stuffed penguin in his tuxedo. She felt an all- encompassing intimacy with earth and sky and sun as she walked, focusing on the vows she intended to keep. Charles ignored her gown with its hand-beaded pearls, skirt of creamy watered silk, did not take his eyes from her face.

His hand shook as he placed the ring on her finger.

After the wedding, guests gathered on the great lawn at the side and back of the house. Platters of shrimp, lobster, aspic and beef sat surrounding a small fountain in the center of the table, hundreds of roses at its base. She looked around at the women from the mill, wearing their homespun Sunday best at one side of the lawn, the wives of the mill owners preening in their silk dresses and plumed hats on the other. Well, she couldn't expect to bridge the social gap on one afternoon. She was just glad so many of the girls she knew from the mill showed up and seemed to be enjoying themselves. She did regret that Nora, who had taught her ribbon weaving, and Flossie and Sarah, two soakers whom she had come to know at lunch time had not come. She turned to Mary and shared her disappointment.

"Oh, but they're here," Mary said. "I saw them."

Eleanor surveyed the guests, could not spot them. Mary must have made a mistake.

She quickly checked the buffet table, noting the roast beef and shrimp were low. The server was busy carving the ham, and it seemed just as simple to dash a few feet across the lawn and into the kitchen and request more.

Sitting around the table with the cook were Nora, Flossie and Sarah.

"What in the world--?"

They stood immediately when they saw her.

"Why are you sitting here in the kitchen?" she said. "You should be outside, with the other guests."

"Oh, we--it isn't for the likes of us to be out there with all them rich people," Nora said.

"That's nonsense. You're my friends. You have just as much a right to be out there as they do. Do you hear me?"

Florrie began to cry, rubbing the dark pouches beneath her eyes. "Don't make us go back there. We don't feel right. They don't want us."

Sarah pushed back the strings that were her hair. "Don't be mad at us, Eleanor. It's just the way it is. That's all."

"But it doesn't have to be. You'll see, all of you. It will be different, better, with Charles running the mill. And I intend to have a say in things too."

"We're hopin' for it." Nora put her feathery hands on Eleanor's shoulders. "We know you wanted us here, and don't think we're not glad of it. But them rich. They hate our guts. Always will."

Eleanor hugged Nora. "In any case, I hope I see you out there later." She smiled. "But I'm not so foolish to think I can tell you girls what to do."

They waved goodbye and she walked back towards the reception after asking the cook for more shrimp, beef. The mill owners and their wives still stood in groups as far from the workers as possible. And the workers sat on the ground or stood huddling at the far side of the lawn.

Dante would have predicted such a division. He had lived through conditions in Europe where the poor had been used to being pawns of the wealthy. He knew how hard it was to throw off the yoke of that experience. She boiled with anger, not sure if it was at the world because of the injustice she saw or at herself for once again thinking of Dante on her wedding day.

"You look like a princess. A real princess."

She did not have to turn to recognize Catherine's voice. She wore a pale yellow dress, somewhat faded, but made especially lovely by the daffodil corsage she fashioned and placed on the band of her straw hat. She touched her collar, embroidered with silk daisies.

"I got the idea from you. I remembered that collar and cuffs you showed me, the ones your mother made and you attached to that dress to make it so pretty."

"I'm glad you came. I want to talk to you about something."

"Important enough to interrupt your wedding celebration?"

"Yes. I want you to come and live with us."

Catherine nearly dropped her platter of food. "Come live with you? And Charles?"

Eleanor smiled. "I'll be living with him, so I guess that's what I mean."

"Why would you ever want me livin' with you two?"

Eleanor had thought about this question a great deal. Although she disguised her feelings, living on Silk Road, being alone in that great house, the possibilities of boredom with Charles gone all day, terrified her. Idleness meant time to think of the past. She also knew she did not fit the pattern of the woman Charles should marry. She needed a companion, someone she could trust, who would save her from herself and the dark memories waiting to seize her every day of her life.

Catherine looked confused.

"You'd have your own room, of course," Eleanor said.

She still did not respond.

"And you know I'll pay you well. What you get at the Alliance. You'd eventually be in charge of the household, if you like. The supervision of meals. Things like that." She could think of no more to offer.

Still Catherine stood mute.

"Is it the Alliance you think you'll miss? You can still volunteer. All you want."

"I--have to think about it."

She watched Catherine turn towards where Charles stood, speaking with Michael Buchanan.

"Is it Charles you're worried about? Don't worry. He'd welcome you. He'll agree with whatever I want." She impulsively touched Catherine's arm. "The truth is, I need you. I'll be all alone in that big house. I'm not sure how it will work out. Please say you will."

Catherine brushed at imaginary lint on her dress. "I need to think it over."

Eleanor sighed, rubbed the slight perspiration that began to bloom on her forehead. She must not show her paralyzing fear of the days ahead. She never dreamed Catherine might refuse.

"Well,then, I suppose that's what you should do." She forced herself to survey the many guests she needed to greet. "You'll let me know. Soon? One way or another?"

"Of course. Soon."

Charles appeared from nowhere.

"I've just invited Catherine to come live with us. Wouldn't it be wonderful? I'd love her companionship, and she could help with the household." She swallowed hard. "Of course, I don't expect any problems in adjusting."

He took her hand in his.

"I understand, my dear. This is a great change for you." He turned to Catherine. "I'd be so happy if you would consider it. You'd be invaluable to Eleanor. And I, for one, would be so glad to see your smiling face each day."

Catherine's face turned the color of the cardinal swooping onto the dogwood above them. "I'll let you know."

"Well, then, that's all we can ask, isn't it?" He studied her hat. "What a lovely idea, putting those daffodils on your bonnet. They look so perfect, and the hat frames your face so well, if you don't mind me saying so. Don't you think so, Eleanor?"

"Why, yes," she said, though she hadn't noticed.

They left Catherine, spoke with the Buchanans, other guests. By the end of the evening she felt sick and tired of smiling at people she had little use for. She watched the mill workers dancing a tarantella, in between approaching the buffet table to pile their plates high with shrimp, lobster and beef. She felt a surge of happiness seeing them enjoy themselves, even if they always drifted back to the far side of the yard.

Dante would be so touched by their happiness. If only he could see her, surrounded by such wealth. She would never want again, never walk with broken shoes, never repair tattered clothes or be so thin she could feel her bones.

Colin would surely write him about the wedding.

Would he know she would forfeit it all, in a moment?

For him.

Darkness descended. Guests said goodbyes. Carriages lining Silk Road began to disappear. Workers lingered, stifling yawns, having exhausted themselves dancing, yet reluctant to leave this opulence. The mill awaited them at 6 a.m.. They finally began to depart slowly, staring one last time at the world they would most likely never visit again.

Charles raised his voice to the crowd.

"May I have your attention? I want to thank you all for coming, and I hope you enjoyed yourselves. We want to share our happiness on this wonderful day. Tomorrow you needn't be at the mill until twelve. Of course, you'll be paid for the full day." He gestured to Eleanor with a sweep of his hand, embraced her. "It's not every day I marry the most wonderful woman in the world."

Everyone applauded.

She could prolong the evening no longer, must follow the tradition of leaving before more guests departed.

They waved goodbye, walked the path in the coming darkness, lanterns lighted here and there, leading to the house.

And the wedding night.

She broke out in a sweat, clung harder to Charles, his face aglow with happiness.

Charles opened the great oak entrance door with a click of its brass handle.

This was all hers now.

Shestaredpasttheentranceway,   intothefoyerwithitsgrandfather clock ticking, monitoring the hours of her life with Charles and the portraits of his grandparents and parents staring down on her. Most likely she would pose for one with him someday. She clasped the carved post, ascended the stairs to the entrance of the bedroom.

Charles must have told the servant to have it lighted. A single pink-shaded lamp bathed the room with soft hues but did not dissolve the ponderous masculinity of the drab walls, mahogany furniture. She immediately envisioned stripping the flocked wallpaper, substituting a flower pattern. The weighty velvet draperies would be replaced by Alencon lace, as she had seen in fashion magazines.

She studied Charles, flushed from the wine, and was suddenly terrified. But she must persevere. It was her duty and her debt.

He kissed her on the cheek.

"Will you unbutton the back of my dress?"

She felt the flesh of his lips on the back of her neck, forced herself to breathe heavily. He kissed her neck. How often had she seen that gesture in films. It seemed so romantic. And now--.

"I can't wait to be unburdened of this heavy dress, I won't be long." She moved towards the bathroom, where she could drink some water, splash her sweaty skin. "Will you douse the light?" He would think her shy, not see her face.

He hastened to the lamp, darkening the room.

When she returned in her negligee she sensed how patient he tried to be, how gentle. She lay in the luxurious bed, let him explore her body, gave appropriate sighs of passion.

"I don't think you could ever imagine how much I love you, Eleanor."

"I love you too. You must know that."

She owed this to Charles. She kissed him long and hard. Suddenly, she remembered her father. His rough, calloused hands. She cried out when he entered her, angry at her inability to control the memories that would not leave her.

"My dear, forgive me." His eyes welled with tears when she looked at him. He seemed to feel the pain more than she did.

He was so tender, so loving. How could she tell him that this act frightened and revolted her?

"It's--all right," she said. "I know it hurts. I've--read about it." She slammed her eyes shut. He thrust into her more slowly, then uncontrollably. She showed a plaster smile after the act's completion.

"I want you to be happy," he said. "More than anything, my dear. Are you all right?"

"Of course. You've made me very happy."

"Have I?" His face, a study in perplexity, gleamed with sweat in the light of the moon embracing them.

"Of course. You must know that."

She was grateful for his near stupor. He never suspected she was not a virgin.

The silence of evening soon pervaded the room. His lids fluttered. She knew he would fight sleep until she condoned it.

She snuggled next to him. "Why don't we get some rest? It's been such a wonderful day."

He struggled to lift his half-closed lids. "You haven't asked about our honeymoon."

"Oh, I thought you'd be so busy at the mill. I don't expect it. I understand. I'll have plenty to keep me busy here--"

"I'm taking you on a very special trip. Have you ever heard of the *Lusitania?*"

"Of course. The great luxury liner."

"I've booked passage on it, for May 7. That will give you enough time to get ready with your packing, I hope."

"I can't believe it. I'd love to take a trip on it. I read all about it in *MacLean's*."

"Well, then, it's settled. Darling, so many of your dreams will come true now, if I have anything to say about it." His eyes closed as he held her. "Let's get some rest."

"You're so good to me."

She kissed him on the forehead. He fell almost immediately into a deep sleep. She had survived her first act of married love. She hoped perhaps they would grow easier.

Hours later she stared at Charles, lying so peacefully, doubting she would ever know such tranquility, wondering what it would be like to get a full night's sleep.

The silver glow of the moon came through the window, fell upon her.

Dante looked up at that same moon. She felt his presence, though hundreds of miles separated them. She began to cry softly, muffled the sound in her pillow. How could she go on knowing she would never see him again?

One thing she did know. When her death came, she would leave this earth still loving him.

Catherine sat on her bed holding her hat fingering her now- wilted daffodils, crying. It had been a few days since the wedding and still her mind churned with turmoil. She looked around the room, its water-stained plaster and chipping paint, filled with acrid smells lingering from her roommates who came and went various hours. She never asked why Mina and Margaret donned heavy make up and spent their evenings elsewhere. Both helped support families in Ireland. Who was she to condemn them? A woman could never surmount her situation in life with only the paltry salary received soaking silk at the mills. She knew that first hand. She had to take what chance offered.

Now her chance arrived. But it was two chances at once. Both were at war with each other.

She had resigned herself to never falling in love, but then she met Charles Lafferty. At first she thought he acknowledged her at the Alliance with more than friendly greetings. Soon she realized kindness lay within his nature, and the other girls received compliments as well. It was that generosity that she loved him for.

At the same time, her loyalty to Eleanor clashed with her feelings for Charles. Even though she owed her life to Eleanor, she had begun to notice flaws in her. She could be brusque with Charles and unfeeling. She did not even compliment her on her new collar or her special idea of wearing daffodils on her hat, until Charles admired it.

How could she be in daily contact with Charles knowing the agony of not having him return her love? He worshipped Eleanor, that much was obvious. But the joy she would experience seeing Charles every day tempted her. All she would ever have of him would be that nearness. She must believe it would be enough.

Certain she made the right decision, she plucked the dead daffodils from her hat, plopped it on, straightened her dress, and walked to Silk Road to tell Eleanor she would move in with her and Charles.

* * *

Catherine's acceptance of her offer was the last thought on Eleanor's mind this morning. Only a few days remained before the *Lusitania* left New York for Liverpool.

She found her issue of *MacClean's*, reread the article about it, savoring the descriptions of its Georgian lounge and Louis Seize dining room, whatever that meant. Outfits she had fitted weeks before the wedding would do quite nicely.

She memorized descriptions of each so if the mill owners' wives complimented her and asked about them she would sound knowledgeable about fashion. She eyed her blue moire coat trimmed with small bands of black velvet and tiny pearl buttons, her stylish silk crepe de chine outfit, fastened from the waist down the center with ivory Venise lace insertions, her emerald dress hat with ostrich plumes and a double row of emerald satin ribbon to highlight her eyes, her embroidered voile dress. She opened her closet, touched her military lace shoes of gunmetal calf with--with some sort of new heels. She frowned, peeked at her listing. Louis heels, they were Louis heels.

She must work even harder to memorize the names of these styles. Charles must not be ashamed of her on the trip, or in their future social life.

Since the first days of their marriage, she had tried to absorb everything in sight. As she dined with Charles, she studied the dinner service. Roses and gold rims encircled the plates. Sterling silver complemented them on each side. Cut glass goblets gleamed at her. She picked up the large spoon on the farthest side of her plate, smiling at Charles, who patiently taught her which forks and spoons to use at various times during the meal.

Tonight he looked somber as he read the newspaper.

"Don't you like the beef?" she said.

He handed the newspaper to her. "I've got some misgivings about our trip. Look at that. In the bottom corner."

She read the ad for Cunard's steamship leaving Pier 54 Saturday at 10 a.m.. "I don't understand. The trip doesn't seem to be canceled."

He pointed his finger at the ad. "Not there. Look at the part below, in the black box."

She read it carefully.

Notice! Travelers intending to embark on the Atlantic voyage are reminded that a state of war exists between Germany and her allies; that the zone of war includes the waters adjacent to the British Isles; in accordance with formal notice given by the Imperial German Government vessels flying the flag of Great Britain, or any of her allies, are liable to destruction in those waters and that travellers sailing in the war zone on ships of Great Britain and her allies do so at their own risk.

The Imperial German Embassy

"I'm cancelling our trip," he said. "I know you're disappointed but I can't endanger--"

"Cancel--How could you? You know how much I want to go. And this is silly." She pointed to the newspaper. "The *Lusitania* isn't a warship. It's the fastest, largest steamer in the Atlantic. I told you I read all about it. So I would know everything for our trip. Why would the Germans attack a luxury liner? Wilson would go to war in a minute. You know that."

"But what we don't know is what the ship might be carrying. Perhaps guns. Or ammunition. And neither do the Germans. Besides, no matter what kind of ship it is, it'll be in a war zone. I'm sorry, I just won't take that chance. If anything ever happened to you--"

She thought of hours spent packing, dreaming of the trip, being on the ocean, wearing her finery. In that instant she hated him, always weighing situations, always rational. How could he be so foolish to think they would be in real danger? If only he could live by his emotions, say they would go, and damn the danger.

"I'm so sick and tired of everybody talking about the Germans and the possibility of war. And now you spoiled my trip!"

"You know I would never want to do anything that would hurt you. I didn't think there would be danger when I booked, you know that. Be reasonable. Please."

She jumped up, swooped in back of him, tightened her arms around his shoulders, her voice low, intimate. "You'd take me if you loved me."

He broke free of her embrace, clasped her hands. "It's because I love you that I won't take you."

She wrenched her hands from his, stomped into the hallway where she saw a servant admitting Catherine and ran to her.

"Catherine, Charles is so foolish. We're not going on our honeymoon. Can you imagine that?"

"But I thought it was all settled."

"He says it's too dangerous. The Germans are warning passengers that those waters will be in a war zone."

"A war zone?"

"Isn't it silly? And now we can't go." She rested her face on Catherine's comfortable shoulder. "He's so foolish not to take me. He knows how hard I've been planning."

"Well, it seems to me if it's a war zone, why, maybe he's right. I'm sure he knows more about these things than we do."

She jolted her head from Catherine's shoulder. "You're siding with him?"

"I'm siding with what I think is best for you."

"I thought if you lived here you'd always be on my side."

"Then maybe it's best I don't live here. I have to go with my own mind too. Although I came to tell you I would move in, if you still want me."

"Of course I do. We both do."

"Charles only wants what's best for you. You know that."

"I do want you to live here. I trust you, more than I can ever say."

"Well, then, it's settled. I'll be movin' in next Monday. I'll give notice. My room will be rented in no time, I'm sure."

Eleanor led her towards the dining room. "We'll be so happy. I know it."

The day the *Lusitania* left New York an article in the Times showed morbid photographers selling photos of the ship, proclaiming "Last Voyage of the *Lusitania*." It stated passengers received ominoustelegrams warning them to cancel their berths, that Alfred Vanderbilt said, "Have it on definite authority the *Lusitania* is to be torpedoed." Yet, others were quoted as saying they felt it ridiculous the Germans would attack for the Central Powers sorely needed American good will.

Eleanor still thought Charles a fool to believe the warnings. She was even more troubled that he could be so decisive and unbending. After what she'd seen in their courtship, she expected he would be malleable in her hands. She wasn't quite sure if she felt glad or angry at his unbending will. What she saw as his weakness had always been a source of contempt to her. Now she found that in a strange way his decisiveness generated a new respect in her.

The usual paper lay on the breakfast table a week after the *Lusitania* left New York City. Charles finished reading it, laid it down next to his plate. He drank his coffee slower than usual, scrutinizing her. She picked it up casually, less interested in world events than local ones, especially the plight of the workers. She was following the unrest beginning in Bayonne, a city near Paterson, involving the Standard Oil Company, wondered if it would eventually become a strike.

When she read the headlines and lead article, she began to tremble.

Lusitania Torpedoed

The queen of Britain's Cunard Line, the *Lusitania*, was torpedoed and sunk yesterday by a U-boat off Ireland, with the loss of nearly 1200 lives, including 128 Americans. The torpedo thudded into the starboard, behind the bridge, to the accompaniment of a powerful explosion. President Wilson's intimate advisor, Colonel House, has urged immediate war in the absence of a full German apology.

She stared open-mouthed at Charles. "I can't believe--- Torpedoed."

She waited for his look of self-satisfaction. It never came. He reached his hand to hers across the table. "Thank God we weren't on it, that I can look across the table and see my beautiful wife."

"You were right. I--apologize."

"That's not important, my being right. That you're safe and sound is what's important." He rose quickly. "I just hope this doesn't mean all out war. The thought of all those young men dying." His eyes misted. "It's heartbreaking. I wish I could go."

"What a foolish thing to say. You know you're needed here. The goods you create, the silk for parachutes, will save lives. You should be proud."

"I am." His mill already produced goods needed for the war effort being sent to Britain. "I've decided I'm going to enlarge the commission weaving, change the way the whole mill is run. Slowly but surely, I want to eventually make most of my profit that way. And the workers will gain too."

She started to speak, hesitated.

"Go on, my dear," he said. "Say what you're thinking."

"Well, I wondered. It seems like a wonderful idea. But will it affect our profits?"

He laughed. "I didn't expect you to take so immediately to capitalism. But no, of course not. I must continue to make the profit I do, if only because the alternative would be to shut down the mill. What good would that do for the workers? And commission weaving, when executed properly, would give me a greater one, and would let me increase the wages of the soakers and ribbon weavers. Men want to have a hand in a business they've helped create. It's human nature. And they'll work harder if they get more and more profit out of it. We can't lose."

She blushed. "I sounded selfish."

"Of course not. You've had such a hard life. I can't expect you not to be happy with the wealth you have now." He smiled. "And want to keep it."

"You know I want what's best for the workers, I do. After all, I was one of them. And I'll never forget it. The strike. The starvation." She stared into space, caught herself. "You must get them better heating in the winter. And the children. Oh, Charles, I don't want to see any children working when I visit the mill." She folded her arms across her chest. "And another thing. We really should think about limiting hours. We can't have them work themselves to death. And--"

"Slow down. All in good time."

Excitement surged through her at the power for change existing in Charles. And now in her. "But I have so many other ideas-"

"And you know I'll listen to them. We'll talk about them, I promise. But now I've got to get to the mill." He grabbed his hat from the hall rack. "Colin's coming tonight. We'll talk then."

She watched him walk down the path. Rushed as he was, he stopped to admire the pink and white tulips embellishing each side of the walk, just opening. He never failed to wave goodbye before alighting into his carriage.

Eleanor's thoughts jumped elsewhere as soon as he left. Colin might write Dante now. He said they no longer corresponded, but he might be excited enough to tell him about this breakthrough for the workers, an actual share in ownership of the means of production at the mill. But Dante might admire Charles for this step, even see him as a decent man.

As she should. As she did. Yet--.

She stood in the doorway, the sunlight brightening her. She tried hard to remove Dante from her thoughts. But she failed again. She had stopped trying to understand the mystery of love, and memory. She knew only that it sustained her life.

That evening Charles made a definite decision to increase commission weaving at the mill, especially after Colin's encouragement. Eleanor suggested twenty-five more workers be offered the opportunity. Colin announced he would give Denham and Whatley notice and work for Charles. Eleanor thought change would do him good and liked the idea he would be closer to Charles.

As the weeks progressed and their idea took root, they began to refine it. Eleanor made a study, found high rates of absenteeism from illness at other mills where workers put in fifteen to eighteen hours a day commission weaving. Charles decided to allow a maximum of ten. The workers complained at first. When they found they were out less from illness and produced less flawed silk because they were less fatigued, they realized the benefit. Other mill owners didn't follow Charles's method, and weavers still worked staggering hours. Word quickly spread about the excellent working conditions at Lafferty's. Soon weavers from other mills applied for employment. Eleanor encouraged Charles to consider expanding. She also visited the mill often, the workers giving her smiles of appreciation that said "Thank you" between clacks of their looms--for benches where they were now permitted to sit during lunch, for fifteen-minute breaks, for brightly- painted walls.

One day Mary examined her privately at the Alliance. She realized her mill visits, her sense of accomplishment, would end.

She sat across from Charles at the dinner table, a smile pasted to her face.

"I have news for you. I saw Mary today. On a medical visit. She told me what I already suspected. I'm going to have a child."

"Darling! I can't tell you how happy I am." He frowned. "Of course, you must take every precaution. You can't be visiting the mill, or anywhere else for that matter."

It was as she had foreseen. Society ruled. She would not be seen in public after her pregnancy became evident. She quelled her anger at the thought of such foolishness. But she would abide by his wishes. She owed him that at least.

Eleanor's disappointment not being involved with changes at the mill lessened with the coming of summer and having her first real garden. She ignored the stifling heat to admire her flowers in streams of glory on the path. Her garden relieved her from inner turmoil. She loved its order, its reliability. Every year her perennials returned; they never disappointed or hurt her. And she passed the summer admiring pink and white hollyhocks reaching for the sky amidst her blue delphinium and Michaelmas daisies, foxgloves in large bell clusters, pink and white peonies, clouds of purple and pink phlox, so many others. Even Charles' rare striped ranunculus and double hyacinths bloomed that summer. She admired his success with rarities. His passion for flowers fed hers and she began to realize how much they had in common.

Almost every evening they walked the garden's paths, admiring their beauty, sharing ideas. She valued Charles' opinion, asked his thoughts on planting more honeysuckle--she loved its sweet, intoxicating smell. He complimented her on her excellent taste, as he always did, and asked her opinion on trying new varieties he'd read about, double-flowered violets and lemon lilies, genuinely interested in her advice.

One evening in late August she confessed her dream to have a Victorian rose walk similar to one she saw illustrated in McClure's, showed him the photo. He studied the photo and matched varieties she would need. He suggested a rambler, 'Alberic Barbier' with large, pale yellow flowers and deep green foliage, a 'Boule de Neige', a white Bourbon rose, to provide the walk with height and form, plus a 'Cecile Brunner' Olyantha rose, which would produce large flowers throughout summer. On the other side he recommended a 'Fantin Latour', a rose that buds deep pink, then opens to reveal white petals with a pink flush, and a 'Madame Hardy', a damask, brilliant with a greenish center he especially loved for its uniqueness.

She frowned.

"Why would I ever want white roses with green centers in my garden?"

"We won't have the 'Madame Hardy' then." She smiled.

Every morning, weather permitting, she visited her garden. Some days she walked with exhilaration, at peace. Other times when the depression that so frequently visited came unannounced, her garden comforted her better than any human being ever could.

Charles pampered her more and more as the child became due. He insisted she not wait for dinner if he were late. If he missed the evening meal with her, he came to the bedroom, plopped down among her movie star and fashion magazines. He yawned often, rubbed his eyes, yet always found time to talk with her.

Tonight he appeared excited. He carried a book by Edith Wharton on Italian villas and spoke of setting aside acreage at the back of the house next summer, perhaps installing a fountain, as in some of the photos, perhaps developing stone and box sculpture. He pointed to statues of Roman gods, decked by paths of green cypress, fishponds and box parterres, gardens planted with medicinal herbs. Eleanor winced at the idea of fountains spewing and fish swimming in ponds. She could see it was a particular idea of beauty, but it was so different from hers.

Charles sighed, and yielded.

Again.

Autumn arrived, trees ablaze with color. Showers of gold and orange leaves covered the lawn. Planting of next year's bulbs began. She wanted to try a new variety of daffodils, insisted on putting them in the ground herself to make them truly hers. When she rose, cramps rumbled through her. She grasped her stomach, crouched over, felt wetness in her underwear. Tom Branigan, their gardener, led her to the house, helped her lie down on the couch. Catherine immediately called the Alliance.

Mary examined her carefully when she arrived, observing the staining in her underwear, then gave her a sedative.

"How many times have I told you not to do so much bending and working in the garden?" She snapped her satchel closed. "You're spotting and I don't like it. And I don't like the idea of those cramps either."

Eleanor's eyes filled. "Am I going to lose the baby?"

"I hope not, if you follow my instructions. Your gestational sac's intact and hasn't been expelled, so that's good news. But your cervix is weak. You'll need complete bedrest to keep this baby."

"You mean I can't get out of this bed these next three months?"

"Not even to go to the bathroom. Catherine will have to bring you a bedpan."

"But I have so much to do. I-"

"I don't want to hear it. If you want this child, you must do as I say. I'll look in on you in a day or so. Have Catherine call me immediately if you feel cramps returning, or if you bleed again."

"Whatever you say. Of course."

Charles burst into the room. "Are you all right, my dear? What happened? Catherine called me at the mill."

"She should be all right, if she follows my instructions and stays in bed." Mary gave her another look of warning. "Remember, complete bed rest. Plenty of liquids. And don't lie flat all day. Sit up and raise your legs now and then. Move them around."

"Why does she need to do that?"

"You don't need to know all the medical reasons, Charles. Just make sure she follows my instructions."

"But I do want to know. I want this child more than anything on earth."

Mary sighed. "Very well. When she's off her feet she's increasing the flow of oxygen and nutrients to her uterus. If she raises her legs now and then, the water will circulate and the flow of blood to her placenta will increase. If she lies on her back all day the weight of the baby will press the same blood vessels delivering blood and nutrients to the placenta. Vital blood vessels are located in her front spinal column and behind her uterus. Lying on her side is good too. Try to shift positions now and then."

His face flushed with embarrassment. "I understand. Thank you."

Mary placed her hand on his shoulder. "Charles, if you want a male doctor from St. Joseph's I won't be offended."

"Oh, nonsense, Mary."

"The only person I want to take care of me is Mary," Eleanor insisted through drooping lids.

"Of course. You look exhausted. Get some rest now. I'll look in on you later."

Eleanor drifted into sleep.

Charles and Catherine walked Mary to the door.

"I must warn you," Mary said. "If she's going to be in bed all this time, she's going to lose that essential flexibility in her vagina when the baby comes."

His face turned white as the narcissus blooming in the vase on the hall table. "Is she in danger?"

"Having a baby is always a danger. Hers is elevated."

Charles felt fear spreading from his stomach to his whole being. "If I had ever known-"

"If you had known, you wouldn't have done anything differently. A child is a precious gift. Women pay the price, but it's well worth it. I'll stop by soon."

Mary whisked out the door.

Catherine put her arm through Charles'as they walked through the hallway. "You know I'll be with her every minute. I'll do all I can."

"I don't know what I'd do without you, Catherine. I mean it."

"That's all I care about. That I'm helping you. It means the world to me. I'll get back to see if Eleanor's sleeping."

She scurried up the stairs.

Charles walked to the library window, lifted the heavy curtain, watched Mary walking the path to her carriage, her back straight as a board, her feet pounding the flagstones with every step. If only he had her self-assurance. But he did feel his ownership of the mill giving him more confidence. He was rising to the occasion of decision-making, demonstrating leadership, helping the workers.

His relationship with Eleanor was a different story. He knew she felt some semblance of happiness, mostly at the material comforts he could give her. If his instincts were correct, soon she would make more changes to the interior of the house. But she took so little pleasure in life. He thought of their love making, the fear so often welling in her eyes, fear she thought she disguised so well. No matter how gentle he was, that fear remained. Was she afraid of passion, of letting go? She fought so hard to stay in control at all times. Would he ever be able to arouse her passion to the point she transcended fear? It was such a mystery.

He had no idea how she would fare as a mother. He prayed she would love the child, grateful to have Catherine, so comforting and kind, at Eleanor's side.

A chilly wind blew through the window. Autumn was settling in full force, the sun beginning to vanish sooner. A purple haze smeared the sky, obliterating what brightness was left.

He shivered, closed the latch on the window, covered it with the heavy curtain, blocking light completely.

As the weeks passed, Catherine became Eleanor's constant companion. She gave up working part time at the Women's Alliance to devote all her energy to Eleanor. Charles gave Eleanor a list of books he thought she would like, and Catherine obtained them for her. She read to her, or Eleanor would read herself, giving Catherine time to study medical books she borrowed from Mary, which absorbed her more and more. She had long outpaced Eleanor in interest and knowledge of medicine. Mary said she had no doubt Catherine would have been a fine doctor as she demonstrated more and more expertise at the clinic.

Catherine even placed her precious studies second to administering to Eleanor--for Charles' sake more than Eleanor's. Nights she lay in her bed in tears, reliving the sight of him catering to Eleanor. She tried to stifle her thoughts, focus on Eleanor's good points, yet could not help but despise her casual treatment of Charles.

She often walked through the house, pretending to be its mistress, imagining Charles would soon be coming home. To her. She lived for the morning, when Eleanor slept late and Charles refused to disturb her. Catherine and he had breakfast together. He inquired about her studies in medicine, about her early life, family. At first she felt shy, a servant being above her place, but he quickly dispelled that feeling with his kindness. They became friends who respected each other, all she could ever expect. She often looked in the mirror, studying her scarred face, thinking of Eleanor's vibrance, cursing the injustice of life.

She hated evenings when she dined alone, Charles up in the bedroom with Eleanor, sharing the day's news, pampering her. Sometimes when her obsession overpowered her, she listened at the door to their conversations, heard them speak of the mill, or a book she read. Charles praised her at every turn. One time she spoke of her embarrassment at not being as educated as he, broke down in tears. He said her desire for knowledge impressed him far more than a college education. Catherine listened in as he patiently explained points in books that Eleanor did not quite understand. He said she must never be discouraged but proud of her accomplishments through reading. That not having a strong school background made her progress even more impressive.

Why did she punish herself by listening to these conversations? She would creep downstairs, have tea, go to bed, and cry. The conflict between the gratitude she should feel to Eleanor and the love she did feel for Charles consumed her. The calm assurance she projected each day withered more and more. She scarcely ate. On rare occasions when she slept, her dreams terrified her. She would decide to leave after Eleanor delivered Charles's baby, then she would see him, savor each crumb of his kindness to her, burn with desire at his nearness.

She could never leave him.

But she must relieve her torment, uncertain how. She knew if she did not her mind would shatter.

Christmas of 1915 began as a dreary time for Eleanor. The day- to-day prison of bed began to splinter her nerves. The more she attempted to relax, the more angry she grew at the pregnancy that robbed her of her new life. And the coming holiday made it worse.

Catherine purchased a large wreath for the oak door. Pine boughs and Christmas holly covered the marble mantelpiece. The new wallpaper, splashed with white hydrangeas and green foliage, seemed to have been created for this time of year. She studied the ponderous drapes glaring at her, still waiting to be replaced. Earlier Catherine looped them back with ties to bring in natural light.

Cold air of evening began seeping into the room, crawling through the cracks around the windows. A brutal night lay ahead, evidenced by the raw sky. Catherine began to draw the drapes.

"Please," Eleanor said, "don't close them yet."

She hated the drapes closed, leaving her feeling entombed. At least the fireplace gave some warmth and cheer. She heard carolers singing "God Rest Ye Merry Gentlemen" immersed in happiness of the season. The thought of such revelry while she lay bedridden unnerved her. She threw her blanket aside, plopped her feet on the floor.

"I'm sick of this awful bed. I'm all right. I haven't had any bleeding for months and-"

"Charles!" Catherine ran to her side.

"Eleanor. Please. You don't have much longer to go."

Eleanor flung her hand to her forehead, her breath fast and strained. Her clumsy body protruded with a giant lump that never ceased to startle her. She tried to stand, wobbled, fell back upon the bed. She had not realized the extent months of disuse would cause her body to lose strength. She hated this weakness, being at the mercy of others for every need.

Charles flew into the room, sat beside her. "Darling. Please. Soon now--"

"I'm so useless and weak, and sick of it all." Tears gushed. She hated herself for crying so easily since her pregnancy began.

Charles put his arm around her. "You're bored. That's what it is. And I don't blame you one bit."

"Whatever you do, don't tell me to read a book. I'm tired of reading, reading, reading. I want to walk. I want to go out in the air. I want to look at our land, see the garden, the snow covering our pine branches and--"

"It's only a little while longer. The baby will be healthy because you've done this. You can't give up now."

"Listen," he said, "I've got an idea."

"I'm not reading more books!"

"It isn't books I'm thinking of. It's the house."

"The house?"

"The decorating. You've worked wonders with this room so far, with the wallpaper. And I'd be so glad if you could do something about downstairs. The dining room. It's so dark and dreary. The rooms haven't been touched in years."

"You mean I can change them? Do whatever I want?"

"Of course. Perhaps start with the living room. Get rid of that awful flocked paper. It's gotten so dark and dirty over the years. And the dark paneling doesn't help. I've seen some designs by a man named Voysey. I could show you his book. Paler colors, the ones you like. And less furniture. Why, that room is so cluttered with that Chesterfield sofa, the arm chair, the ladies' easy chair, that massive chiffonier, it amazes me I haven't broken my neck falling over all the furniture."

She laughed. "Why didn't you say so? I have to confess I was thinking about redecorating. Can we have a decorator come to help me? The one Catholina Lambert has? I know what I want, but I do need some help."

"Of course. I'll enquire next time I'm at the club who Catholina had."

"Will you go soon?"

"Probably Thursday, as usual. Is that soon enough?"

She swallowed hard, knowing he would go that very moment if she asked him. "Of course."

She turned to Catherine who sat quietly observing in the chair across the room. "Will you get my drawing pad from the bottom drawer? And my colored pencils. Right next to it."

Colors must be decided, furniture, drapery, tiling, flooring. She wanted a newer look, one of stylized elegance. The cornice in the living room with its elaborate foliage and gilding must be replaced by a plainer one. Thick curtains and dusty velvet drapes would be removed. Wall surfaces would be light and simple. Perhaps the door panels could be decorated with a single motif, a spray of flowers she would paint. She must have a French ceramic Art Nouveau fireplace installed, like the one in Catholina Lambert's home.

She pulled her colored pencils from their pouch, began drawing. The house would become a reflection of herself, offering her hope and refuge, immersing her in beauty.

She sensed Charles scrutinizing her, the panic-stricken look on his face gone. "You must always tell me what's on your mind." His hand felt strangely warm, comforting when he touched hers. "Whatever is in my power to give you, you know it's yours."

"You're so good to me."

She burst into tears, struggling to understand why she could not love him. He was good, through and through.

"Now, now." He kissed her cheek. "And when you're up and about, I'll take you to Central Park. You'll love it. Frederick Law Olmstead's masterpiece. And we'll go to the Metropolitan. I know how you enjoyed Catholina's collection of paintings. The Italians, the Dutch. And the Impressionists you loved so much."

"Yes, he said I must visit the Met."

"That's the first place we'll go after the baby's born. As soon as you're up to it. The paintings will open up a whole new world to you." He hesitated. "You know I don't want you to feel the baby will be a-- hindrance--in any way. You can still pursue your interests. You'll have Catherine to help you. Or we can get another nurse, if you like."

"Oh, Charles, you're so much smarter than me. All you know about art. And artists. Everything."

"Eleanor, I'm the one jealous of you. All the new worlds you'll experience. Why, you're opening like the flowers you paint so beautifully." He rose from the bed. "Now get some rest. Tomorrow Catherine can get you more supplies if you need them, do your leg work. Won't you, Catherine?"

"Of course. I'd be happy to."

Neither observed Catherine's face drained of color.

The last weeks of her pregnancy Eleanor sat amidst color charts, decorating books, fabric samples. Catherine trudged up and down stairs, then to various shops ordering furnishings as prescribed by Eleanor. The decorator, a thin man with a pock-marked face round as a pie, complimented her upon her modern approach to design, her love for the neo-Georgian furniture, less dependent on 'that horrible stuffing,' as he phrased it, her penchant for the style of the Arts and Crafts movement. She had no idea what he meant, but she did know exactly what she wanted.

She sat in bed, her body so ponderous she could hardly move, placed her hand on the giant mound protruding from her stomach. The size of her body terrifed her. Her heart chilled when she thought of the bulb of flesh grown into a human being within her. She feared the delivery, worried her child would be deformed, terrified at the thought of the excruciating pain. As usual, she refused to unburden her fears to others, sat in self-enclosed exile, her heart pounding from constant anxiety.

One morning she felt brief, irregular contractions in her abdomen. Her water burst. The baby was ready to be born.

Mary soon arrived. The first thing she did was throw Charles out of the room.

Mary and Catherine sat counting intervals between contractions. Hours passed. Eleanor lay, pain arriving at intervals, penetrating like a searing iron. She clenched her teeth against her lower lip. Blood trickled down her chin. Catherine unclenched her mouth, pushed a cloth between her teeth.

She lay near a precipice of unconsciousness, felt cold on her forehead, saw fuzzy outlines of what must have been Catherine and Mary.

"Push hard," someone said. "It'll be over soon. Push!"

Hours later, the baby finally moved down through the birth canal.

She saw a blur that must have been Mary's form. She mustered more strength, attempted to thrust the baby from her spent body. She would not discard nine months of her life, deny Charles this child.

Her effort failed. The baby did not move.

Someone put a mask smelling like alcohol over her nose, taking her to a netherland where she dwelled in and out of reality. Then something sliced across the area below her stomach. The heaviness of her body abated. She lay uncertain what happened. She finally saw the blurred shape of Mary holding her child. Mary placed the baby in her arms.

"A beautiful boy."
She heard her child's cry of life.
She smiled weakly. She had given Charles a son.

* * *

Eleanor quickly forgot the pain of birth. She held her son, a perfect baby, his only flaw a birthmark at the side of his forehead. But that would eventually be covered with hair when he grew older. She spent every possible moment with him, studying his fingers, rubbing his toes, examining the fingernails like translucent shells, stroking his dimpled arms and legs. She liked to brush his tuft of auburn hair, downy as feathers. She especially loved to look into his gray eyes. Her eyes.

He began to smile very soon after his birth. Catherine said he laughed at seeing the angels hovering over him, but Eleanor believed he smiled at her, that already he recognized his mother.

Charles felt an equal pull at his heart when it came to his son. He and Eleanor rhapsodized on and on as they took turns holding him. He said he felt glad the baby looked so like Eleanor instead of him, and was so healthy. They talked about the baby's future, wondered if he would take to running the mill, then laughed they should have such thoughts with him still an infant in the cradle. They named him Robert. It was not only Colin's middle name but also that of Elizabeth's father. Her mother would have been pleased.

By spring she felt completely revived, wallowed in the splendor of its balmy days, sitting Robbie outside in his carriage while she worked or sat in the garden. Her child stirred within her a happiness she never imagined she could feel. She would watch him sleeping in the shade of the giant oak tree at the side of the house while sitting in her garden.

But as time passed she became restless. She found herself wanting to visit the mill to see how the commission weaving was working out. Did the white paint she suggested last year make a difference in the somber room where the men and women worked? Was Charles obtaining the best quality silk, or were dealers still now and then attempting to pass off inferior products--as she discovered when she helped at the mill? She knew silk's quality from her own experience ribbon weaving. Did he have any statistics yet on the health of the workers now that their hours were lessened? Had the screens she suggested last year been installed so they could have fresh air now that spring arrived?

That evening she dreamed of the silk strike once again. Dante appeared, walked with her through the mill, admired the white walls, the clean-swept floors, the smiling workers. He put his arms around her. Then his eyes filled with tears.

She awoke, shaken. Why did he always show sorrow rather than joy? She left the bed, checked Robbie's bassinette, watched him sleep so peacefully, a smile on his face creasing his dimples. She ached to hold him in her arms, controlled her impulse.

She never told Charles how her nights were still haunted by the gaunt faces of the workers.

And of Dante.

Colin turned fifty in September. She decided to have a small celebration in honor of his birthday, as well as break up the routine beginning to stagnate her again. It would be fun to have a beautiful vanilla cream cake, her favorite, and decorate the house with fall motifs. She placed yellow and white mums in vases throughout the first floor. Catherine helped her adorn the fireplaces with ribbons of leaves.

She hoped the birthday gathering would lift Colin's spirits. He brooded constantly since reading of the Easter Uprising in Ireland. Colin knew Tom Clarke, one of the leaders. He once came to visit the United States. She would not have been surprised if somehow Colin managed to meet him in secret. She always suspected his involvement in the underground movement to free Ireland.

She remembered the stories Colin told her about Parnell, the great Irish leader, Patrick Pearse, the poet and schoolmaster, and James Connelly, the trade union organizer. He especially revered Pearse, who believed in the need for blood sacrifice for Ireland. Colin was obsessed with Irish politics. She wondered why he stayed in Paterson, grateful he did. She loved him dearly.

She and Charles discussed the Uprising when it appeared in the papers. The plan of the Uprising was to take over strategic strong points in the center of Dublin, but things went awry from the beginning. Pearse, Connelly and Clarke, other leaders, were forced to evacuate the burning post office where they had their headquarters. The newspaper account said Pearse surrendered. Colin refused to believe it. When he received a letter from his friend Paddy verifying it, he fell into a depression that had not abated. Over and over at dinner gatherings he came back to the topic of Pearse's surrender. Hadn't he been the man who called upon the people for the need of a blood sacrifice?

On the day of the party, Colin arrived at the door with his hair greasy, moustache untrimmed, dark circles under his eyes.

"Hello, darlin'." His voice sounded thin as water. She smelled liquor on his breath.

He revived at the sight of Robbie. Eleanor had dressed him in a creamy silk outfit, collar and cuffs finished with scalloped embroidered edges. His throne consisted of Charles's lap on the rare occasions when Eleanor let him leave her arms. Charles squeezed his finger and mumbled baby talk to him. Robbie smiled, gurgled.

"When do you think he'll get more teeth?" Charles said. "Do you know about when?"

Eleanor laughed. "It won't be that earth shattering, I assure you. Besides, it'll just mean he'll be able to bite you."

"I don't care if he bites me. Everything about my darling boy is earth shattering to me. It is."

"He certainly knows he's the center of attention." Eleanor smiled. "And he deserves it."

She touched the tips of her fingers to his chin, tickled him. He gurgled again.

Charles bounced him up and down. "He's going to get all the attention in the world." He turned to Robbie. "You're my darling boy, aren't you? Yes, you are. Just wait until I take you to the mill. Show you off."

"The mill? Charles, it's too soon for that. All those germs."

"It's never too soon to show him what will someday be his, is

it?"

"I don't think at his age he'd notice, do you? I forbid you to take him. And that's that."

Charles sighed. "I suppose if you insist--"

"I do. Promise me."

"All right then. I promise."

Eleanor noticed Colin spoke little as they discussed the baby, but his smile told her Robbie comforted him.

Catherine appeared, carrying a chocolate cake gushing with layers of chocolate icing, gleaming with candles.

Eleanor scowled. "I thought I said I wanted a vanilla cream cake."

"Don't upset yourself, darling, Charles said. "Chocolate is my favorite."

Catherine smiled.

Eleanor relented, knowing Catherine worked hard helping her prepare for the small gathering.

"To the glory of Ireland." Colin dutifully blew out the candles, cut the cake, passed it around, taking only a tiny piece for himself.

Catherine was more subdued than usual, eyes darting from Colin to Charles, back and forth, again and again. Silence dangled uncomfortably between Eleanor's attempts at continuing conversation.

"You all seem so gloomy today." She turned to Colin. "Is it Ireland? Have you heard worse news?"

"Nothing since what I told you already. I should get another letter. Soon I hope."

There was another bout of silence. Eleanor clicked her tongue. "We haven't gotten the paper three days now. I don't understand it. I'm going to wait for the boy who delivers it and complain. I miss my morning papers. I like to keep up with what's happening in the world. And I miss my gardening and recipe column."

No one commented. Their thoughts seemed elsewhere as they stared at the cake, the tablecloth, the baby.

"Why is everybody so quiet tonight? Catherine spent so much time making the cake, hoping we'd have a good time. Is something wrong?"

"Of course not." Charles turned to Catherine. "Any cake Catherine makes is always exceptionally delicious."

Catherine blushed.

"I think it's just that we're all tired. I've had a long day." He turned to Colin. "I know Colin has a great deal on his mind."

No one wanted seconds of cake and coffee. The cream on the cake began to sag. Catherine began to remove the candles. Robbie fell asleep, leaving no one on whom to focus harmless small talk.

Charles rose. "Colin, may I see you in the library?"

Eleanor pushed her chair back, began to rise. "I'll go too. I think it's about time I started getting involved again with the mill. I've told you that. Catherine won't mind doing the dishes alone. And Robbie's fast asleep."

"No. I need to see Colin alone."

"But-"

"I said I need to see him. Alone."

They disappeared down the hall into the library. Catherine began gathering plates, saucers, spoons. Eleanor remained in her seat, perplexed. Charles so rarely spoke that way to her. Well, whatever they talked about in the library she would be privy to. He might just as well be put on notice now she planned on being back at the mill soon, next to him at the helm, helping with decision making.

"I think I'll have some more coffee. If there's any left."

Catherine poured it for her. As she walked towards the buffet to put it back on the stove, Eleanor deliberately turned over the silver milk pitcher, its contents spilling.

She rose immediately. "Look what I've done. I'll just go and get a towel to clean it up. And get some more cream while I'm at it."

Catherine clenched her arm. "I'll get it."

Eleanor glowered. "What's wrong with you? I'm sure I know where to find cream in my own kitchen."

"Stay here. Robbie--"

"Is fast asleep. You can watch him a few minutes, can't you?"

Catherine sat down. "Come right back."

"Why wouldn't I?"

Once she left the room, she turned down the long hall towards the kitchen area, out of Catherine's view, bustling to the library. The door was open.

She smiled and stood closer to the door.

"I don't know what to do about Eleanor and the mill." Charles' voice.

"I thought it would happen sooner or later. After a time I knew the clothes, the decoratin', the doodads would wear off. Her heart is with the poor, the workers, though sometimes I think she doesn't even realize how deep it goes."

"I suppose I'll have to give in. And now this. I'm sure you realize Eleanor doesn't know they caught him."

"Of course. The dirty bastard. Drink did him in. Braggin' revenge. Lucky the bartender followed through on it. Now I see it all clear, but why didn't I put two and two together faster? Like you did. I suppose it was the shock of her death.I couldn't think. The whole day I've been fallin' apart all over again. The memories--"

She heard Colin's voice crack, what sounded like someone blowing his nose.

Why hadn't they told her the monster who killed her mother had been caught?

"If only they'd put the bastard in prison when he attacked Eleanor," Charles said. "But lawyers, you know. The weasel got off."

Clegg? She braced herself against the wall, rooted to the spot, compelled to hear.

"Well, justice will finally be served," Charles said. "I don't know how Eleanor will fare when she finds out it was a revenge crime. You know how she loved her mother."

"And didn't I?" Colin's voice cracked again. "You're right. Elizabeth would never want her to live with that burden."

"I don't know how long Catherine will be able to keep the newspapers from her. And there are always busybodies who may speak of it to her. Although I've passed the word as best I can through the mill owners to warn their wives of the delicacy of the situation."

"She'll have to find out sometime."

"I know. But these dark moods she has. She's been through so much. If only I knew how to help her, but she closes herself off. At least I can try to save her from more suffering as long as I can."

She ran through the hall to her bedroom, caught her breath. Better to have let Angus Clegg rape her rather than live with this knowledge. She envisioned what should have been, her mother downstairs, laughing and talking, probably knitting a sweater for Robbie. Married to Colin.

She must compose herself. If she could salvage anything from this horror, she must let them, in their compassion, believe she knew nothing.

She went to the basin, washed her face with cold water.

"Eleanor, are you up there? Colin's leaving."

Charles, calling from the bottom of the stairs.

She straightened her dress, went to the top of the stairs. "I think I had too much cake. I feel awful."

She descended, grateful for the bannister.

"You needn't have come down, darling. Colin would understand."

Charles put his arms out. She fell into them.

"Why, you're shaking," he said. "I hope you're not getting the flu. Or worse. So many workers have been out sick lately. It's back upstairs you go as soon as Colin leaves."

Colin said his farewells. They ascended the stairs, Charles supporting her. She turned at the top of the landing and surprised Catherine staring at her.

Catherine must have guessed she listened at the library door. She felt touched at her desire to shield her from knowledge of the cause of her mother's death.

But she couldn't think about Catherine now.

She ran through a dark tunnel. Footfalls pounded behind her, louder and louder. A wart-covered beast she didn't recognize followed her, tried to grasp her with its talons.

She finally came to the end of the tunnel, but it was a stone wall. She battered it until her hands bled. She tried to run away but her body was sinking in quicksand. The beast confronted her.

Her mother appeared in the distance. "Come to me. I'll save you."

The beast slashed her throat.

She screamed.

"Eleanor!"

She opened her eyes, saw the blurred face of Charles. He tightened his arms around her, rocked her body with his. "It's all right. Only a dream. You're safe and sound." He caressed her face, wiped the sweat from her face. "There, there. It's all right. It's over. There's nothing to be afraid of. You're safe at home. With me."

Her foggy mind began to clear as she looked around. "Another nightmare?"

"You're having too many of them lately. I wish I knew what's causing them. Is motherhood straining you too much? I thought Catherine would be sufficient as help, but you know we can get a nurse. You're not overly worried about Robbie, are you? He's as healthy as can be. You know that."

"I--don't know--what causes them. But I'm fine now. Really. I don't want to talk about it."

"Well, I do. I'm going to ask Mary for some sleeping powders for you. For a while. Until whatever's bothering you hopefully improves."

"But nothing's bothering me."

"I've been reading about dreams, a book by a doctor from Vienna, named Sigmund Freud. He says often our fears go back to frightening experiences in childhood and we relive them in dreams. Can you remember anything disturbing about your childhood? Or anything about your dream?"

She turned from him. "No. Nothing. I told you. I'm fine now." "My dear, I'm not so naive to think there's no reason for these nightmares. I just regret you won't share what's troubling you with me. You know I'd move heaven and earth to help you."

"I know, Charles, but I don't need help."

Charles remained true to his word. Mary prescribed powders which did help her sleep.

But her world had changed.

She wandered through the house in a daze, studying rooms she wished her mother could have seen, searching for refuge in her son's face, fingering his hands and toes. She sat in the chaise longue for hours, her only comfort Robbie, clinging to him, weaving his soft hair through her fingers, touching and petting him.

How her mother would have loved him.

When they dined, she imagined her sitting across the table, sharing delicacies she had never known during the years with her father. She stared at her Limoges, knowing she would admire its rose pattern. She visited the library, the world her mother introduced to her, remembering their years together visiting this refuge from her father, finding salvation in books. Almost everything she did reminded her of her mother. And herself as causing her death.

She watched Charles look more and more drained, felt pained by it. Yet she was completely unable to emerge from the depression clutching her.

One morning she noticed Charles at the window, watching Tom Branigan trudge across the yard to the greenhouses at the back of the property.

"I've decided to close the greenhouses, Eleanor," he said.

She thought at first she'd heard incorrectly. Charles's passion for plants was just as great as hers. One greenhouse was devoted entirely to growing rare species he cultivated.

"The greenhouses?"

"It's too much to ask Tom to maintain all the property, plus the greenhouses as well. With the management of the mill, I can't get out there as I used to. We'll need more help if we keep them, and I can't see the added cost. I'm not sure how commission weaving will work out, if it'll give us as substantial a profit as we think. So the greenhouses will go as my first step at conserving."

She sprang from the chaise. "Why, Charles, you can't do such a thing. How will we ever have plants for spring? And our wonderful vegetables. Everything would sit there, lifeless, empty. They--"

"I've made up my mind. It's not sensible to maintain them with the outstanding debts I'm holding."

"But surely they aren't that costly to maintain."

"You'd be surprised. The water alone--"

"Well, I'll help with the greenhouses. I can't let them go. I can't." Tears filled her eyes. "I've lost so much already."

Early the next morning she donned her galoshes, tacked her hair back with a snood, put on her muslin dress. She found Tom in one of the greenhouses. He smiled at her through a leathery face covered with wrinkles from hundreds of hours in sun.

"Well, if it isn't Mrs. Lafferty. I'm glad to see you out here. So much to do. Always is."

"I'll help you again, if I'm not in the way. Just tell me what to do. If you don't mind."

"Mind? I'd be pleased. You have the touch, you know. The daffodils you planted came up wonderful, didn't they? I never did have luck with that delicate variety."

She followed his instructions to the letter. Inside the greenhouse she scrubbed all the equipment, seed boxes, and pots, killing lurking insects and fungal spores with phenolic disinfectant. When she finished, she carried them outside, placing them in the sun to sanitize in its rays.

Her mind filled with the task of sowing pansy and viola seeds. Then she remembered that the suckers from her cinerarias must be removed, could not imagine her garden without them. And stock she helped Tom sow in the nursery areas outdoors before she took to her bed must be potted and brought indoors.

The day moved along quickly. Tomorrow she would work on the vegetables. The tomato seed must be sown, and the cauliflower and lettuce Charles loved so. Fumigating was also essential. Tom showed her how to scatter mist on the foliage with his bellows-like sulfurator. She became absorbed in her work.

The greenhouses must not be closed down.

At the end of the day her feeling of suffocation disappeared. Why did she feel so exhausted, yet exhilarated?

Charles watched her crossing the garden to the greenhouses, a study in transfiguration. It had worked. He knew the earth would save her, give him back the tiny speck of herself that belonged to him. He buttoned his jacket, ready for his trip to the mill, carrying with him a weight of sadness she never suspected, his constant companion when he thought of Eleanor and their marriage.

Temperatures fluctuated erratically through October. The odd changes affected Colin, who came down with the flu, and was slow to recover.

The workers constantly asked about the baby. Some kept sending little hand-made socks and hats, even months after his birth. Eleanor hoped to feel well enough to have a Christmas gathering to thank them for their generosity.

Then, after all her care not to expose him to germs keeping him within the confines of the house or garden, Robbie got sick.

She studied him, asleep in his crib, touched his flushed face, its heat penetrating her fingers. But he slept soundly. She felt glad Catherine would be home from the Alliance soon to give her opinion on whether she should call Mary. She advanced so much farther than Eleanor had in medical studies, had practically become Mary's assistant rather than nurse's aide.

She hoped the situation would not get to the point of calling Mary. She hated to frighten Charles. Last month they had nursed Robbie thru a cold, and Charles had been terrified. This time Robbie seemed worse. But Catherine would know what to do.

She heard Catherine click the front door open.

She went to the kitchen, packed chicken soup, pot roast, potatoes, string beans, readied herself to slip over to Colin's apartment and rush back to Robbie. She didn't relish leaving him for an instant, but with Catherine present she felt secure. She loved Colin dearly and owed it to her mother's memory to do all she could for him.

Catherine looked gaunt when she entered the kitchen. Eleanor had noticed she was losing weight and had tried to talk to her about it, but Catherine simple wanted to be left alone.

"Have something to eat, will you?" she said. "You look so tired. I've just packed some food for Colin. I'll just run over and be right back. I'm glad you're here. I want you to look at Robbie."

"How is he?"

"Asleep. His forehead's very hot and I don't like it. I think we should call Mary, yet I hate to see Charles get so upset. And you know so much more about these things. Will you look at him, see what you think? We'll decide when I get back."

"Of course."

When Eleanor closed the door behind her, Catherine nearly hurled the teapot at it. How could she possibly leave Robbie even for a short time to bring food to someone who, after all, was not family?

She trudged up the stairs, a skeleton of the girl she had been when she moved into the house, thinking of what she felt was Eleanor's mock compassion in suggesting that she eat something, the pretense that Eleanor cared for anyone but herself.

She approached the crib, looked at Robbie, his lace outfit pale in comparison to his beauty. For the thousandth time she examined his golden lashes, chubby cheeks, dimples creasing the side of his mouth as he slept. Once again she imagined him hers, Charles her husband. She could make him happier than Eleanor ever would. She saw the sadness on his face each time he tried to nurse Eleanor through her depressions.

She felt drained, clenched her thin fingers. Always on the sidelines, nursing the baby who should be hers. She knew she should feel sympathy for Eleanor. She certainly listened at the library door the night of Colin's birthday gathering, must have heard the truth about her mother's death. And Eleanor most likely saved her life when she aborted Clegg's child what seemed so long ago. Yet, exhilaration swept through her knowing Eleanor suffered. She hated the ugliness within her justifying her elation. Yet, she could not help it.

She studied Robbie long and hard, turning from her obsessive thoughts about Eleanor and Charles. He slept soundly.

Too soundly. When she and Eleanor nursed him thru a cold a few weeks back he cried ceaselessly. This constant sleeping sent a chill thru her. She watched his tiny chest rise and fall, his face flushed.

A suspicion grew in her she dared not give a voice.

She touched his lips with her fingers. He did not awaken. Her heart beat faster. She bent closer, unclamped them with her fingers, opened his mouth wide. There it was, a thick, gray membrane on the roof of his mouth, covering it to the back of his throat. Diphtheria. He must be brought to the hospital immediately.

The clock on the mantel chimed. Eleanor would be back any minute.

She paced back and forth, her mind like tangled wire, waiting.

PART III

The Return

Colin sat up on his cot, better physically but heartsick. His beloved Ireland was being lost before his eyes. He held a letter from Paddy O'Hara. The more he read, the more he wished he had been part of the Easter Uprising. He sickened at the thought Ireland would lose its heart and soul if it were up to the British. He read Paddy's letter once again:

Dear Colin,

It is with a heavy heart I write. I should have sooner, but my heart and soul was in mourning, and is still. They killed Tom Clarke, who did so much for the Rising. Tommy MacDonagh is dead. And we mourn Patrick Pearse, our beloved poet and Commandant-General. May he rest in the hands of the Lord. What you may not know from the papers in America is they killed Willie, for no other reason we can see but that he was Patrick's brother. God, I can see his youthful face standing there at St.Enda's School, laughing and having such a good time with me. And surely you remember Joey Plunkett.

He's gone. And Eddy Dale and Michael O'Hanrahan. And Eamonn Ceannt, Michael Mallin and Sean Heuston we used to play stick ball with. All gone to their reward now. I only mention the boys we knew. There were others. Their blood will forever glorify the name of Ireland.

I end my tragic list with having to tell you one of your dearest friends, James Connelly, is dead. He could not stand because of his terrible wounds and so the bastards executed him as he sat in a chair.

Amidst all the tragedy here, you may think me crazy but I still feel hope. There's still a group of us, strong and determined to continue this revolution. We are setting up an Irish Republican Brotherhood network, led by a man we respect and admire more and more each day, Michael Collins. I know you get tired of me saying it, but I wish you would follow your heart.

Come back to us.

The money you manage to send from America has been a great help. But it's you we need.

I know your heart may be torn because of the life you have there, but the cause of Ireland could be no less great than whatever holds you to Paterson.

Write me soon. And think on what I have written.

Yours in Irish brotherhood,
Paddy

The door creaked. Eleanor arriving with some food. He placed the letter under his pillow, would not share the latest sad news just yet. She had enough to face each day.

Eleanor removed her shawl, laid it on the kitchen chair, rosy- cheeked from the briskness of cool October air.

"I hope you don't go and catch a cold bringing me food," Colin said.

"Oh, don't worry yourself about that. I'm glad to see you sitting up finally." She turned to the kitchen counter. "I'll heat up the food I brought."

"I'd be most appreciative, my girl."

She found a pot easily enough in the mess of the kitchen area. Dust began to cover the table and stove. Plates she hadn't washed the last time still sat in the sink. She must come back and straighten up once she was sure Robbie was well. She opened the drawer of the small cabinet next to the sink, pushing about for another fork and spoon, easier than finding and cleaning ones already lying in the sink under piles of plates, pots, utensils.

She noticed a bundle of letters, many with post marks of Ireland. She rustled thru them, immediately recognizing others in Dante's pointed lettering. Many were post marked much more recently than the last one Colin shared with her and her mother.

She seized one at random, dated June 1, 1915. Colin must surely have written around this time about the wedding.

Dear Colin,

My heart is so heavy I can hardly hold my pen. Eleanor dead. You know how much I loved her, although I was never foolish enough to think my love for her and life with me could ever have made her truly happy. I see her face and form before me constantly, this starving girl who meant more to me than I can ever say. To think we must go on without her pains me beyond belief. She showed such courage and strength during the strike. If only I had told her how much she meant to me. Why did I not speak? I keep thinking of the lines from Wordsworth:

"What though the radiance which was once so bright/ Be now forever taken from my sight;/ Though nothing can bring back the hour/ Of splendour in the grass, of glory in the flower/ We will grieve not, rather find/ Strength in what remains behind."

Forgive me. I can't continue.

Dante

Tears welled in her eyes, spilled down her cheeks.

He loved her.

But why did he think she died? Had Colin said such a thing? She re-examined the date on the letter. It came to her. He must have written telling Dante she planned to honeymoon on the *Lusitania*. He assumed she had taken the voyage. She didn't know whether to laugh or cry. Did he have to think her dead, sunken to the lower depths of the ocean, asleep in the briny deep, before he would declare his love?

Colin surely must have written later, saying she was quite alive.

She stuffed the letter into its envelope, searched for the one with the most recent date, found it. October 1, 1916. A few weeks ago.

Dear Colin,

The months drag on. Standard Oil Refinery does not move but the parrafin workers may be entering the strike soon. They are presently making $2.20 a day as unskilled workers.

Skilled earn $3.20 and they did not receive a raise in the 1915 strike here. We're hoping about 600 workers from Vacuum Oil will join us in sympathy. The fifteen members of our committee are still involved with attempting to voice our demands. A fair pay increase, an 8 hour work day for everyone, an unbiased system for firing, and 20 minutes lunch. Does that sound unfair to you? Does it sound familiar?

The superintendent at Standard, George Hennessey, at this point, has rejected our demands. We will continue to negotiate, but things do not look good at all.

Please continue to send me clippings on the strike here from *The Call*. I'm always interested in how they report on the IWW, always misunderstood.

I can imagine the pain you feel hearing the latest from Ireland, the executions I read about in the papers. But remember, you are doing important work in Paterson. You must continue to remind Eleanor of that as well.

Wherever we are, if we fight for justice it is our reason to live. We have found something greater than ourselves that gives our life meaning.

Sincerely,

Dante

P.S. Tell me about Eleanor and her son. Are they well? Is she happy?

She read the first paragraph again to be sure she understood correctly. Standard Oil. The strike in Bayonne. Dante was only about an hour from Paterson by train. She tried to recollect what she read in *The Call* about the strike, didn't remember a settlement being mentioned as of a day or so ago. He must still be in Bayonne.

Why hadn't he come to her?

She folded the letter, placed it in the drawer.

She turned. Colin stood before her, his face colorless.

She lunged at him. "I hate you! He never stopped loving me. He didn't. And you--"

He grasped her wrists. "You should not of read those letters. You're a married woman now. Married to a good man. And you have a child."

"But he loves me. Don't you know what it was like to think he didn't? That no one did? That no one ever could because--"

"Darlin', how can you--" His voice cracked. "You're surrounded by people who love you, always have been."

She slumped onto the kitchen chair. "Who? Who loved me?"

"Your mother--"

"Mother's dead. Because of me."

He blanched. "Oh, Eleanor, we tried---"

"I know."

"Charles. You know he loves you dearly."

"He doesn't know me. He wouldn't love me if he knew--" Something was breaking open in her.

"Eleanor, how can you say such--I know you. And I love you."

"Like you loved my mother? How much good did your love do for her?"

"I don't understand--"

"You're a coward, that's what you are. You should have claimed her for yourself years before my father died. But you let him keep hurting her."

"Hurt her?"

She smashed the tears from her face. "Oh, don't tell me you don't know. You think she limped because she fell? It was because he threw her against the wall one night. When he was filthy drunk. And you left us to him. Is this the love--"

"Are you sayin'--I didn't know, truly I didn't. If I had--"

His face froze. Not with anger or grief but with something cold and hard.

"Eleanor," he said quietly, "what did he do to *you*."

Fear blossomed within her again, huge and dark.

He gripped her shoulders. "Tell me, girl. What did he do?"

"No--I can't!"

But it was too late. She was there again with him coming to her cot and her unable to understand what he wanted. And he said if she cried out, he would beat her mother.

"If I had known--," he said softly, "I'd of killed him myself."

"Is Dante in Bayonne? Is he?"

"Yes."

"I'm going to him."

"You'll make the mistake of your life if you do."

"I'll make the mistake of my life if I don't." She grabbed her shawl from the chair, faced him.

"I will never forgive you for not telling me. You will not come to my home again. Never. When I see you in the street, I will walk past you."

He moved towards her.

"You are dead to me," she said.

She slammed the door in his face.

Colin stared at emptiness. He went to the cabinet, hands shaking, took out a bottle of wine, gulped down a large drink. Eleanor. He never dreamed--. Surely Elizabeth could not have known, yet, knowing her, she might have rather lived with the shame than reveal it. She had told him she and Michael had less and less of a physical closeness. Did she think that might have caused him to turn to Eleanor? Or had she convinced herself it never happened?

And how had he been so blind?

He drank more wine. Why hadn't Elizabeth told him? Was it fear if she did he would kill Michael? He surely might have.

Eleanor.

Lost to him.

He finished the wine, took out Paddy's letter. "The cause of Ireland could be no less great than whatever holds you in Paterson."

What held him now?

He stumbled to his cot, pulled out the suitcase he brought with him from Ireland to America, rubbed its worn surface, remembering. He packed some clothes and a few cherished mementoes, snapped it shut, placed it on the cot.

He could take the train to New York, find out when the next boat left for Ireland. He longed to return to his friends, fight with all his strength for Irish freedom. Yet, did he dare have a glimmer of hope Eleanor might reconsider, forgive him?

He sat a long time, then finally made his choice.

Eleanor hardly noticed where she walked. The air had chilled.

Wind blasted as she ran. She pulled her shawl tightly around her.

Dante.

She relived the contents of the letter over and over. He loved her. He was near.

A trolley trudged along Market Street. In her distraction she did not notice its approach, almost stepped in its path. She jumped back just before it swept past her, stood a few seconds after it passed, struggling to catch her breath. Then once again she ran.

She would see him, face him. Once and for all. If he saw she would leave the world she knew for him, he would finally believe in her love.

She approached the house on Silk Road, breathless but undaunted, ran up the stairs to her room, pulled her small suitcase from the closet, began packing a few changes of clothes, some personal needs.

"Are you all right?"

She turned. Catherine stood in the doorway.

"I'm leaving. I'm leaving Charles. Dante Ravelli. He's in Bayonne. He could leave any day. I have to get to him before he goes. It's my last chance. I love him. I'll always love him. And I know now he loves me."

"But what about Charles and--"

"You wouldn't understand. You could never understand what it is to love someone so much you'd risk everything to have him. Everything." Catherine slowly stepped back towards the doorway, clutched its frame. "I don't know how it will work out. All I know is I have to go to him. Find out. In time Charles will let me see Robbie. He--"

Her words faded in mid-air. Had she lost her mind completely? Robbie was ill.

"Robbie. I'm not thinking." She placed the suitcase on the bed. "How is he?"

"He's--better. Much better. The fever. It's broken. He was smiling. I think it's just the sniffles. It doesn't seem anything much. After all. Such good news."

"Better?"

"Yes."

The sniffles. He'd just survived them last month, back to normal in no time. With Catherine there, he would easily recover.

She paced the floor, trying to decide what to do. But she knew the answer. She had known it as soon as Catherine spoke.

"I'll leave then," she said, "if he's all right. You'll take care of him, won't you? I know you will. And when I'm settled, I'll be in touch with you. Charles is too kind not to let me visit him." She threw her arms around Catherine. "I know you can't really understand. What it means to love someone you'd give up everything for him. You must promise you'll take care of Robbie."

"Of course."

She grabbed her suitcase and jacket. She paused in the hallway, outside Robbie's room. Her child. How could she leave without holding him in her arms one last time?

Catherine followed her. "If you go in that room, you know you won't leave."

It was true. She would stay. And lose Dante forever.

She did not enter.

She kissed Catherine goodbye, held her hard. Catherine was trembling. She ran the stairs, disappearing into the Paterson evening.

* * *

Catherine went into the kitchen, made some tea and removed the vial of laudanum she kept in her pocket. It was almost empty. She went to her room to the drawer where she kept her nightgown and undergarments, felt beneath them for the new full bottle she had taken from the Alliance. She filled the vial, careful to put the stopper on tightly, hid the precious bottle at the back of the drawer.

Her tea waited in the kitchen. She placed a few drops of the blessed opiate in the cup, the exact amount to bring euphoria. She savored the tea, the laudanum permeating her as she waited for Charles. It was the second Thursday of the month, the night of his monthly gathering with friends at the Bellevue Hotel. It would be hours before he returned. She would bide her time. The house did not feel empty with Eleanor gone but full.

Full of her own presence now.

A few minutes after the clock at City Hall chimed midnight, Catherine heard Charles turning the latch of the door. She straightened her dress, her hair, ran down the stairs.

"Charles! Thank God you're here. Robbie seemed fine, but now he's relapsed. I checked his throat just a minute ago. I'm afraid it may be diphtheria. We've got to get him to the hospital. Right away."

His face drained of color. He attempted a semblance of composure.

241

"Bundle him up. Immediately. I'll call the carriage back." He stopped at the door. "Eleanor. Where's Eleanor?"

"I'll explain everything in the carriage. We can't lose time." She touched his arm gently. "Remember, I'm here to help you, Charles."

Catherine bundled up the baby, relishing the shock that would overtake him as she told him Eleanor left him for Dante Ravelli.

He listened, stunned, confused, as she explained the events of the evening while he held Robbie to his heart.

* * *

When Eleanor entered the Bellevue Hotel she breathed a deep sigh of relief. One lone gentleman sat by the fire immersed in The Call.

The desk clerk shot a momentary glance of surprise when she asked for a single room. He must remember her from having come in often with Charles for dinner. They had to pass the reservations desk to reach the dining room. Perhaps he thought a disagreement had arisen between her and Charles, and she left him.

She caught herself, checking her paranoia. Surely women stayed overnight at the hotel for other reasons, times when they must make trips alone.

"I need information on travel to Bayonne, please."

She tried to sound casual.

He eyed her behind his steel-rimmed glasses bouncing light from the lighted ceiling fixture. "I'd be happy to give you that information, madame. You need to take the Erie to Jersey City. From there hitch up with a trolley. That'll take you right in."

She spent a restless night, rose early, and caught the Erie. Luck smiled on her. She had only a ten-minute wait to catch the trolley to Bayonne.

She had not been to Constable Hook in Bayonne, which had been one of the most fashionable and popular resorts on the east coast, since childhood, when she visited with her mother to see her friend who eventually died of cancer. She remembered the city with its clear waters and ragged coast line, readily accessible to shipping. Her mother said it was called the "Newport of the East," although at the time she had no idea what that meant. Through the years she read articles about its beauty in women's magazines and newspapers in the library. Now stories of strikes prevailed. The great industry leaders were beginning to leave their impression on Bayonne, slowly transforming it into a city of smokestacks, refineries and polluted air.

She sat on the trolley approaching Constable Hook, observing how Standard Oil's refinery demolished the natural landscape, saw for herself what The Call said was the longest pipeline in the world, stretching from Oklahoma to Texas.

She alighted, walked towards the area of the Hook. Before her lay the first view immigrants entering New York harbor beheld. Over two thousand inflammable acres of stills, cracking units and storage areas at Bayonne and nearby Bayway, all owned by Standard Oil.

She walked down a street that looked somewhat familiar to look for the church she visited with her mother now and then when she was a child, near the neighborhood where her mother's friend lived. The area had been razed. In its place were gigantic tanks. Manufacturing and refining plants stood in silence.

She heard no sound of water lapping near the shore, no birds squawking, hovering over the harbor. The stillness told her the strike remained unsettled. Dante must still be here. Soon his face and form would appear and entwine her in the comfort of his arms.

She knew the dangers in entering Bayonne. She had followed the previous violent strike of 1915 carefully, always drawn to the plight of workers. City officials feared taking action against Standard Oil. Accounts she read said guards shot to kill, not wound. In response the workers on strike rioted. Some of the strikers and an innocent bystander, as well as a police lieutenant, died. She remembered it so vividly because Charles had important business in Bayonne at the time. He had to take the Central Railroad and told her he and other passengers were ordered to lie down in the cars when the trains passed 22nd Street, to avoid strikers throwing dangerous stone barrages.

She watched the trolley disappear into the distance.

Less than a block away crowds of strikers milled about, held in control by what must be special police marching on duty near the Hook. She turned in the opposite direction, towards the end of East 22nd Street. The downtown area was a shambles. Garbage was strewn over the sidewalks, mixing with goods previously behind broken store windows. She stepped into a small storefront, the last on the block. A scarred counter with stools bolted to the floor in front of it faced her. The glass mirror behind it still possessed a few shards stuck in place, and a torn Coca Cola sign hung on the wall opposite. This must have been a sweet shoppe or luncheonette.

A heavy-set man, stomach resting on his belt, emerged from the back room. He eyed the ruffles on her silk blouse, the workmanship of the suit she wore, the rich leather of her shoes. He frowned.

She slid onto a stool at the counter, brushed back tendrils of hair dangling in her face. "What's happening out there? Can you fill me in? Please. I've come from Paterson and there's someone I have to find. Involved with the strike."

"I got no use for owners. And I got no use for anybody part of owners. You get me?"

She glanced at her clothing, back to him. "Oh, but I'm not on their side. I'm on the workers' side. Please. Believe me.I'm looking for one of the leaders of the IWW. Dante Ravelli. Do you know him?"

"I know of him. But he does not find time to see you. He is with workers. I am sure of this. Two dollars and twenty cents a day I made. A crime when you think of money Standard Oil makes. That is why I take a chance, start my store. It is very hard. And look what they do."

She gestured toward the wreckage of his store.

"Please, don't give up. I was in the Paterson silk strike. I thought it would never end, but it did." He studied her clothing again, then shrugged. "You want coffee?"

"Yes, please." She nodded towards the door. "I saw what looked like hundreds of strikers, down at the end of 22nd Street."

"It started with only fifty, you know. But now six hundred more is gone out in sympathy. From Vacuum Oil. Plus now close to two thousand, they walk out at Standard. That is what you see out there."

She paid for her coffee, then turned to the door, ready to face whatever lay ahead in the crowd.

"I would not go out there. It is very bad. The police. All over."

From the doorway, she saw dozens of police, arms linked, forming a line down East 22nd, trying to separate the strikers from the armed guards within Standard and Tidewater Oil. A group of strikers rushed the police line. Shots rang out. Three patrolmen fell to the ground. Minutes later the police retaliated with clubs. Scores of strikers fell to the ground. How could she ever find Dante in this turmoil?

She felt the hand of the shop owner on her shoulder.

"Come with me. You see here what they did last riot. They could come down this street again." He led her to the back of the store. "My name is Paul. Elsa, come here. It is all right."

A blue-eyed woman, blonde braids crowning her head, appeared.

"Hello. I'm Eleanor."

They shook hands.

"This lady needs help," Paul said. "Can we let her stay here tonight? She wants to find Dante Ravelli."

"Of course. Of course."

She led Eleanor to the back of the store, motioned to a cot. "That was where my son slept. But he is married now. You can sleep there, if you don't mind a cot."

She remembered the cot she had lain on most of her life.

"No. I don't mind a cot. I'd be grateful if you let me stay here tonight. Do you know Dante Ravelli? In the IWW?"

"I heard him speak. My sisters and brothers, they are still in the refinery. He gives them such hope. I know he is on the committee for the strikers, so you will never find him. He must be with it all hours I am sure. It is very bad." She touched Eleanor's arm gently. "You should go home."

She had left her husband and child for him. How could she just go home? "I can't. Not now. I've come too far."

"You look so tired. Try to rest a little. See what morning brings."

That night she lay on the cot, listening to the mob shouting in the streets and the shop owners tossing and turning on the other side of the partition. They must have been terrified their store would be vandalized again, even set on fire. Their lives, now hers, lay in danger.

In the morning she quietly left the store before the owners awoke, not wanting to disturb their sleep, knowing they would only encourage her again to go home. She walked to the end of 22nd Street, stopped a freckle-faced boy running from the crowd.

"What's happening?"

"Don't go down there. You'll get hurt," he said. "There's thousands, all out of control." He kept running.

She heard a commotion behind her and turned. Hundreds of angry workers marched down the street, shouting for the release of those arrested the night before. They stopped when they reached the police station. She mixed in with the strikers. That would be where she would get word of Dante.

The chief of police stood at the top step of the station facing the mob, his gun pointed in the air. Then a tall man with stooped shoulders who must have been one of the union leaders climbed the step next to the chief. His arms flapping, he shouted to the crowd. "Go home! Go home! This won't be settled by blood in the streets. We're negotiating. Have patience and go home!"

She looked around, trying to pick out other IWW leaders. Dante was not there.

She stood amidst a crowd permeated by the savage emotions of the workers' fury. She was trapped in the chaos. And she felt a fool. What could her love mean to Dante amidst this turmoil, his life's blood the justice he fought for with his every breath?

She pushed through the crowd, walked away, her thoughts splintered. She had given up her husband and son for this one chance at true love in her life. But Dante was willing to lay down his life for the sake of justice.

Could she make a sacrifice? Live without love if she found him and he rejected her, endure the hard core of loneliness at her center for the rest of her life? Could she make that sacrifice and survive?

She decided to return to the sweet shoppe. Perhaps the owners would let her stay another night so she might collect her thoughts, sort her way through her confusion.

The store owners did kindly take her in again. That evening, amidst their protestations, she decided she must return to the crowd. She knew the danger but was obsessed to see Dante.

Minutes after she arrived, the emotions building all day exploded with a force and power that enveloped 22nd Street. Hundreds of strikers carried firebrands, light from the flames glowing upon faces racked with anger. Someone threw one onto the platform of the Lehigh Valley Station. Others followed. The blaze ripped across the wooden floor.

Fire trucks screeched into the crowd, but the strikers attacked them, cut their hoses. One fireman's face gushed blood after a striker smashed it with a stone.

Another group of strikers set fire to a saloon on East 22nd Street. Flames inundated the block. She heard a child crying, looked up, saw a baby held by a man standing next to a woman in the window of a second floor apartment. Tongues of flame licked its facade on the first floor. The frightened couple and their child disappeared from the window. A few minutes later she saw them standing on the roof.

Somehow word got to the firefighters at the railway station. Ten or so arrived on the scene, began trying to set up a ladder.

Then Eleanor spotted a young woman watching the fires from her second floor apartment at the corner building on East 22nd. She must have seen the strikers moving east from the station and leaned out the window to warn the firemen on Avenue F of their approach.

A shot pierced the air. The girl's body plunged onto East 22nd. Panic stricken, fearful of reprisal, strikers ran in all directions. Eleanor froze. In a moment she was back in the silk strike watching the Italian immigrant, Modestino, shot and wounded.

This time she did not run.

She darted across the smoke-filled street, knelt beside the bleeding woman, who was clutching her chest. She held her hand. Her fingers reddened with blood.

"Don't be afraid. Help is coming. You'll be all right."

It was not true, of course. Eleanor could see nothing could be done. She squeezed her hand harder, looked into the woman's eyes. They began to glaze over, stare at nothingness.

A man ran towards her, knelt down, held her in his arms. Her blood soaked his shirt.

"Eva! My dear--"

He held her harder, his face filled with shock, confusion.

She felt the warmth of a hand touching the back of her shoulder. "Her husband is here. Please. Let me help you."

Dante. The voice she would know from all others. Always. She could not move.

"Please. Madame. You have been so kind. The ambulance is arriving. You must come away from here. You are in danger."

His voice was like light enveloping her. She must try to stand, look upon his face, etched in her memory every day for so long. But still her mind would not permit her body to move.

"Let me help you."

He grasped her arms from behind and tried to lift her from the ground. She gathered every ounce of strength she could muster and rose with him.

He turned her around, stood before her. She realized he did not recognize her. She despised her foolish upswept hair, her silk blouse, expensive jacket, fine leather shoes. He would hate what she stood for now. She bowed her head.

"You were so kind to help this poor woman," he said. "But you can do no more."

She finally lifted her head, struck by how he'd aged. Small lines had deepened around the corners of his eyes, dark circles rested below them, gray had begun to creep through his black hair, his face a study in exhaustion.

And then it lit with recognition.

"Eleanor? My God!"

She embraced him, held him hard. She continued to hold him, the ambulance blaring around them, the strikers watching from their hiding places, the fire flaring in the buildings in the near distance.

At first it seemed she held a stone, then his shock passed and he held her close.

"I had to see you. I love you. Still. Always. I had to come to you. You'll be gone soon, I know it, and I--"

"Do you realize the danger you have put yourself in? You have been through a strike. This one is even more violent than Paterson."

"I don't care, I had to come, I--"

"You must calm down." She heard strain in his voice. "We must not be the center of attention of these crowds. Come with me."

They made their way through back streets he seemed to know well, avoiding East 22nd where strikers once again converged along with special police still trying to quell them. The air chilled. She began to shiver.

He removed his jacket, placed it around her. It was the same one he owned in Paterson, even more frayed at its neck and cuffs. She held it close, as though spun from gold. She stared at him often as they walked, his face drawn, yet still emanating strength. The touch of his hand on her arm suffused her with hope.

The streetlamps lighted as they walked, bathing the tenements they passed in an artificial glow and softness they did not truly possess.

He led her down an alley to a building of wooden planks, its windows so filthy she could not see inside. They entered a door with a broken lock, stood in the hallway. Peeling paint surrounded her on both sides. Plaster missing from some of the walls left holes here and there. They ascended squeaky steps to the third floor, then passed two doors, one closed, the other occupied with what must be wives of strikers with their infants. She paused momentarily, glancing at the blankets strewn upon the floor. One woman nursed a child. Another ate what looked like gruel from a saucer.

She smelled cigarette smoke and cabbage.

Dante stopped at the third door, pushed his key into a shiny, newly-installed lock. The door squeaked open.

"This is it. Where I'm staying."

A woman around Dante's age sat at a table, her skin like pink porcelain, her heavy black hair pinned back in a chignon, her eyes focused on piles of paper before her. She wore a plain muslin dress, clean and ironed, patched here and there, scattered with faded blue flowers that matched her eyes.

Eleanor's heart sank. How foolish to have imagined him alone, with no time to fall in love with such a beautiful woman dedicated to his cause.

"Eleanor, I'd like you to meet Sophie Krebinski. She is very important to us and our work here."

The woman blushed, smiled at her.

"She takes my words in English and translates them into Polish so the strikers can understand them. And all of the strikers' demands in Polish she translates for me into English." He smiled, touched her shoulder, "Without her I don't know what I would do."

The woman immediately returned to the translations so crucial to him and the strike's success.

"Sophie's husband is one of the most important men on the Strikers' Committee. People listen to him. He is my right hand man. They both have my greatest respect."

Eleanor sighed with relief realizing theirs was a working relationship.

Dante scrutinized the papers lying on the table. "How are the flyers coming?"

"I'm finished. Yes. I have a copy. Here."

She handed a paper to him. He read it slowly.

"I take it to Paul, and we will print. Right away, I know. With government men coming tomorrow."

He nodded, smiled, handed her the paper back. She held his gaze a moment.

"Good luck, Dante. Tomorrow. I will not see you until after. You are our hope."

She closed the door quietly as she left.

She faced him. He encircled his arms around her. She responded, her love unrequited so long. He held her hands, kissed them. She felt consecrated by his love.

"I love you more than life, Dante."

He sighed, moved her away gently.

"You should not have come here. The danger. And your husband and child. They need you."

"I've made my decision." Her voice sounded shaken. "I want to be with you."

He began to pace, stopped at the window, looked out on the street.

She approached him, refused to embrace him. He must be the one to act.

"I will not take advantage of your love."

She thought to tell him she read his letters but decided not to. Instead, she studied his profile, his body a portrait of restraint.

"And now your foolish principles will keep you from me?" she said at last. "I've thrown away mine coming to you, but I have no regrets. Do you think it's wrong that I love you? Do you think I can help it, can stop whenever I want? I wish I could."

She turned from him, folded her arms across her chest. "Before, yes, I was an inexperienced girl who wore her heart on her sleeve. I'm not that young girl anymore. And I love you even more than I did when we were together in Paterson."

She began to pace the floor.

"You won't admit you love me, will you? You'll hold onto your principles at all costs, damn you!" Try as she might she could not hold back the tears ebbing in her eyes. "I'm throwing my heart at your feet. If you don't want it, then I'll leave. But I won't regret it. Not one second. Because I have more courage than you, after all. The courage to love, no matter what happens."

She walked to the door, a journey of a thousand miles.

"You will regret it, if you stay."

Her fingers touched the knob.

"Stay," he said softly.

He walked toward her, removed her hand from the knob. Warmth from his touch shot through her.

He led her to the cot, slowly undressed her, and she him.

For Eleanor every part of his body felt sacred during their lovemaking. Her fingers explored his face, chest, arms. His hands, which she had seen so often lifted in strength, empowering thousands, now responded only to her. He had waited so long to make her his. He explored her body, touched her where the heart of her womanhood lay. He kissed her there, his lips exploring the secret places she never realized a man could know so well. There was none of her father's brutishness or Charles's timidity. She savored every second of his lovemaking.

"Eleanor."

She sensed urgency in his voice, the rasping sound of desire. His flesh bonded to hers. She gave herself to him, all fear dissipated, and they consecrated their love. They became each other.

Afterwards, she slept in his arms, her passion spent. If rioting, shouts in the street, blaring of sirens and fire engines resounded, she remained oblivious, protected in his arms.

The despair lying in wait for her all her life had finally been swept away.

The brightness of morning awakened her.

She gently moved away from him, glad he slept soundly. She could guess how little he usually slept. She wondered whether he liked to rise early or late in the morning, what he enjoyed for breakfast. These mundane questions became paramount. She must learn his likes and dislikes as they shared life together.

She quietly rose from the bed, dressed, filled a sauce pan with water to make tea. She found bread in a drawer, munched a piece. She knew she should wake him. She remembered Sophie saying the government man arrived today and that must surely mean federal mediators. But she didn't have the heart to just yet. She wanted to give him just a few more minutes of peace, free from concern about the pain of the world, sheltered from being its conscience.

She studied his face, at rest, and smiled.

She had lived without any hope of being with him for so long she had never considered what their life together would be like. It would certainly be different from the one she knew with Charles. But now that they were together and he finally acknowledged his love, she would convince him to pursue a more stable life. She knew he must always be involved with the workers. She would help him. She never cringed at hard work. But she would have to be near enough to be able to see Robbie. That would be a certainty. And if he wanted children that would be wonderful.

She forced herself to stop thinking of the future, focused on looking for more food. If she could find eggs, she would make him French toast as a surprise.

He stirred, sat up quickly.

"What time is it? Do you know?"

"I heard a church bell ring eight a while back."

"Is it eight o'clock then?" He rubbed his eyes and began to throw on clothes. "I must get to Nydash Hall. We have so much to go over before the mediators arrive."

She sat down beside him. "I'm making some tea. And there's bread. If you have eggs--"

He rose, tucked his shirt into his pants. "I'm afraid I don't have time."

"Can't you stay with me just a little longer? Don't leave yet. Please. We have to talk. There's so much to--"

He sat down, held her hand, kissed it.

"How thoughtless of me, to act this way. After last night."

He embraced her. But she sensed his mind was far away. He gently broke his hold on her.

"We have been working toward this day for weeks. You understand. With the mediators coming. I need to get to the hall. I'm scheduled to speak to the strikers, within the hour."

"But we'll talk when you get back, won't we? About after? What we'll do and where we'll go after the strike." She spoke somewhat hesitatingly. "You won't want to get involved in another labor dispute right away, will you? It takes so much out of you. Can you take some time off? Maybe we could go away, the two of us. Just for a while, and then--"

His face stiffened. He stared at his hands, averting her eyes. She waited for him to speak. He did not.

Finally, she forced herself to continue. "Why, if you don't want to do that, of course, I'll go with you. To your next assignment. I'm not afraid. I've been through enough in Paterson for you to know that."

Still he did not speak.

She waited.

Finally he looked up. His eyes met hers. "I know where I am going after the strike here is ended. And it is not a place for you."

"Not a place for me?"

"I'm leaving the United States. For good."

"You're--what? Leaving the--?"

"I am going to Russia. A great revolution is near. The Czar is no longer effective. The people cry in the streets for bread. It will not be long before they rise up and take what belongs to them. It is the only way. I am certain Russia's greatness will finally come to flower now. Soon. And I must be there."

He rose from the cot, his face animated. "I have met Trotsky. He was here, in the Bronx, in May. Can you imagine this? I am overwhelmed by his greatness. Yes, a movement is building force. Karensky will emerge as its great leader and I want to be part of it. To finally be with the people in that glorious day when they claim what has been due them for so long." He raised his hand, pointed his finger at her. "Russia is where victory will be. Never in this country. This country stinks with capitalists who will never be overcome. The masses are too weak."

"But in Paterson you didn't feel as--I don't remember you feeling this strongly."

"I had not seen what would happen with the strike in the beginning. After, I realized how little was accomplished. And then I saw--Ludlow. The senseless deaths." His face filled with sadness. "The massacre. Women. And children."

He thrust his hands into his pockets, began pacing back and forth again. He wound up at the window, looked down at the workers whose low voices she began to hear below.

"And here. Do you know what suffering these men go through? Men in the refining department working staggered hours, day and night shifts, for an average of eighty-four hours a week. Eighty-four! And the high death rate of the lead burners in the sealing department? They get lead colic, that's what they call it." He slashed his fingers through his hair. "And the still cleaners. I saw them. Wearing iron shoes, wrapped in layers and layers of sacking, entering the stills in turns. To break out the red hot coke left by the oil. My God! The temperature in those stills. Over two hundred degrees. They can only stand it three, four minutes at a time. And the bosses make them work furiously!"

He pulled her to him, his fingers pressing hard into her flesh.

"I can do--nothing."

"Dante. Please--let these things go. Let them go. You're doing all you can."

"Is that your solution? Stop thinking of them? So easy. Erase them from my mind. Like that." He snapped his fingers in mid-air. "Is that what you have done?"

"How could you ever think that? I'll never forget what the strike did to me. But I can't dwell on the past. I can't!" Her face became rigid. She pushed herself from him, sat on the cot.

He stood above her.

"The day I was at the factory a man collapsed in the still. They rescued him. His clothes, they were all on fire. Do you know what the average life of a still cleaner is? Ten years. You take a twenty-year-old Polish or Lithuanian immigrant. Comes to the great promised land. Big, strong, healthy. At thirty he will be a bent old man. Or he will be dead. And you ask me not to think about these things?" He clenched his hands. "I think about them day and night. I hardly sleep thinking about them. I-"

She lunged at him. "Stop it! I don't want to hear about suffering. I'm sick of suffering!"

He pushed her back onto the cot, sat beside her, forced her to look at him."You fool yourself trying to forget. You won't. It will never die."

"I won't listen. I won't!"

But his anger compelled her to listen.

"Oh, you have a different life now. Safe and free. All you desire. Do you know what I have? Memories. Burned bodies of women and children who died in the iron strike in Colorado. The young skeleton of you near starvation. Men working in those blazing stills. I am haunted by them. Haunted!"

He covered his face with his hands. She instinctively reached for him, held him in her arms. She felt the explosions of his heart against her chest. She held him tighter. He remained spent, did not move. Finally his breathing became more controlled. He looked at her, his face ashen.

"What have I done? What have I said? I frighten you. I don't mean to frighten you."

"It's all right. It's all right."

She placed her steady hands into his trembling ones. If only she could take his pain, endure it for him.

"Forgive me." His voice became stronger as he attempted control. "Forgive me."

"I'll go with you. To Russia. It will be all right."

He tried to smile. "You would never be happy. After the life you've known? You think because you would be with me it would make everything right. But can you really imagine yourself in the cold rooms you would live in, the small amount of food? And me. Gone most of the time." He shook his head. "I will not offer you such a life."

"If we were together, I would be happy."

"So easy to say, to believe. But love is not all. You do not understand that yet. And there is your son. Never to see him again?"

She had lost so much of Robbie in going to him. But to be in Russia. Never to visit him, hold him in her arms, touch his flesh.

"And there is Charles."

"Charles? Why would I ever regret leaving him?"

"Because he loves you. To be loved by another involves great responsibility, you know. It is not to be taken lightly. I think always one loves more than the other. And perhaps one love can make two."

"What do you mean?"

He closed his eyes. "I am tired. So tired. And I have such a long day ahead."

"Tell them you're sick. You don't have to go."

"You know I can't do that. We have worked toward this day for weeks, I must go. When I return, we will talk more. I promise."

He walked toward the door, hesitated, looked back. She brightened. Perhaps he would stay.

But he just stood, absorbing every aspect of her.

"What are you thinking?" she said. "I never know what you're thinking."

"I was remembering something I read somewhere. That man is forced to choose the perfection of the life, or the work."

"I don't understand."

He smiled at her. The same smile she remembered from the night they met, when they sat in freezing rain on the bench by the Falls.

He unbolted the lock, and left.

The room felt hollow. She dragged herself to the window. Hundreds of workers rushed towards him when he appeared. He embraced them, blended with them, marched down the block to Nydash Hall. He soon disappeared in the crowd.

She grasped the window frame, relived his words, hacked to the bone by the sudden realization her love for him was ignited by delusion. She would never be first in his life. His passion for her would never transcend the one he felt as the conscience of the workers.

A vision flashed before her of the bleak existence she would lead in Russia. She loved him with emotions so powerful she nearly obliterated herself. But not enough to leave her child, her life in Paterson, become part of a revolution in a country so alien to her.

She stood at the window a long time, the street and room quiet as dust.

Finally, she gathered herself together, walked to the station to catch the trolley connecting her to Jersey City, then board the Erie to take her home to her son. And Charles.

The area was quieter than she expected as she waited for the trolley. Most of the workers must be at Nydash Hall, though a few waited for the streetcar.

"Missus! Missus!"

She turned to see a woman waving in the distance, though she could not imagine anyone in Bayonne who knew her. As the woman approached, Eleanor saw it was Elsa, the wife of the shopkeeper who took her in. She was breathless and carried a loaf of bread.

"I got one of the last." She pointed down the street to a shop in a soot-streaked, brick building. "It's the only place I know now to get it."

Eleanor had been too paralyzed to realize until she looked more carefully that people stood in a line filing around the block.

"Did you find him?" the woman said.

"What?"

"Dante Ravelli. The man you looked for."

She met the woman's questioning look.

"No. I--never did."

The trolley approached from the distance.

"Well, goodbye, missus."

Eleanor half heard her, shaken as she boarded. Then she straightened, lifted her head high. She found a seat as the trolley began clacking along.

She saw one last, fleeting image of Dante standing on a platform surrounded by strikers in front of Nydash Hall as the trolley rattled past him. His arms were raised high, his hands still reaching toward heaven.

To her surprise, she realized that the shock was fading, replaced by a sense of peace. He was where he belonged. She fixed her gaze on him, craned her head as the trolley began to disappear, absorbing every aspect of him one last time.

She finally looked straight ahead, facing Paterson.

And home.

She had only a half-hour wait after debarking from the trolley at Jersey City to catch the train to bring her to Erie Station in Paterson, the roar of the locomotive reminding her of the booming of the giant looms in the silk mills as it chugged on and on. She studied her reflection, blurred in the glass.

She felt exhausted, spent from the emotions that exploded these past two days. But she finally understood. A life with Dante in Russia was impossible. And though she would never know the same passion with Charles, she could still have a life with meaning as his wife.

And she would have Robbie.

And it came to her now that she understood what Dante meant about love and responsibility. Charles's love was a dependable love. She would make amends to him, ask his forgiveness. She surprised herself at the profound longing she felt for his kindness and understanding, qualities she had so foolishly taken for granted.

Until now.

The train pulled into Erie Station on Market Street. Ash from the smokestack filled her nostrils as she descended and she rubbed soot from her eyes with her handkerchief. The last signs of autumn enhanced the street. Leaves still refused to give up their color completely. The streets of Paterson, the familiar homes on her block, the hemlocks that weathered the years, the oaks that endured the century, comforted her by their permanence. She felt the October chill and welcomed it. Catherine, always cold, would surely have a fire in the hearths in the library and living room.

She sighed with a contentment she had not known for a long time. She grasped the handle of the door, her door, hastened through the hall. The warmth of the rooms struck her. She smiled. Catherine, so predictable, had the fire going. If Charles were home, he would be in his world of solitude and study, the library. She tried to stop her mind from fragmenting, formulating what she would say to him as she approached the library entrance.

He was not there.

Catherine sat before the fire, her shawl wrapped tightly around her, though its blaze made the room stifling. A small suitcase sat by her side. She was rocking back and forth, staring at the flames, oblivious to the click of Eleanor's heels on the oak floor.

"Catherine?"

Catherine looked up, stared at her.

"Catherine, where's Charles?"

She lifted herself from the couch as though arthritic. "You're-- back."

"Are you all right?"

"You're back."

"Where is Charles?"

"With Robbie. At the hospital. I came to pack a few things for him. He's been staying overnight."

"Overnight? At--. What happened?"

"Robbie. He's got diphtheria. He's at St. Joseph's."

"But you said he was all right! That he would be fine."

"He--seemed better when you left, but then--after--he fell back to sleep. He wouldn't wake up. I examined his throat. It was covered with gray--"

"When did you bring him to the hospital?"

"The night you left."

"Diphtheria?" She slumped into the chair, still not completely comprehending. How could this be? It was a contagious disease. The farthest Robbie usually got was the garden. She had been so careful with him. So careful. Overly protective, Charles had said. But what did these thoughts matter now? She wasted precious time.

She ran to the door. "I'll go to him."

"Wait. I'll call for your carriage."

"No. I've lost too much time already."

She bolted through the door.

Catherine listened to the sound of Eleanor's footsteps pounding the floor as she ran, their echo disappearing into silence.

She would not allow this change in events to upset her plan. Charles would never forgive her for leaving him and his sick child. He would still be hers.

She went to the liquor cabinet. A drink never hurt anyone. She added a dose of laudanum, settled in the soft leather of a chair, wondered if Eleanor would suspect her betrayal. Of course not. Eleanor trusted her completely.

The soothing liquor spread through her. Her heart thumped less wildly. She studied the flames consuming the logs in the fireplace a long time.

She cringed. If the priests were right, she would burn in hell for what she had done.

She gulped the rest of her drink, poured another.

Soon remorse was swept away, replaced by oblivion.

St. Joseph's Hospital was only a few blocks away on Market Street. Eleanor ran down Mill to Market, Robbie's face emblazoned in her mind. His soft skin, his new tooth popping from his upper gum.

She had dropped her guard, assumed he would be all right.

Because Catherine encouraged her.

She should have called Mary. How could Catherine have made such a disastrous mistake, with her advanced medical training? But she didn't have time to think of that now.

She approached the hospital, stood a few seconds, gasping for breath.

A visitor to Paterson might easily have passed it by, for no sign hung outside. But she knew a great deal about St. Joseph's. Her mother had sometimes gone there to volunteer. She told her in the early days the nuns often took in laundry or begged for pennies at the factory gates to purchase food and medicine for those who sought their help. No one was ever turned away. Mary could not speak highly enough of the Sisters of Charity who ran the hospital. She placed serious isolation cases in St. Joseph's, with its much larger facilities, and the hospital staff felt grateful for the Alliance for often alleviating their case loads as well. And Charles's contributions to the hospital had been partially responsible for opening the first isolation ward for victims of terrible epidemics that wracked Paterson from time to time.

Surely he never dreamed their child would ever need to be in that ward.

The stucco building emanated peace and quiet. At its top sat an ornate cupola, above its spire a gold cross. Eleanor would never be a believer; but as she looked up at the cross before entering, she found herself hoping that if God existed, He watched over her child now.

She approached a nun at the desk, the woman a study in cleanliness and efficiency. She directed her to the end of the hall, and left, to an area marked "Isolation Ward."

She heard the quiet clicking of her heels, the echo of her steps, the shuffle of her dress, as she walked towards the ward.

Charles sat hunched in a chair in the hallway, his hands to his head, elbows resting on his knees. He looked up at the sound of her footsteps.

"Charles?"

His eyes were bloodshot, cheeks and chin bristled with stubble. He stared back at the floor. She was not certain he truly saw her. Perhaps the doctor had given him a sedative.

She wanted to take him in her arms, comfort him and feel him console her. But she still didn't know how it was between them.

She knelt in front of him. "Charles. Please. Look at me."

He bobbed his head, looked up, appeared unable to focus. His eyes looked scraped by red lines, bruised.

"What did the doctor say? Will he be all right?"

He did not answer.

She gripped his arm. *"Please."*

"We have to wait. But I've been waiting and waiting. Waiting and waiting. He's having such a time breathing, you see."

"My poor Robbie," he said, his voice oddly high-pitched. "They think it's affected his windpipe--and if it has--" He clenched his knees. "My darling boy--"

She bowed her head. "We'll wait, Charles. Together."

He did not seem to hear her, kept clenching his knees.

She yearned for Charles' comfort, always unfailing. Robbie was her son as well. She longed to throw herself at his feet, beg his forgiveness. He made no effort to touch her, speak further.

But this was not the time to think of her foolish self. There would be time to sort things out when Robbie recovered.

And so, isolated, she sat next to the shadow of her husband, waiting for news of her child.

She did not know how many hours she sat with Charles mute beside her. Another couple arrived, waited, holding each other's hand as the nurse carried their crying child behind the closed door. Then another older couple, the husband carrying a boy, perhaps seven or eight, approached the nun on duty. Soon a nurse came, brought him into the ward.

After long hours a nun emerged from the door, her rosary clicking at her side as she walked.

"You'd better come," she said.

They donned masks the nun gave them, walked an eternity down the corridor to the isolation ward. Curtains separated each patient. The nun paused when she reached the middle of the room, gestured to a crib.

"You understand--he's been through so much. Poor baby. It's the end now."

They stood beside the crib, looked down at a child she did not recognize. Charles's look indicated he felt the same way.

She breathed a sigh of relief. The nun had brought them to the wrong crib. This baby was the color of putty, his eyes slits, his body swollen.

She turned to the nun. "You've made a mistake."

"No. I'm so sorry. This child is your son."

Eleanor examined the baby again. She forced herself to touch his skull, divided the hair on the side of his scalp.

She froze. Robbie's birthmark. The one she worried about, the one defect that would be covered as he grew older.

As he grew older.

She would never know that time, never warn him of the danger from carriages in the street, never show him how to plant flowers in the garden, never walk with him his first day of school. She stood, impaled by myriads of lost moments.

He made a grating sound, then gasped.

Then silence.

"My darling boy," Charles whimpered.

She buried her face in her hands.

"You both have my deepest sympathy. He's with God now." The nun embraced them, attempted to lead them away.

She leaned on Charles, longing for what she had known so many times before, the refuge of his arms.

He pushed her away.

And so she stood alone, shattered by grief.

Many people told Eleanor afterwards Robbie's funeral was one of the largest gatherings of tribute in Paterson's memory. Even larger than the funeral of Thomas Rogers, who founded Paterson's locomotive industry. All of Charles's associates, their wives and families, along with thousands of workers from his mill and others paid their respects. Twenty-four thousand struck in 1913. Now they showed their sympathy in tribute to a man who gave them dignity. She knew they hoped their gesture and comments would comfort her and Charles, lessen their grief.

It did not.

Just the sight of the facade at St. Joseph's brought a flood of memories of her childhood, of her mother holding her hand, teaching her to make the sign of the cross, explaining how to genuflect. She remembered Elizabeth's laughter the first time she genuflected, clunking both knees to the ground instead of one.

She descended the carriage, clinging to Charles' arm, insensate as wood. Past the mourners crowded outside the church, silent as stones. Down the path to the great oak door. She smelled the grass, newly mown, walked past the waxen gleam of magnolia trees, sentinals guarding each side of the door. They had always amazed her, should never have survived this far north. But they did.

Robbie's casket lay on the altar, adorned with white violets, sprigs of rosemary. For remembrance, Charles said. They dragged down the aisle. Color from the stained glass windows caught light from the sun, transfiguring them with artificial brightness as they walked past the other mourners. She sat next to Mary who held her hand, attempting to comfort her in her grief. The "Alleluia" resounded. The congregation bowed their heads as Father Garrity lifted the communion wafer. She did not bow hers. She sat with eyes riveted upon the casket, thinking of Robbie, alone in darkness.

She stood mechanically as the priest recited the Gospel:

"At that time Martha said to Jesus, "Lord, if Thou hadst been here my brother would not have died. But even now I know that whatever Thou shalt ask of God, God will give it to Thee." Jesus said to her, "Thy brother shall rise." Martha said to Him, "I know that he will rise at the resurrection, on the last day." Jesus said to her, "I am the resurrection and the life; he who believes in me shall never die. Dost thou believe this?" She said to Him, "Yes, Lord, I believe Thou art the Christ, Son of God, Who has come into the world.""

If only she could believe, find hope in those words.

She clung to Charles' arm, knowing he would not push her away. He did not seem aware she was there at all.

After the service, droves of workers walked behind them as they rode in the hearse to Holy Sepulcher Cemetery. They passed the Falls, the splendor of their roar permeating her. They drove past the mills. Black bunting draped the facade of Charles' mill, closed today, quiet as breath.

They entered the main gate. Colors and textures of the sugar maples and birch mixed with the Virginia creepers' pink and scarlet leaves. Now and then a bird chirped, flew into the sky.

They reached the grave site.

Father Garrity droned on.

"May the angels lead you into paradise. May the martyrs receive you at the coming and lead you into the holy city of Jerusalem. May the choir of angels receive you, and may you have eternal rest with Lazarus, who once was poor."

Charles' assistant, Stephen Kosinski, and the gardener, Tom Branigan, lowered the casket. She was filled with regret at Colin's absence. He should have been one of the two to carry it. Yet, she understood his inability to face this day.

The casket thudded into the earth. Charles buckled. Catherine and Kosinski steadied him. He buried his head on her shoulder while they led him away, his legs unstable as broken sticks.

Every mourner eyed Eleanor as she scattered soil on the casket.

Except one.

During the service Mary studied Catherine. She had been in turmoil since hearing of the circumstances of Robbie's death. Catherine had treated so many cases of diphtheria at the Alliance, knew the disease inside and out. How could she have missed the symptoms in Robbie?

Mary remembered the times Charles had dropped by, the look of worship in Catherine's eyes. She believed the situation to be harmless. Catherine would live her days in unrequited love for Charles, and perhaps be none the worse.

She studied the look of adoration in Catherine's eyes when she looked at Charles, thought of the blame he surely placed upon Eleanor for leaving Robbie--and of Catherine's expertise as a nurse--. She could only arrive at one conclusion.

But she must be sure. She would call Sister Margaret at St. Joseph's from the library as soon as they arrived back at the house. Sister Margaret would have the information she needed.

Mary stood lost in thought beside Eleanor at Robbie's grave. She watched her touch her child's coffin one last time, walked with her to the carriage, their steps leaden.

They rode in silence all the way home.

Eleanor felt fortunate to have Catherine's friendship at this time. She took care of all the post-funeral arrangements, serving a buffet in the back garden for everyone who offered their condolences. Catherine's work left Eleanor free to focus on graciously accepting everyone's sympathy, knowing it came from love. She spoke to each person, in part to thank them, in part to delay having to face Charles. He was still dazed, unwilling to speak to her.

She noticed the empty cake tray but it seemed an insurmountable task to rise, walk to the kitchen. She waited, looking for Catherine who was no where in sight. Finally she forced herself up from the chair, took the tray and plodded across the lawn.

She heard shouting and stopped in the doorway of the kitchen.

Catherine stood with her back to Eleanor. Mary faced her, filled with anger.

Mary's eyes widened when she saw Eleanor, but she did not stop speaking. "So you let Robbie die, thinking Charles would never forgive her. That he'd be yours. How can you live with yourself?"

Catherine sank into the kitchen chair, her back still to Eleanor. "Don't you know how much I hate myself? But, God forgive me, I'd do it again. If it meant I'd have Charles."

Eleanor dropped the cake tray. It hit the floor like a clashing cymbal.

She lunged at Catherine. Mary held her back. "What will that do? She lied to you. Knew Robbie had diptheria. I called the nun on duty that night. His throat was almost closed when they arrived after midnight. He was already near death from suffocation."

"After midnight? But--"

"When did you leave?"

"When did--?"

"It's important. Think."

"About five? Six? I had come from bringing Colin dinner. So it must have been closer to six." She confronted Catherine again. "You told me he had improved. That he was even smiling. All those hours passed. You waited. Until--"

"Charles won't believe you. Never."

"Keep telling yourself that." Mary towered over her. "There's nothing more to be said here. It will be my evidence against you. And my word."

"You will leave this house. By morning." Eleanor's anger boiled. "I'll see you in prison for this."

"Charles--"

"Get out."

Catherine ran through the door.

Mary placed her arms around Eleanor.

"I can't say how sorry I am it came to this. But I had to find out the truth. For all our sakes. I know you loved Catherine. Trusted her. But you see now, don't you? You weren't responsible for Robbie's death. You didn't know he was a dying child."

"But I left him."

"Would you have if you'd known how sick he was?"

"I swear I would never--. Never."

"Don't you think I knew that without even asking? You need some rest. I'll tell Charles. He needs to hear it from me since I'm the one who uncovered it."

"All right." She straightened her dress, pushed back the wisps of hair that had loosened. "I have to get back to the guests. They came out of kindness. I can't let them down."

"Are you sure you'll be all right?"

"No--but I'll have to be."

She lifted the cake pan from the floor, washed and dried it, cut wedges of cake steadying her right hand by clenching her wrist with her left. Then she returned to the guests.

Catherine was nowhere in sight.

After the last mourner departed, the depth of Eleanor's isolation grew heavily upon her.

She retreated to the upstairs back bedroom, her mind whirling.

She paced back and forth, back and forth, uncertain whether to confront Charles now or wait until morning. Neither of them would sleep. Too much of the sound of Robbie haunted the house-- her wondering if he would wake up crying in the middle of the night, leaving her bed to hold and soothe him. Was he getting another tooth? Is that why he cried so? Once it burst from his gum, he would sleep better.

She caught herself. Was she losing her mind? She shook her head hard, though she knew it would never expel memories within her.

She sat on the bed realizing in her state she could not wait through everlasting night until morning to confront Charles. She must find the strength to confront him now. She wrapped her woolen robe around her, its warmth encompassing her. She began to pace the floor again, her breath heavy.

She tightened the belt on her robe, attempted to compose herself. The cold door knob sent shivers through her. She walked down the oak stairs to the library, each step the sounding of a knell.

Charles sat staring at the ashes in the hearth, a bottle of whiskey open beside him. He held a glass. His hand shook as he lifted it to his lips, pressed it against his lower one to quell his tremor as he drank.

She decided to leave. The night would be sleepless, but she could not face him this way. She turned to go.

"Eleanor."

His voice sounded low.

"I thought maybe we should talk," she said. "But it can wait until morning."

"I'd rather talk now. It's better to get it over with."

"I'll start a fire."

"No. I don't want one."

He seemed to be speaking to thin air.

"I had to tell you, Charles. It doesn't do any good, I know, but I have to say how--how sorry I am. For everything."

She stood in front of him, above him, for he had not risen. His head jerked as he tried to look up at her, his skin ashen.

"Has Mary told you? About Catherine?"

"I don't want to believe it. But the facts force me to." He stared at her through hollow eyes. "And now that I know, what do you want of me? I've given all I can. With Robbie gone, there's nothing left."

"*We're* left."

She sat down, facing him.

"So Dante left you, is that it?"

"Not one day will pass I won't remember what I did leaving Robbie. You know now, you must believe now, I had no idea how sick he was."

"Is that the point then?"

"I don't understand."

"You had no right to leave him under any circumstances. You left your child. Not to mention me, of course."

He frowned at the ashes in the hearth. Finally he looked at her, through her, from a place of emptiness she could not penetrate. Her heart thumped so hard it hurt. Her vocal chords felt twisted. But she knew she must try to make things right.

"I was a fool. Living in a foolish dream Dante could love me more than his work. But now I know, he didn't love me as much as you do, Charles. The workers and justice and all his high ideals, that's what he loves. I refused to believe I would always be second. I think he may have been trying to tell me that, in Paterson." She pressed her fingers to her temples. "Yes. As I think of it more clearly, he was. I finally understand. And now his whole life will be the revolution."

"The revolution?"

"He's going to Russia. He says there'll be a great revolution there. He must think the peasants will revolt, then be equal finally. Something like that."

Then she heard the sound she least expected. Charles laughed, a robust laugh she had not heard for so long. She surprised herself by smiling, glad at some kind of reaction, even at her own expense.

"Something like that?" he said, "No thought of what's happening in the world. Certainly not about a coming revolution in Russia. I'm sorry, but that is so much you." He controlled his laughter. "But I know why. It's because you needed every ounce of strength to survive in your own world. I put up with it because I understood that. Because I loved you. So much. Even though I knew you didn't return my love."

"That's not true. I do care about people. I made you change the work loads. And I encouraged commission weaving, didn't I? And benches for the workers. I--"

"Perhaps I was too harsh in saying that. I don't know anymore." His eyes met hers, all sign of laughter gone. "Let me ask you something. If Dante Ravelli were not leaving for Russia, for his revolution, and asked you to stay with him, what would you have said?"

Her face flushed. She rose.

"I won't answer such a foolish question."

"You're refusing to answer?"

"I don't know. I don't know what I would have done."

"You would have stayed with him. You know it."

She sank back down. "But that didn't happen! It's all in the past anyway. I want to start from where we are now. Charles, listen to me. It can never be the same for us in some ways, I know that. I've been so horrible taking advantage of your love. You've been so good to me. I understand now. Love can be so many things. And your love is a dependable love. I can rely on you being there. For me. First in your heart. That never would have been true of Dante. I see that now. I swear it."

"So I've become your knight in shining armor at last. Not plain looking? Not weak?"

"Why do you have to say things like that about yourself?"

"Only because they're true. I was weak, when it came to you. And I'll never be a handsome man. I accepted that a long time ago." His face darkened. "Dante Ravelli. I never knew, do you believe that? I suspected, of course, that you loved someone else. Someone was always between us."

"Charles, I think you still love me. You do."

The comfort of the whiskey had overtaken him. He slumped, ran his fingers through his hair.

She felt encouraged he didn't respond. Surely that might mean he still did care. They would leave the past and useless recriminations.

A calm came over her. For the first time she realized she stood before a good man with whom she might find the happiness that had eluded her all of her life. Her realization of how much she cared about him flowed through every vein of her body.

"We can begin again. I believe that with all my heart. Do you?"

He did not respond.

She knelt before him. "Charles, you can forgive me. I know you can."

"But can I ever forgive myself?"

"Yourself? Why, you were a perfect father. I was the one who--"

"I'm responsible for Robbie's death."

"What are you saying?"

"The mill. I brought him to the mill. To show him off. My son. I was so proud--." His voice trailed into a whisper. "I killed him in the end."

His betrayal of her trust flared within her. "But, you gave me your word--"

"Dear God, don't you think I know that?"

"You knew? All this time? Why didn't you tell me?"

"Because I hated you for leaving us. God forgive me, I wanted you to suffer."

Her moment had come. The hours of anger seething at his ignoring her since she had returned, when she needed him so. Now this revelation, which put in place the last pieces in the puzzle of Robbie's illness. She raised her hand to thrash his face--and saw desolation carved on every feature.

She lowered her hand, swallowed her words. She could not hurt him more.

"Why are you telling me now?"

"When I found out you didn't know how sick Robbie really was, I had to stop punishing you, tell you the truth. I should have told you immediately. But I was so overcome by my own guilt, my anger--" He sighed. "Knowing you've never loved me. So much of our life together has been a sham." He dropped his arms to his sides where they hung like puppets'. "Our physical relationship. A sham. Pretense. All pretense."

She felt as though a giant worm slithered through her, gnawed her. She must overpower it, destroy it, no matter the cost. She could not let this honorable man who made the mistake of loving her blame himself for a failure not his.

"No, Charles. I won't allow you, to blame yourself for our poor-- sex life." She bent down, pressed her head against his knees, uncertain she could face him.

Finally, she did.

"The failure was mine." Her face reddened. "My father. The memory of--what he did to me. It comes back worst--those times."

"Your father?"

Her throat felt constricted. But she must find the courage to speak. "He--came to my bed drunk. So many times. When I was--a little girl."

"You mean he--hurt you? You mean--"

She nodded. The stain embedded within her all these years finally became visible.

And he did not turn away.

"Charles, I killed him for it. And for my mother. He beat her so hard. He crippled her." She twisted her fingers as she spoke, her voice almost inaudible. "I--fixed the railing. So he would fall. We had to be free of him. We had to. I never told anybody. Until now."

He stared at her. Finally, his look softened. He touched her face.

They rose together and he held her in silence.

"All this time," he said presently. "Why didn't you tell me?"

"I couldn't. The shame. You would have thought I was-- unclean."

"Don't you know by now it wouldn't have mattered? I knew there was something. But I never imagined--God, the thought of--. I always felt you were a woman possessed with such courage. But coping with--this. Inside you. All these years."

They remained silent a time.

"Do you think we can try to begin again, my dear?" he finally said.

She stared past him. "It's nice to think we'll live happily ever after, isn't it? But we've done such terrible things to each other. And I have to be honest. I can't come back until we both come to grips with what you did." Her eyes filled. "I'm not going to lie to you, say right now I forgive you. I wish I could."

"You've been through so much. More than I ever imagined. Forgiveness comes hard for you. The shell you've developed to protect yourself from hurt. I understand."

"I don't need my feelings explained. The point is how I feel right now. I trusted you. You gave me your word--." She turned from him. "And what about you, hating yourself, day after day? I can't live with the ghost you are now. Believe me,

I understand guilt. It tries to destroy you at every turn. Don't let it win."

"Perhaps we do need time. But why can't you stay? We can both try to work this out."

"Sometimes when two people's lives are shattered, they need time to be apart, to think things out. It's the only chance they have to build a life together again. I'm probably not making sense to you."

He hung his head. "I'm afraid you are. It's just that the thought of you leaving--"

He took her hand, pressed it against his cheek.

"And I need time to heal. To sort things out. I know that now. That I could tell you--everything. And you didn't turn away. It means the world to me."

"I'd give my life for you. You must know that."

They stood, guilt penetrating them. She understood they deserved to feel it. But she realized what he did not, that their separation was the only chance they had for recovery, for the day to arrive when Robbie's death would not be the major event that bound them.

"I can never express the guilt I feel from abandoning you and Robbie," she said. "We both have to get to the point we can forgive each other. And ourselves."

"I'll do whatever you wish. Anything. I can not lose you."

They stood silent for a time.

"I thought I'd have a memorial built for him," he finally said. "At the back of the property. By the perennials." He attempted a smile. "They're so reliable. Blossom each year. Never fail."

"I like that." She pressed his limp hand in hers. "I hope the time comes when I come back to you as the wife you deserve. That is all I can offer now."

"I will live for that day."

"I'll leave then. In the morning."

She walked towards the door. She did not say goodbye but looked straight ahead.

She packed the next morning, filled her suitcase with essential needs. Then she removed a bag she kept in the back corner of the armoire. She opened it and studied the shoes she wore during the strike, soles worn thin, tongues torn away, eyes and hooks broken. She held them to her heart, lost in thought. Then she placed them in the suitcase.

She went to Catherine's room before leaving to be sure she was up and packing. Let her live in the streets for all she cared.

She found Catherine fast asleep.

Her anger flared. Catherine's betrayal struck her all over again. And she was able to sleep. She would shake her hard, wake her from her sick, peaceful slumber.

Catherine lay facing the window. Her quilt bulged from the outline of her body in a fetal position. She had unpinned her hair. It spread across the white pillow case like a black web.

She approached the bed.

Something was wrong.

Catherine's face was colorless.

She lifted the coverlet and tried to shake her. Her limbs were stiff in *rigor mortis*.

She scrutinized the night table holding Catherine's medical books, a romance, an unopened box of chocolates, a hair brush, comb. And a laudanum bottle, emptied of every drop.

She stared at Catherine's body for what felt like a long time, letting her thoughts sort themselves out. One feeling emerged, a sense of victory. But such a hollow victory.

She closed the door.

She walked the path of the garden to the greenhouses, doted on her plants, safe from the cold of the brisk day. She touched the faces of her flowers, lingered over each, forced herself to leave.

The memory of her argument with Colin gnawed at her. She had to apologize, try to make him understand she was out of her mind at the thought of Dante nearby. It would be a good first step in a new direction.

She passed the rattling mills, facing another day, reached his apartment, began climbing the stairs.

"Was it a room you wanted, miss?"

She turned to see Mrs. O'Hare, his landlady, a wren-faced woman, all aflutter.

"Oh, excuse me. It's you, Mrs. Lafferty. I didn't know you from the back and without me glasses. Is it Colin you wanted?"

"I have to speak to him. It's early, I know."

"Ah, but he's gone."

She stopped dead on the stairs.

"A few days now. Went back to Ireland." She clicked her false teeth with her tongue. "And now the room needs rentin'. Though I don't expect a problem. With all's need rooms. But it won't be easy to get a renter as nice as him."

"How do you know?"

"That he went back? Why, he told me. Left most everything up there. Said he only wanted to take a few things he needed. His dresser, the bed, even some of his clothes, they're still in the closet."

"Is it--all right--if I go up?"

"I don't see why not. I'll just get the key." She turned to leave, then faced her. "Oh, there's a letter he left for you. On my kitchen table. I'll bring it. Anything from his room you can take, I suppose, you two bein' so close. Of course, it's a plus if there's furniture. For when I rent it."

"I don't want--anything."

She returned with the key, the letter, then left.

The room looked as Mrs. O'Hare said. It seemed Colin still lived here, he had taken so little. She sat on a kitchen chair and studied the letter. It had a return address of Paddy O'Hara in Cork, Ireland. Her hands began to shake so much she could hardly open it.

My dear Eleanor,

I could not stay and know you would never speak to me again. I have to break a promise I made to your mother the day you were born. Michael was not your father. I am. You are my little girl.

Your mother, she never wanted you to know.

She had her reasons. Sin was the biggest. As you can guess. I should of told you years ago. Spoke up no matter what. But love does strange things. It makes us weak. If I had spoke up right at the start, he could never of done those awful things. I swear I never knew he did those awful things. I would of killed him and not you have to if I found out.

You did right to kill him.

I will be at the place I wrote on the letter a few months at least. It would mean everything if you write to me. That you tell me you forgive me.

Your father

She stared at the letter.

How had she not known? Her mother's last words. All that time she thought Elizabeth might have condemned her for killing Michael, implying she repent. Instead, in her last moments she confessed.

Colin, a man with a heart pure as light.

Love created her.

Of course she would write. Why, she would even ask him to come back to Paterson. He might.

Hope surged through her.

She ran down the stairs, gave Mrs. O'Hare two months rent, told her to hold the room. She stood speechless, watching Eleanor descend the stairs.

She wandered the streets of Paterson for hours, absorbing her city and the places she knew so well, as much her friends as any man or woman she had known. She sat on a bench, the Great Falls cascading before her, spewing power to run the mills, as they would long after she lay in the earth.

She walked past McNamara's Bar, heard coarse voices of men singing:

Meet me tonight in Dreamland
Under the silv'ry moon.

She remembered her happiness as that song played at Palisades Park when she rode the carousel.

With Charles.

She walked along her block in the tenement area, studied the window where she had so often viewed the street. Darkness made the curtain look like a shroud. She studied the window a long time, seared by memory.

But she didn't live there anymore.

She kept walking.

She approached the Women's Alliance. Impulse propelled her to climb the stairs, peer into the window.

Mary sat at the far end of the room, stethescope in hand, checking the heart of a boy no more than eight or nine. What was wrong with him? Did he have parents? Were they from the mills? She imagined the coolness of Mary's hand as she touched his face, shaken by the thought of what Robbie might have looked like at that age.

She stood in the doorway. Sickness and death hovered in the air. They always would. She studied the patients in their beds, some resting, others tortured with pain.

She decided in that moment she would return to the Alliance, where she belonged. She was filled with uncertainty about her future. Yet, she must hope that within this sanctuary she could strive to overcome the suffering of her past and try to find forgiveness through the sacred act of healing others.

Mary waved to her.

She waved back.

She entered the room.

EPILOGUE

He studied the drifts of snow, then left the window. Loss penetrated him. He read his letter once again:

> February 25, 1917
> My dearest Eleanor,
>
> I am a fool. I have written to tell you that you are in my thoughts every day. I know now you are the center of my being, the one fixed star that gives meaning to my life.
>
> I want to come back to you. I know I ask so much. You would be giving up Charles and your beautiful child. But I can not live knowing that you exist in this world and I am not by your side, that I have lost you.
>
> Elizabeth Flynn writes, tells me there is always work with the IWW there. It would be a harder life for you than the one you have now, I know. But we will have our love. Will you forgive a man who foolishly threw it away?
>
> I will wait each day for your reply, and hope.
>
> Thine,
> Dante

He folded the letter carefully, addressed it, placed it in his pocket, decided to mail it at the post office near the Tauride Palace.

He approached the area, heard shouting. Thousands of people engulfed the Palace. He smiled. Three hundred years of the Romanov regime was ending before his eyes. His revolution lay before him, and beyond it a nation dedicated to justice.

Then he noticed the bodies scattered across Znamenskaya Square. It took a moment to realize what they meant. Then he began to run with the others.

The bullet struck him in the stomach.

He clutched his gut and fell to the ground. Blood gushed over his hands. He heard tramping, bellowing of hundreds of people surrounding him, marching to Tauride Palace, engulfing it. He saw a blur of the armed detachment of Bolshevik Red guards, factory workers, students, sailors of the Baltic fleet, Bolshevik sympathizers among the military garrison running through the streets and Nevsky Prospekt.

Above him the sun's splendor refracted on the gold, onion-shaped dome of a church. He drifted toward unconsciousness.

"Eleanor---"

No one heard.

Dmitri Orlov dismounted next to another victim and kicked his body hard. No response. He was dead.

He knelt next to the body. Threadbare clothes, not worth much.

But he might have rubles. He began searching his pockets. "Echt!"

He removed only a few rubles from his pocket, noticed a letter, soaked with blood. He went through his wallet, ignoring his red- stained gloves. Inside he found an identification card in what might be English.

And a photograph, worn by touch.

It depicted a girl, thin as air, wearing a plain dress. She looked directly into the camera. Sister, lover, wife? What did it matter?

He threw the photo to the ground, watched it trampled in the furor around him.

A wooden, horse-drawn wagon was nearby, picking up the dead. He caught the driver's eye, gestured for him to approach. He helped him pick up the body. They threw it in the cart with the others, and moved on.

BIBLIOGRAPHY

I owe a great debt to those writers whose books and research were so helpful and inspirational and wish to acknowledge them and their work.

Primary Sources

Without the historical research of Steve Golin and his book, *The Fragile Bridge: The Paterson Silk Strike: 1913*, I could not have written this book. Another great help was *Silk City*, edited by Philip B. Scranton, and the essays it contained: "The Unity and Strategy of the Paterson Silk Manufacturers During the 1913 Strike," by Steve Golin; "Fantasy and Realism: The Manufacture of Silk at Pelgram and Meyer, 1872-1928," by Patricia C. O'Donnell; "The Battle for Labor Supremacy in Paterson, 1916-1922," by David J. Goldberg; "Labor Conflict and Technological Change: The Family Shop in Paterson," by Philip J. McLewin; "An Exceedingly Irregular Business: Structure and Process in the Paterson Silk Industry, 1885-1910," by Philip B. Scranton; and "Technology Diffusion and the Transfer of Skills: Nineteenth-Century English Silk Migration to Paterson" by Richard D. Margrave. Eileen Van Kirk's book Silk was very helpful. Kathleen Middleton's *Images of America:* Bayonne, gave me an understanding of the strike against Standard Oil.

Secondary Sources

Abels, Jules. *The Rockefeller Billions*

Andrist, Ralph K.. *The American Heritage History of the Confident Years: 1865-1916*

Bukowczyk, John J, "Hegemony and Polish-American Politics in Bayonne, 1915-1929" (thesis, Wayne State University)

Chernow, Ronald. Titan: *The Life of John D. Rockefeller*

Consumers Union of U.S., and *Consumer Reports* editors, *Funerals: Last Rites (Appendix 6)*

Flynn, Elizabeth Gurley. Rebel Girl (The speech she made to the workers during the Paterson strike is exactly quoted, page 159 of the International Publishers paperback edition of her autobiography.)

Gambino, Richard. *Blood of My Blood: The Dilemma of Italian Americans*

Gargiulo, Vincent. *Palisades Amusement Park: A Century of Fond Memories*

Hales, Diane. *The Encyclopedia of Health, Pregnancy and Birth*

Harr, John Easor, and Peter J. Johnson. *The Rockefeller Century*

Haywood, Bill. *Bill Haywood's Book*

Herbst, John A. and Catherine Keene, editors. *Life and Times in Silk City: A Photographic Essay*

Hill, May Brawley. *Grandmother's Garden: The Old-Fashioned American Garden 1865-1915*

Llywelyn, Morgan. *1916*

Miller, Kirby and Paul Wagner. *Out of Ireland*

Millies, Stephen, "The Ludlow Massacre and the Birth of Company

Unions," *Workers World,* 1/26/95 (Internet)

Murphy, J. Palmer and Margaret Murphy. *Paterson and Passaic County: An Illustrated History*

Murrin, Mary R. *Women in New Jersey History*

Neill, Kenneth. *An Illustrated History of the Irish People*

Olian, JoAnne, editor. *Everyday Fashions 1909-1920*

Pipes, Richard. *The Russian Revolution*

Reagan, Leslie J. *When Abortion Was a Crime*

Rose, Graham. *The Classic Garden*

Russell, Vivian. *Edith Wharton's Italian Gardens*

Semchyshyn, Stefan and Carol Colman. *How to Prevent Miscarriage and Other Crises of Pregnancy*

Salisbury, Harrison. *Russia in Revolution*

Schnitzler, Henry. *As They Were: Bayonne and New Jersey*

Schermer, David. *World War I*

Sinclair, Gladys Mellor. *Bayonne: Old and New*

Marilyn Hering

The Call (Paterson daily newspaper)
Undset, Sigrid. *Kristin Lavransdatter*
Women's Project of New Jersey. *Past and Promise: Lives of New Jersey Women*